REN-SHEN

HALF SPIRIT

CHRIS MILANKO

Copyright

To the original Lion and Priestess

Mitcho (Dad)
Rina (Mum)

Contents

Book One - The Quickening

A thought became a ROAR.

Chapter 1 - The Early Years

Steve Nedelkin always seemed a little older than he actually was. He physically matured early and had an intellectual maturity which older people would always embrace. Perhaps it was due to the fact that he lost his mother when he was just six years of age. It wasn't long before young Steve was doing the necessary tasks around the house for both his father and himself. He enjoyed reading, exercising and absolutely loved playing his guitar.

Born in Adelaide, Australia, the son of Macedonian immigrants who left poverty and a civil war behind in what is now part of Greece, Steve was always taught to be proud of his Macedonian heritage. "We Macedonians ruled the world," his father would sometimes say. He'd often remind Steve that his family used to be important once upon a time and say, "Even the mountains used to have our name!" Of course none of that made a great deal of sense to Steve because his people arrived in Australia penniless and worked as labourers for most of their lives. They only sought to measure themselves against their fellow immigrants and the suffering they endured from their endless toil seemed a badge of merit. Watching relatives compare employment related injuries seemed very peculiar to him.

His father was a lion of a man with immense strength and an enormous capacity to explode with a rage which others would fear. Steve vividly recalled seeing his father's violent nature when a local gangster made an uninvited entrance to a function held by his local Macedonian community. While most of the community members didn't want any trouble, Steve's father couldn't bear watching the criminal try and intimidate his family and friends. The tough guy was removed from the community hall by the scruff of his neck. When he tried to square up and fight Steve's father, he was rewarded with a backhanded slap across his face. The kind which only a strong man who worked with his hands all his life could deliver. After he picked himself up off the ground, the gangster sprinted away to safety - never to be seen again.

As a young child, Steve quickly learned how his father's demeanour changed around what he called "shpioni" or spies. Those people were treated with caution and a sense of trepidation by his father. The "shpioni" were the people from the same region back in the old country who had ties to the new Greek government. They had the potential to make life a permanent misery for any relatives back home if there was any indication of Macedonian patriotism enthusiastically displayed in his warmly embraced new country. Words and actions were always measured carefully in the company of those people. The hidden agendas and purposeful double meanings conveyed in such meetings were often a source of intrigue to a young Steve who quickly learned to read between the lines.

School was pleasant enough for Steve. He had an uncanny ability to quickly grasp concepts and easily maintain a solid B+ average. He certainly wasn't the smartest in the class, but nobody doubted he could have given some of the brilliant student minds a run for their money if only he pursued anything academic with real vigour. A constant theme in his report cards was the potential ... the potential ... the potential.

He played numerous team sports yet didn't particularly excel. He didn't seem to enjoy the actual games very much and always wondered if he should enter the fray at the expense of another team member. All of the sports were about chasing after a ball and, quite frankly, it didn't go unnoticed his pet dog Rover enjoyed chasing balls far more and would have been infinitely more up to the task. Nevertheless, Steve did enjoy the social interactions and the numerous sports allowed him to move effortlessly between a number of school cliques.

One notable event occurred at an Australian rules football training session when Steve was fifteen years old. The team was playing "Red Rover all Over". They were split into two teams with one team halfway along the football field and the other level with the goals. The other team had to run and tackle Steve and his teammates and drag them to the ground. One of the faster boys managed to grab Steve and tried to wrestle him to the ground. He did everything right, his arms managed to wrap around Steve with particular attention to his centre of gravity. He dropped and tried to drag Steve down with all his might. Much to his dismay, he was flung off Steve as though electrocuted. This prompted others to attempt the seemingly inevitable takedown. The first few were ejected in a similar manner, then finally all of the opposition managed to lay a hand on Steve. Yet he couldn't be dragged down. Hilariously, the entire team then attempted to drag him down and they simply couldn't do it no matter what they attempted.

Steve glanced at the coach who couldn't understand what kind of crazy force was stopping this rather average team player from being dragged to the ground! Everyone, other than Steve, was perplexed. The physics was quite logical to Steve. In fact, the entire team pushing and pulling in every direction created a hedge of sorts. All of their frenzied physicality and desperation was there to be utilised and Steve let them all "help" him stand upright amongst it all.

Steve was rather nonplussed by the event, yet his colleagues seemed to treat him differently from that time on. It was simple and logical to him, the right kind of angle of deflection, a twist, a push and people could be controlled physically. One of his friends suggested he should develop his natural abilities further and join a nearby Karate school. It was 1985 and the film Karate Kid had been released a year earlier to huge box office success. Karate had enjoyed a phenomenal resurgence in popularity and finally managed to claim the crown from Kung Fu which the legendary Bruce Lee singlehandedly made famous in the 1970s.

The instructor, Sensei Mike Fergusson, was an ex-Vietnam army veteran. He was incredibly strong. A tall man with long red hair and what seemed a tattoo for every occasion painted over the exposed areas of his body. Long before tattoos were a necessary fashion accessory for the modern Millennial, the tattoos seemed to tell a story as they wound around his muscular frame. A glimpse of a phoenix, a snake, a dragon, a fish ... all of them oriental in design. Not even a hint of a bawdy sailor's tattoo on the huge man. The tattoos were impeccably done and only added to the mystique of Steve's second mentor. His first mentor was clearly his father.

Sensei Mike would command attention by his mere presence and all classes were conducted in Japanese. There was no choice. Not a single word was uttered in English. The language transformed Sensei Mike, as soon as he stepped into the Dojo and commanded his students, his energy infused everyone in the room. The Okinawan Japanese is regarded as a dialect and is constantly changing as it slowly continues to transform into the standard modern Japanese language. Sometimes Sensei would use more archaic Okinawan words usually reserved for the elderly in Okinawa. Steve's enthusiasm for his karate extended to embracing the languages immediately and it would prove to be extremely useful in the near future.

In the early 1970s, Sensei Mike felt abandoned by Australia. The Vietnam veterans never received the appreciation and reverence that other returned war veterans received in earlier wars. In fact, they were often despised by the younger generations for their participation in what they believed to be an unjust war. He left his home country and moved to Okinawa where he quickly recommenced his training in Karate that had been abruptly curtailed by the Vietnam war. The style of Karate was Gōjū-ryū and was popular in the region. It was formalised over two generations under the eager and competent minds of the likes of Higaonna Kanryō and subsequently the spiritual founder Chōjun Miyagi. Sensei Mike was hardened by the war but found comfort in dedicating himself to his training. In the ten years he was in Okinawa, he managed to impress his masters with his ferocious strength and understanding of the complexities of the softer forms of the art. He earned his godan (or 5th dan level of black belt) in record time and was well known in many circles for his fierce combat style. However, events he was reluctant to describe forced him to flee his beloved and idyllic Okinawa and return to Australia.

Steve was enormously parochial about his martial art style. No other martial art could be better than Gōjū-ryū and no other instructor could possibly be better than Sensei Mike. Though it wasn't too long before Steve learned how the great founders had each travelled to China to learn such exotic Chinese styles such as Luohan and White Crane and how inextricably linked Gōjū-ryū was to the southern Shaolin Kung Fu styles. Indeed many Gōjū-ryū katas would exhibit the Chinese influence with their hard and soft movements. These distinguishing features were often more akin to Shaolin Kung Fu styles than other contemporary Karate styles.

The training felt glorious to Steve. There was no room for doubt about what he had to do and no waiting for other team players to have his turn. He was blessed with strength and coordination and was "man-sized" at 15 years of age and close to six feet tall. The training comprised excellent body conditioning and strengthening exercises. Flexibility came quickly and practise was infinitely rewarding. While most students often had to

train for years before they were even allowed to train the Sanchin Kata in the most traditional dojos, Steve left his Sensei no
choice. He was allowed to begin learning it after two months.
He had done everything asked of him and excelled - it was as
though every essence of his being was created for the purpose of
karate.

Sensei Mike would say, "Sanchin means 'three battles' and I
understand this as a battle to unify the mind, body and spirit.
The untrained eye sees the Sanchin kata as a sequence of extremely slow movements combined with a look of intense determination. Don't kid yourselves. It's a battle on all fronts. The
entire body anticipates every defence and attack and the mind,
body and spirit combine to create the perfect technique. It anticipates, it readies, it absorbs, it breathes, it lives, it sees and
hears and smells and senses everything that is happening and is
yet to happen. It is a meditative form of combat that only the
mind's eye can see, yet it manifests itself in such a way that an
average person sees nothing particularly remarkable. Make no
mistake, the essence of a man, his soul or spirit or reason for existence can be crushed with this kata's intent and fervour."

Steve understood the intent of Sanchin as a baby knows to
suckle the breast of its mother. It was natural, it was the only
way and any other way was indirect and futile. It simply made
perfect sense to Steve and he was of the resolute belief he was
born for this. Some students never fully mastered the Sanchin.
It was the alpha and omega. Steve's form was faultless within six
months.

Sensei Mike knew he had found someone special in Steve who
was worthy and who would honour the style. Naturally, good
students were good advertising for Sensei Mike and he needed
every dollar after returning penniless from Japan. Classes continued to grow and it wasn't long before Steve was teaching
some sessions and demonstrating his outstanding, remarkable

martial skills. Two years later, Steve was awarded black belt status. His ability demanded the acknowledgement of the black belt and his respect and admiration and servitude to his Sensei made it a pleasure for Sensei Mike to bestow the honour on his prized student within record time. Most importantly, Steve had earned the respect from his hero, his Sensei.

At seventeen years of age, Steve had few peers who were able to match his fighting prowess. The way he embraced his katas allowed him to transcend the normal instinctual reactions most people respond to in violent situations. Steve understood the only true enemy was himself and it was essential to be able to harness every aspect of his being to make him the complete fighter he so wanted to be. Sensei Mike was the only fighter whom Steve could spar with, and be challenged by, with every move. Steve had a repertoire of moves which would work without fail with lesser adversaries. But Sensei Mike typically had an answer for every one of Steve's moves. On the rare occasion Steve managed to find a way past the fearsome guard of Sensei Mike, the sheer elation of the "win" would end up being a Pyrrhic victory as it would distract Steve for a microsecond before Sensei Mike returned the favour tenfold. The little "wins" for Steve began to grow into more frequent occurrences and the joy from Sensei Mike was obvious. His protege was getting very close to being as fully trained by Sensei Mike as possible. Only further tuition in Okinawa under the great masters would help Steve realise his full potential to become a Gōjū-ryū master.

Sensei Mike knew Steve would honour him and stay with his dojo forever if necessary. Such was their bond and Steve's dedication. But he saw so much potential in Steve and wanted to see how far this young man could go. He saw greatness in the young Macedonian warrior. Sensei Mike wanted to see how Steve would progress with a life free from the pain and suffering he himself had endured. He believed it would allow Steve to flourish and become one of the most enlightened masters in the style of Gōjū-ryū. But first there was one thing, a tournament! Steve needed to take away someone else's right to win. He needed to take it from them. He would learn that things a man dreams of sometimes come at untold cost.

Chapter 2 - Whispers

The timing couldn't be worse. The tournament Sensei Mike had enrolled Steve in was only two weeks away. An event open to all styles of martial arts from anywhere in Australia. A national title!

There was a complication. Training for the event was not the problem. Steve was impeccable. His two years of single mindedness and commitment to his art was obvious. He was seventeen years old and had the muscularity and fitness most men would never enjoy in their entire lives. He was more than physically prepared to fight, he was made for it. The complication was the upcoming school exams, which were set to finish a day before the tournament began. The exams were weighted towards eighty percent of his end of year result and facilitated admission to university. That they were somewhat important was not totally lost on Steve.

Steve had coasted through his final year of schooling. He wasn't doing badly but his mind was clearly elsewhere. His martial arts training rewarded him with wins on a nightly basis and studies would only possibly reward him one day, if he got enough marks, if he studied the right course at university and then if he found the right job. Naturally his Macedonian father wanted him to be a doctor or a lawyer as if to counter the millennium of peasant farmers in his bloodline back in the old country.

Steve had indeed become smarter over the last two years of training. His mind was a sponge and he learned to sense everything about his environment. The training helped him in every way. Everyone could see it. Even his father!

He started furiously swotting for the exams. There wasn't enough time - but, to Steve's surprise, his training gave him a clarity of mind and focus so he could work his way through the syllabuses and gain the necessary understanding to tackle the exams. In fact, he did better than he expected in the exams. He was focused enough to complete them competently but his spirit was gearing itself up for battle!

After the exams, Steve sat down for yet another talk with his father. They used to be more akin to lectures, but as Steve grew older, the lectures became more a battle of minds. They would often talk until late at night about the future and about life back in Macedonia. Steve was indeed his father's son in many ways. He had the same ability to communicate with people and his strength was an obvious inheritance although he didn't have quite the same rage as his father. Perhaps the alcohol was a distinguishing factor. Steve abhorred any drugs and thought alcohol was just as wicked as any other substance people would consume to reduce the clarity of their minds.

After talking about the old country (yet again) with his father, Steve was curious about the family name, Nedelkin. "Dad, would we be able to trace our family history?" Steve asked. His father just waved the notion away. He then explained that the ending of the name was a clue about the difficulty of tracing anything. Having "in" as the ending of a name in Macedonian is indicative of an ancestor being a "domazet" which means a son in law who takes on the family name of the wife's family. This often happened when the wife's family didn't have a son to carry on the name. So if Jack married Jill Smith in this example, Jack would then become Jack Smith<u>in</u>. The "Nedel" part was even less thrilling. This probably meant some ancestor was born on a Sunday as "Nedela" means Sunday. Steve's father laughed and said one of his aunties was called "Dosta" which means "enough". This was fair enough as she was the sixth daughter! "Besides, we were Ottoman slaves for five hundred years and then the Greeks destroyed our records anyway. Our lives begin here in Australia. Now it's up to you to make our name something to remember," he said.

Steve asked, "But what about the mountains with our name?" Steve's dad replied, "Ahhh, they're just myths mixed in with a bunch of half truths. But everyone knew our people back in the old country by the nickname Tsareto which is a cute way to say King. So I'd always joke about my royal lineage when I was harvesting or collecting the cow shit for fuel!" It seemed the further Steve wanted to go back, the worse it became for his lineage. "Shit! If I win this tournament, it's gonna all begin from here," he thought, as he allowed his mind to explore the thrill of such a thought.

Steve's father shared one of his own childhood memories with his son.

> "Stefche, Let me tell you about something that happened to me when I was a kid back in Macedonia. The Greeks called it the Greek civil war. But our people knew it as the Macedonian war for independence and our people were fighting for their freedom. A bunch of powerful men in suits decided to split Macedonia between Greece, Bulgaria and Serbia in 1913. Our people went from almost five hundred years of slavery under the Ottoman Turks to end up copping it for decades from the Greeks. At least the Turks let us speak our language!

> "Anyway, after the second world war, Greece was a mess and our people thought they might have a chance to control their own fates. But nobody gave a shit about our

*people. They were terrible times. So many children were
sent out of the region to live in other countries while
the madness was happening. As an orphan, nobody really
gave a shit about me, so I just hid in the mountains. I was
six years old and a little burned orphan girl showed me
which plants I could eat. I'd come down from the mountains sometimes and try to steal some food at night. It was
the scariest time in my life. I'd see these red eyes glowing at
night and I felt like they were always looking for me.*

*"The Greeks or Americans were using napalm on us. It
was the first time it was ever used. They knew people were
hiding in the mountains and they used the napalm to
kill or flush out the enemy in the mountains. Half of the
mountain range was set on fire in seconds and the Greek
army was coming up the mountain to pick off the poor
bastards trying to get away from the fire. As I was running down the mountain, a Greek soldier caught me and
dragged me down to his camp. The Captain wanted me to
tell him where others were still in hiding. I was young
and stupid and I told him to piss off. Even though I was
young, I knew what happened to traitors. I could never let
my people down. The soldiers took turns threatening and
slapping me. Finally, I was on the ground and one soldier
aimed his gun right at me. I don't know what happened.
I was so scared! I screamed as loud as I could and something strange happened. The entire mountains trembled
and they lit up a bright orange colour for a brief moment. I
don't know if it was a bomb nearby or something else. But
the soldiers ran away from me and not much after, I ran
away from Macedonia.*

"That changed me forever and, when I became older, all I

ever wanted to do was have children of my own and pro-
tect and love them and save them from ever having to deal
with the shit that I had to deal with. I will always sup-
port you son. I'm so proud of you. I know you're gonna do
well."

Steve had never heard the story before and he was finally able to
gain a fraction more insight into where his father's pain and rage
had originated.

The night before the fight, Sensei Mike cancelled the training
and invited Steve to come over to his place. Cancelling training
was unheard of. It simply never happened and reinforced how
important Sensei felt the tournament was. Steve wasn't particularly nervous about the tournament up until that point, but
that all changed with the invitation! It was the first time Steve
had actually been inside Sensei's house. Steve would often visit
the house and offer to mow the lawns for his Sensei and ask if he
could assist in any other way. But he never ever thought about
going inside as he felt it was a violation of their relationship
founded on duty and admiration and respect.

Sensei Mike invited Steve to sit down in his living room. Steve
bowed as he entered Sensei's home in the same way as he would
when he entered the dojo. He was overwhelmed by the sim-
plicity of the room. There was no television to be seen anywhere. There were the most exquisite prints and paintings of
beautiful Japanese landscapes which seemed too nice for the
walls they adorned. There were some little Daruma dolls which
looked like nice souvenirs from Japan. Books were everywhere
and the titles didn't even seem to align with the kind of man
Sensei Mike was in Steve's eye. Books on Shinto and Taoism,
Japanese Kami, Nikola Tesla, a few about Kung Fu styles, books
on spiritual transcendence, another with pictures of puppies

.... "What", Steve exclaimed as he noticed what seemed out of order, "I can understand why you have the puppy book, but what on Earth are you doing with the Kung Fu books?" Steve exclaimed.

Sensei Mike laughed. He said "One day, in order to become the true Master of yourself, you will have to grasp the essence of the Five Ancestors of Shaolin and learn the real Kung Fu. You might consider going to China in the same way our spiritual fathers of Gōjū-ryū did over one hundred years ago." Steve was confused, he thought nothing could ever be better than Gōjū-ryū. Sensei Mike made it clear that a true warrior is simply on a path to enlightenment. A warrior must master himself and a pilgrimage to China under the tutelage of a great master would fill any gaps in the warrior's development. Sensei Mike reminded Steve he would need to learn more under the Okinawan greats first and he would know when he would be ready to receive the path to China.

Steve was flabbergasted. For the first time he saw Sensei Mike in a new light. He asked him: "Have you been to China and, errr, completed your path?" Sensei Mike replied: , "My sensei said, a person never completes his path and, if they're lucky, they might receive clues about their destiny and truly righteous path. Anyway, enough about that. My path was cut short a few years ago and maybe I've lost my chance to find it in this life!" Steve needed to know why and demanded answers. Sensei was his hero and he couldn't fathom why he hadn't pursued the path with the same determination he'd shown through every utterance and action since Steve had met him.

Steve saw Sensei Mike change in that moment. He wasn't the superhuman Steve looked up to and aspired to become. He was normal and not unlike his own father. Just another man trying to make sense of the world. Sensei looked older and less assured in that moment. As if some memory was taunting him and running its blade across him, just enough to draw blood. At any point, the blade would surely kill him. Sensei Mike said, "Yeah okay, I'll explain why, but first we must drink tea."

Sensei brought the tea into the room and looked extremely sombre. Following etiquette was not difficult for Steve. Sensei Mike had already shared the necessary rituals with the senior students in his classes. Knowing when to bow, when to consume the traditional sweets served with the tea, how to pick up the bowl, which hand to use when placing the bowl and the precise ninety degrees clockwise turn of the bowl. The occasion was extremely serious and poignant precisely until Steve realised Sensei Mike was wearing a T-Shirt emblazoned with the cutest little puppies you could ever see. He couldn't believe he hadn't noticed it before. Perhaps it was the solemnity of the occasion or merely because he was actually inside his Sensei's home. It wasn't often he would joke with his Sensei, but seeing this huge man with his long red hair, muscles, vascularity and exquisite tattoos juxtaposed against the cutest puppy T-Shirt one could possibly imagine - well, it was too much for Steve! He laughed out loud and almost dropped his tea. Sensei immediately understood why Steve was laughing and briefly smirked as he washed the tea utensils and returned them to their appropriate place.

Having concluded the ceremony, Sensei asked Steve if he liked his T-Shirt and whether everyone should wear them to Karate classes from now instead of their Gi. Steve wasn't used to Sensei being humorous and began to wonder if he had offended him. He apologised, "I'm sorry Sensei, it's a cool T-shirt but I think it's probably best if it's only worn at home, I think it would probably be better if we just keep wearing our Gi at the dojo." Sensei Mike laughed louder at Steve's serious reply and said "Perhaps this would be better." He took off his T-Shirt and it was as though the room shrank and Sensei Mike grew in every direction. The full picture of his tattoos was revealed for the first time to Steve. His body was in fact a work of art, tattoos full of intricacies, exquisite colours and, on the middle of his chest, that tattoo of a severed head with a knife in its mouth. It was utterly gruesome, offensive, frightening and yet Steve couldn't look away from it. He was gobsmacked. It felt like minutes before anything was said.

Sensei Mike broke the shock of silence in the room,

"You've seen some of my tattoos before and now you see the rest. You asked earlier about my path. I haven't told anyone before but I might as well confess to you, my best student, in the hope you never make the same mistakes and learn from my tragedy. These tattoos are my Japan. They are my pinnacle, my regret, my love, my despair, my brother, my enemy, my shame, my destiny, my failure, my direction, my undoing, my win, my loss .... my life.

"I was lost before Japan found me. I was like you before I went to war - eager, optimistic and full of determination. But the war changed me. I did terrible things in the name of war and I lost myself in Vietnam. I couldn't accept what I did in the name of a war I didn't need to be part of. I came back to Australia and was hated for it by the people I cared about. The country rejected me and I just left it all behind. Karate was once my only source of joy so I thought I could go to Japan and try to find some happiness. I did, for a while. It was idyllic in so many ways. Okinawa was beautiful and uncomplicated. My Sensei was amazing, a diligent and thoughtful man. He mastered the gentle way and found his path.

"I had a training partner, Hiro, and although we didn't

have much in common to begin with, we both honed our art together and became the closest of friends. Hiro was as tall as me with a lean physique. Whatever extra strength and muscularity I had to my advantage, he countered with speed and grace. He was so charismatic, liked and feared in equal proportions. He could have been anything with his charming demeanour and intelligence but he was always attracted to the dark side. His associates or friends never seemed to look appropriate around him. When I arrived, I think he enjoyed the temporary change of scenery in his life. He enjoyed the purity of our training and our idealistic pursuits during those times. I'm sure they were an uplifting distraction at a formative time in his life.

"He introduced me to his sister, Chiasa, and I fell for her the moment I saw her. He told me how they were left to fend for themselves from an early age as their parents died in a car accident when they were young. He grew to love me as a brother but told me he could never accept me as a brother in law. Too many Japanese conventions would be violated and his sense of honour forbade it. Love being love, I had no choice but to pursue Chiasa. Her name meant "a thousand mornings" and every day I saw her it was a blessing in my life. I felt if I could have those thousand mornings with her, all my past would be washed away and replaced with her gentle beauty and warmth.

"Hiro and I progressed through our ranks at precisely the same pace. We were training partners and brothers in our Gōjū-ryū family. My secret from my dear brother was the love that was blossoming between Chiasa and myself. I was willing to do anything to endear myself to my brother Hiro. I thought that time would be my friend and he would accept me as his brother in law. He would call me in the middle of the night and ask me to help him drop off some boxes. I would help without question. Sometimes we needed to sort out some lowlife thugs who were harassing some important people of Okinawa. I did all of this without question. Nothing was questioned. I thought he would understand that I was necessary in his life and his sister would be blessed to have me as a husband.

"By this stage we were both extremely competent in our martial arts. I was the fittest I'd ever been and we were both so finely tuned with each other's abilities that nobody dared to question us on our beloved Okinawan island. It was then that Hiro introduced me to Kumicho. It didn't take me long to figure out we were already serving him and he was the leader of the most powerful Okinawan Yakuza clan. I knew precisely what was happening and I was powerless to stop it, I was being inducted into this mob of gangsters with my brother Hiro. I just couldn't disappoint Hiro, I was almost ready to ask him if I could marry his sister again. But it just wasn't the time to create any new tensions. I gave myself to Kumicho willingly.

"The same feelings of war dread started to enter my spirit. I had almost forgotten how damaged I was thanks to the warm love of Chiasa. I did terrible things to undeserving people and it seemed my body wore the mark of all of those terrible deeds. Each time I thought my shame couldn't be worse, I was rewarded with another tattoo. My body became a diary documenting my atrocities. By the time this severed head, the Namakubi, was tattooed on my chest I was the same war machine I was back in Vietnam and my karma was permanently damaged. Yet this beautiful *woman still loved me, she believed in my goodness, she welcomed me and washed my soul time and time again.*

"My Sensei was less forgiving. He saw me for the man I had become (again) and it was not long before both Hiro and I were banished from the dojo in the most degrading way. We were both stripped of our fifth dan grades and our names were wiped from all records held at the dojo.

"As anyone who knows the ways of the Yakuza, my devotion to Kumicho was absolute, I had no choice. Nothing was more important than Kumicho and everything else was secondary in comparison to Kumicho. I was resourceful, capable and useful as a foreigner in my often specialised role within my clan. Hiro and I became quite important within the clan and we both had managed to retain all of our fingers, such was our strict devotion to Kumicho. Others in our clan were less lucky. Offending Kumicho was a grave matter and surrendering a finger or two was often necessary for atonement and to affirm loyalty.

"My world crashed around me when I was ordered to kill my Sensei. My Sensei had been causing problems for Kumicho by undermining his authority in the region and making the drug issues on my beloved island prominent to the local government. That lovely man who showed me the beauty in our martial art. The man who showed how a pure life can create harmony and positive energy with the power to heal. I knew I couldn't do it but I bowed without hesitation to Kumicho.

"What would I do? I'd call Hiro and tell him. I thought I would have his support and we would work out a solution. If I was truthful to myself, Hiro and I were not as close as before. We were both capable men who did terrible things. I was doing things I wasn't proud of but I was robotic in comparison with Hiro. He seemed to relish the power and pain he inflicted on the recipients of his poisonous ways. We were equals in our Karate but he had surpassed me in his desire to inflict misery and seemed to grow with every act of evil.

"I was shocked with his reaction. I was sure he'd support me. Our Sensei used to be a breath of fresh air in both of our lives and always tried to shine the light on our paths. I was positive he'd understand why I couldn't do this. Instead Hiro grabbed me and questioned my allegiance to Kumicho. He pulled me close and spoke in the old Okinawan language when he told me he would kill both me and Sensei if I couldn't do it. He said 'because we are friends and brothers, I will pretend you didn't disrespect Kumicho. Just do it and don't question Kumicho's authority again! That old man deserves to die for what he took away from us anyway.'

"I knew I wasn't going to do it. I wanted to leave, I needed to warn Sensei and I needed to hurry Chiasa away from this madness. I rushed to Chiasa and told her my intentions. My sweet love wept so deeply. She was ready to flee with me but she knew she would never be able to see her beloved brother again. I went and gathered a few necessities and took Chiasa with me to warn Sensei. I was uneasy, something wasn't right. If I searched a moment

longer within myself, I would have known Hiro was trac-
ing my every step. When I reached my dojo, my Sensei was
standing alone in the middle of the dojo looking calm and
peaceful as always. It gave me a warm feeling of comfort
just being in his presence again. I was holding Chiasa's
hand and pulling her along with me as we were running
inside. I managed to quickly bow as I crossed the threshold
to the dojo and, as I raised my head, I was horrified to see
Hiro was already there with a gun pointing at our Sensei.
Hiro looked crazed, his eyes were black and his voice was
screeching as he spoke in a combination of old Okinawan
and Japanese and every word was nothing more than hat-
red and pure evil. I knew that look, war had taught me one
thing, this man was too far gone and somebody was going
to die that day. I shouted at Hiro to draw his attention to
me and hopefully stop those possessed demonic ramblings
of his. He turned his pistol towards me and Sensei began
to whisper to Hiro. It was a whisper but it was as though
he was summoning the wind around him. We were all
inside this vortex and Sensei drew the attention of Hiro
once again. The gentleness had left his eyes and was re-
placed with a look I had never seen on his face before. In
fact, it was a look I had never seen anywhere before. His
gaze was fixed upon Hiro and it felt like he grabbed us
all by our souls when he commanded Hiro with his deep
whispers .... 'Hiroooo, today you choose to show your-
self? Today you get to decide? People who love you must
see the path you choose for yourself? Who is your master,
Hiro? Who will you kill first? I am ready to die, but are you
ready to kill? Leave now and find your true and just path.'

"*The whispered vortex shook me also and I felt my own*
guilt well up within while Hiro's ramblings also ceased.
Perhaps he also felt guilty for a moment. This man

had shown us nothing but compassion and gave himself willingly to us. And this was his reward? But Hiro managed to collect his thoughts, he stepped forward towards Sensei and fired. In the same instance, Sensei whispered something incoherent and performed what was the simplest move in our style and the vortex seemed to amplify and somehow the impossible happened. The bullet missed Sensei. Hiro seemed as surprised as myself and Chiasa were. I launched myself at Hiro and managed to kick the gun from his hand. We fought for an eternity. He was faster before, when he was training every day and wasn't drinking as much, and my attacks managed to find him a few times. I was always a bit stronger than Hiro but his rage helped balance the ledger this time. I had never seen him like this before. I attempted a take down so I could control him and talk to him yet again, but he managed to evade me and jumped completely over me to reach Sensei's family sword. A beautiful and deadly heirloom which had been in his family for more than 400 years.

"Chiasa ran crying and pleading towards Hiro and I ran to pull her back. My arms managed to wrap around Chiasa and I started pulling her back. Hiro turned around with the blade in his hand looking at me with blind rage. He didn't even see his sister in front of me as he moved forward. Before he realised, the blade had pierced his sister through her heart and pierced my lung.

I fell to the ground on my back with my beautiful Chiasa lying on top of me as she drew her last breath with Sensei's sword lodged in both our bodies. I don't remember what happened after this. But I vaguely recall the whispering vortex and Hiro's shrieks as my world faded.

"I was hidden away in recovery when Sensei came to see me. My lung was doing fine but my spirit was broken. Sensei had been checking on me for weeks, he would place his hands on my chest and whisper words I never could quite understand. I could feel his purity of spirit enter me through his hands, it humbled and shamed me. He told me he had tried to summon Luohan (one of the Shaolin Kung Fu Five Ancestors) to counter Hiro's demonic rage. Sensei was despondent and equally inconsolable about the death of Chiasa as I was but he also felt the same about Hiro. He said, 'I have not fully mastered the Luohan and I'm sure I damaged Hiro during the summoning. And I am damaged now also. They are inside me and are growing. I feel them.' None of this made sense to me and none of it mattered. All of my clan would try to kill me and there was nothing keeping me there. I soon left Japan. Perhaps now you understand more about why I lost the path and why I can never return there to finish my training."

Steve was not ready to hear his Sensei's life story. It was too much. Yakuza, Luohan, Chiasa, Hiro .... Whispering Vortex??? It was all too much for him and he remained speechless. Sensei Mike said, "That's enough for one day and maybe a lifetime! Steve, your first real test is tomorrow at the tournament and it's time for one last thing before you should go home and rest." Sensei Mike walked over to the kitchen benchtop and returned with a large envelope and gave it to Steve. "What's this?" Steve asked. Sensei Mike looked quite serious and said, "Well, it's definitely nothing to worry about, please open it now." Steve carefully opened the envelope and extracted the contents. A very official document or certificate written entirely in Japanese, an airplane ticket to Japan and another smaller envelope addressed in Japanese. Steve could recognise a few characters but none of it made sense. He asked his Sensei what it all meant.

Sensei Mike said, "Steve, I've never had a student like you and I have never seen someone with your ability to learn such concepts with the ease you have shown. Your path must continue in Okinawa. You must find my Sensei and beg for his instruction. The small envelope contains a letter to my Sensei pleading for him to accept you. I have also given you a certificate for your grade. Please show it to my Sensei. It means nothing in terms of your formal level. In fact, it is a certificate confirming I have nothing else to teach you. You have learned all I have and taken my best instructions, I am honoured to have you as my student and I know you will be a great man in the future. You've helped me cleanse my spirit. I'm finally ready to try again to find my path. I am very grateful to you for this. I will organise my affairs here and then go to China and try to find the way of the Five Ancestors.

"Steve, If you want to wait and go to Japan after University, I understand and we can change the ticket. But I just think now is your time while you have such momentum in your training. My suggestion is for you to go as soon as possible. I expect you will win the tournament tomorrow. I'd almost prefer it if you lose because you might learn something in the process, but I can't imagine anyone equal to your ability. Please go home and rest and be ready for some fun tomorrow! Actually, there's no way I want you to lose! Oh, and take this Daruma doll for good luck and perseverance."

Steve bowed deeply to his Sensei before accepting the gifts but Sensei Mike would have none of it. He hugged Steve and they both thanked each other. Steve had no idea why Sensei Mike thanked him but he did notice a lightness in his master that he had never seen before. Steve ran home without even touching the ground.

This night was a revelation. Steve had absolutely no chance of sleeping that night. There was a whole new dimension to Sensei Mike that Steve could never have imagined. There was a future in Japan that Steve had not anticipated. Numerous thoughts played through Steve's mind, "How can I leave my father alone? How can I leave my friends and dojo brothers? But Sensei Mike believes in me and says now is the best time! Let me think about it after I win the tournament! But I want to go! But Dad?"

Chapter 3 - The Tournament

I t was 6:00AM, Steve had barely slept all night. So many thoughts competed for attention. Sensei Mike's tragedies, the upcoming fights, Japan .... too much to think about and he needed to focus. His uniform, mouthguard and groin guard were ready. Most importantly, his Walkman had fresh batteries and his favourite mixtape was ready. It was 1987 but Steve was still lost somewhere in the 1970s with his choice of music. From Deep Purple to Led Zeppelin to Black Sabbath and Free, if there wasn't a guitar tearing it apart with some wicked licks out of a Marshall stack, then it surely wasn't worth listening to! He did make one concession to the 1980's though, a new band called Guns & Roses had taken the world by storm and he could feel the adrenaline rushing every time he heard the guitar solo in Sweet Child O' Mine. The mixtape was masterfully created and no matter where the tape was up to, a blistering guitar solo was always nearby and ready to prime Steve for a fight!

Steve's father usually slept in on Saturday mornings. His working week was tough and he usually needed the entire weekend to recover. But he was also awake on this occasion. Steve sat down with his father and told him about some of the things Sensei Mike had done. He was careful about what he told his father. Steve's Dad didn't like men with tattoos, he thought they were all criminals. And he certainly didn't like anyone who had that much influence over his son. But he had a healthy respect for Sensei Mike. He saw how his son had transformed under his tutelage. Steve wasn't ready to tell his father about Japan. He thought perhaps after he won the tournament his father would see his son's potential and let him pursue his dream.

Steve's father talked about some fights he had in his youth, "It wasn't easy coming to Australia back in my days. I was picked on because I couldn't speak the language when I first got here. But I didn't take any shit from anyone, even as a kid." He was convinced the mountains made him strong back in Macedonia. He never lost a fight. He looked Steve in the eyes and said "I don't know what that tattooed hippie has taught you, but listen to me, you've got my blood and you're as strong as a bull. Control their balance and keep hitting them until you only see the white of their eyes!" Steve couldn't actually disagree with his father's approach. He thought to himself, "Sensei Mike always talked about taking away the opponent's balance. Everyone's on the same page today. It's gonna be a great day!"

Steve and his father could barely eat. A bit of toast and some juice. Steve's dad insisted on a drink together before they left. The drink was a Macedonian staple called Rakija. It probably wrecked more lives in the Balkans than any war in the region. They toasted to each other's health "Na Zdravye" and Steve's dad smiled and shouted "Stefo Tsareto" or Steven the (little) King! The liquid fire burned Steve all the way down and, according to his father, he was finally ready for battle. Steve hated the alcohol, but he enjoyed bonding with his father.

With his Walkman playing his favourite music and his Dad driving, Steve could feel the adrenaline pumping through his body. He was completely ready to fight! Ritchie Blackmore, Jimmy Page, Tony Iommi, Paul Kossoff and Slash all agreed. Their guitar playing was the soundtrack for the mayhem Steve was about to unleash on his opponents.

They arrived and quickly found Sensei Mike and proceeded to the registration area. The tournament organisers had a problem. This was an adult's tournament and Steve would not turn eighteen until a few days after the tournament. Technically he was underage and he would need authority from a parent or guardian in order to fight. That was solved quickly as Steve's father authorised his son. There wasn't much else to do but get ready to fight!

Numerous martial arts clubs representing all styles from all around Australia gathered in their groups around the stadium. There were more than two hundred fighters registered for the event. Formalities were completed quickly and it wasn't long before the fighting was ready to begin. Steve had a couple of his club brothers who were also competing and they all sat together with Sensei Mike wondering who they might face in the first round.

A late arrival entered the stadium. It was a group of ten fighters all dressed in black and their trainer who was wearing a hooded top and sunglasses. They were all noticeably muscular, with one even more muscular fighter who was as tall as his hooded trainer. Compared to the others in the stadium, they looked infinitely more serious! Even Sensei Mike seemed to reposition himself trying to get a look at them. Steve managed to read their club symbol. A simple Kanji character meaning Sakura or cherry blossom. Steve, perhaps to comfort himself and his team, said "Look at those losers, other teams are called Karate Warriors and Kung Fu Dragons and Taekwondo Knights, and those guys in black are the Cherry Blossoms, hahaha." Sensei Mike quickly changed the mood and reminded everyone, "Cherry blossoms are a very powerful symbol to the Japanese. They symbolise many things but often mean 'Life is short' and have a whole lot more meaning than some of those other silly names." He pulled up his sleeve to remind his team of the cherry blossoms tattooed on his arm. The black team was already in Steve's head and Steve's father also noticed them and pointed them out to Steve with a simple raise of his eyebrows and tilt of his head toward them.

Three of Sensei Mike's team were to fight and, as luck would have it, Jake was in the very first fight. Jake was almost Sensei Mike's age and had practiced other martial arts before starting with Sensei Mike. He was a strong man and good fighter but sometimes he would lapse back into his older styles which were inferior to Sensei's style. He was up against one of the Cherry Blossoms! Steve and Sensei Mike were both eager to see how the "Cherry" style would measure against their style. Judges sat in each corner of the designated fight area. They held two flags of colours which matched the belts given to each contestant. Jake was given a blue belt to wear and the "cherry" was given a red belt. The referee in the middle gave clear instructions;

"This is full contact, no gloves are worn, kicking to the head is allowed but punches to the head are not, no kicks to the groin and fighting must stop as soon as the referee yells stop. You will fight two 4 minute rounds with a 1 minute break in between."

The fighters understood and bowed to the referee and took their positions. The referee instructed the fighters to bow to each other. Jake assumed the normal bow and his opponent who was simply called "Cherry Blossom 7" did an unusual bow. He was already in his fighting stance but his bow was nothing more than a momentary drop of his hands to his sides while lowering his head. His eyes never left Jake. The referee ordered the fight to begin and Jake was amazing. He charged forward with a perfect front kick which crashed through "Cherry 7's" defences which seemed to surprise him. He bounced right out of the designated area and the judges in the corners held up the blue flags to unanimously award Jake the point. Jake's entire team was elated and even Sensei Mike seemed to look a little more relaxed. The fighters were brought back to their starting positions and ordered to fight again. Jake attempted the same front kick and this time Cherry 7 simply moved to the side and did a roundhouse kick straight to Jake's head. The judges all raised their red flags to acknowledge the point. Jake was a strong man and he managed to stay upright but he looked a little shaky. At that point, Cherry 7 was well aware of Jake's condition and proceeded to pummel him with a fury of punches. Jake seemed to lapse back into his old styles and lost the ability to absorb and deflect. The fight finished quickly, Cherry 7 prevailed and was awarded the win when Jake could no longer continue.

Jake returned to the group and apologised to his entire team. He knew he let the team down. Sensei Mike comforted Jake briefly and said "You did well in the beginning Jake, that fighter was very good. Don't be too hard on yourself, learn from this." Jake was despondent and the team definitely lost a little enthusiasm and confidence for a few minutes. Steve put his headphones back on and tried to regain his focus. It didn't help seeing the Cherry Blossoms dominating the ensuing fights.

Soon enough it was Max's turn. He was an excellent fighter. He only started training one year earlier and was showing great promise. He was a Polish boy from the same neighbourhood as Steve. Even though he was a couple of years older than Steve, he was Steve's younger brother in the dojo. They got on very well, even outside of the dojo. The Polish and Macedonian boys were often surprised to learn their languages shared many similar words. Steve would jokingly call Max the "Crazy German" when he wanted to annoy him during sparring sessions. Nobody understood better than Steve how upsetting it was to have doubt thrown at you about your own identity.

Max's kata was not so well developed and Steve wondered if Max's fighting form would hold up when placed under pressure.

He needn't have worried. He was fighting against one of the "Karate Warrior" fighters. The fight went the full two rounds only because Max was enjoying it too much. His skills were far too advanced for his opponent. Even though he had only been training for one year, he fought like a seasoned professional. He finished the fight without even a scratch. Sensei Mike, surprisingly, was not completely pleased with Max's effort. He said "you wasted techniques on your opponent and you were lucky he wasn't fitter. If you started to get tired, he might have actually had a chance to beat you." He still patted him on the back and said "Well done though, a very good effort, especially for someone who has only trained for one year!" Steve was ecstatic for his "Crazy Polak" dojo brother.

They were all sitting together in a group when a Cherry Blossom fighter was up. He was Cherry Blossom 1 and he was scheduled to fight against one of the Taekwondo fighters. Both were tall men and looked equally matched in muscularity. This fight was going to be fun! The fight started and the Taekwondo guy was amazing. He jumped in the air and completed a perfect spinning kick. For any martial artist, it was a delight to watch. His foot landed perfectly on Cherry 1's face and knocked him straight on top of one of the corner judges. The chair broke into pieces and the judge needed some medical attention. Cherry 1 didn't look too bad after the hit. In fact he looked the same as before the fight started. He was menacing. The Cherry Blossom trainer moved out of the shadows for a moment and motioned over to Cherry 1 to whisper in his ear. It was still impossible to get a good look at the trainer and it started to irk Sensei Mike a little. He thought it was somewhat disrespectful to be covering his head and wearing sunglasses inside the stadium. The fight was ready to start again. The referee started the fight and the Taekwondo guy went straight in for another kick. He chose to deploy a roundhouse kick. Cherry 1 immediately stepped in towards his opponent, blocked the kick as if to swat a fly and punched his opponent in the chest. It didn't look particularly amazing but everyone in the stadium heard the hit. The reaction was immense. He seemed to knock the will to fight out of his opponent. He dropped to the ground clutching his chest and, unable to breathe, he was carried off on a stretcher to the medical room for attention. Cherry 1 proceeded to the next round.

After a few more fights it was Steve's turn and, if normal people had butterflies in their stomachs when they were nervous, then Steve had an entire butterfly farm inside his stomach. He had so much nervous energy and Sensei Mike grabbed him to help him centre himself. He said "Steve, this is just another lesson, you'll be fine. Just don't stray from our way. If you follow what I've taught you, you'll be fine. The other guys didn't follow our way fully. I know you will."

Steve was up against a Cherry Blossom. Cherry Blossom 2 was almost as big as Cherry 1. Jake and Max both encouraged Steve to finish him fast. Steve was impressed with every single one of the Cherry Blossoms. They were militant in the way they dealt with their opponents. The precision and power they displayed looked like they were trained by Sensei Mike himself! Steve managed to squeeze in a quick listen to one more inspirational guitar solo by Ritchie Blackmore of Deep Purple and had "Smoke on the Water" playing in his head before making his way to the fight area. Sensei Mike walked with him and Steve saw his father following closely behind his Sensei. Steve said "Dad, I'm not sure if you're allowed to come to the fight area. I think it's only for the fighters and instructors." His father surveyed the area and looked at Sensei Mike and said "Son, I'm pretty sure nobody would dare try to stop me!" Sensei Mike smiled and seemed to enjoy the obvious love and connection between father and son.

Cherry 2 was closely followed by his hooded trainer. It looked as if his trainer was floating next to him and whispering instructions. Previously the trainer always stayed back away from his fighters and away from the strong lights, but this time it seemed as though he also wanted to be part of the fight! Sensei Mike noticed this also and seemed to grow increasingly uneasy and Steve was feeling the tension from every angle.

It was time to fight. Steve had been training so hard and Gōjū-ryū had been his waking thought every day since he started .... and that was after dreaming about it every night! Steve lined up and Cherry 2 faced him with a menacing glare. Steve, in contrast, returned a humble look and what may have even been a hint of a smile. There was no point in giving his opponent any indication of his intent. If Cherry 2 knew Steve's intent, he would have long gone out of the stadium already! They bowed to the referee and then to each other. Cherry 2 didn't even lower his arms from his fighting stance, he just bowed his head ever so slightly at Steve as if only to comply but certainly not respect the rules.

The fight started and Steve unleashed in a way that shocked everyone in his club, including Sensei Mike. They had never seen such ferocity in Steve before. Steve was always kind and respectful in the club. He meted out his attacks with precision and humility in the dojo. There was no point in getting angry with his fellow students and there certainly wasn't ever going to be any sign of disrespect to Sensei Mike. But the fight was different, Steve allowed himself to unleash that power within him. He charged forward with nothing more than a simple side-kick but his kiai, the short shout made during an attacking move, created a virtual tidal wave. A normal kiai would come from the diaphragm and attempt to connect the martial artist's energy to his technique. In this case, it seemed to come from somewhere even deeper and everybody in the entire stadium reacted to it. Steve even looked like he was riding on that tidal wave when he kicked Cherry 2. Steve's opponent didn't just fall backwards. He was propelled into the stadium seating where all the spectators were. The referee stopped the fight and waited to see if Cherry 2 could come back to the contest. He was helped back into the arena and looked pale, yet stable enough. The referee gestured in a way to indicate the fighters should return to their starting positions. Steve turned away from his opponent and, at precisely the same time, he heard the Cherry trainer spitting words he actually understood from Sensei Mike. These were some old Okinawan words that Sensei would joke and say when they were sparring together. But in this case, they sounded utterly evil and almost demonic. Before he realised what was happening, he heard a shriek and felt a slap to the side of his face and he couldn't see out of one eye. His opponent had attacked him from behind, before the fight had even recommenced. It was highly illegal and all the corner judges immediately thrust both flags in the air in a crossed formation. Cherry 2 was disqualified for his action.

Meanwhile, Steve was on the ground cupping his eye with his hand. The audience started to boo him, they thought perhaps he was dramatising the event a little too much. He stood up with his hand over his eye to see the audience turn on him. By that stage he had collected his thoughts and the pain had subsided. He removed his hand covering his eye and then became increasingly concerned after the audience's boos and hisses turned into oohs and ahhs. He saw all the blood in his hand and realised his face was covered in blood. His eyebrow had been split apart.

He was taken to the medics immediately. They laid him down and cleaned up the wound. He heard two people nearby talking and one said stitches would be required. He then heard another say he wouldn't be allowed to fight if he had stitches. Steve screamed "no stitches, no stitches!" He needed to fight and redeem himself! The medics had a solution, they taped the wound together and bandaged him up and said he would be able to continue to fight.

Steve was truly devastated. He had too much to prove and

wasn't allowed the chance to show his sensei and his father how strong and capable he was. The combination of adrenaline and shock and disappointment was too much for him. He couldn't return to his group and he couldn't even look at his father. He felt ashamed. He shouldn't have turned away from his opponent and he should have understood that trainer's hateful intent immediately.

He sat quietly in the auditorium and quietly cried to himself for a moment. He couldn't understand why he was feeling so bad. The last time he felt so bad and empty inside was when his mother died. Such a long time ago. It was almost as terrible to him and he couldn't understand why.

A little girl whom he hadn't even noticed before poked him in the leg. She was sitting on his right hand side next to him. She asked him "What's wrong, why are you crying?" Steve looked at her, initially he saw only the left side of her face and remarked to himself "So cute, she looks like a little angel!" She had blond hair and was tiny and her voice sounded like a little bird to Steve. He summoned a smile and said "Oh forget it, I'm just a little upset with myself, I should've done better and I shouldn't be injured now and I think I let everyone down ….." So many words fell out of Steve's mouth. The little girl kept poking at his leg and Steve stopped. She said "Listen, I saw you fight and you looked so strong. Everyone said you looked like you would win the entire tournament. You have no reason to cry. I cried for years when this happened to me." She turned her face fully towards Steve and showed her burn marks on her face. It almost looked like she had been branded. The entire right hand side was disfigured and certainly not pretty as on her left side.

She continued, "I cried because this really hurt, my whole family cried because they couldn't help me. I was trying to help my family and I got burned. It really hurt a lot. It still hurts. So I don't think you should cry. I think you should be proud of how strong you were in that battle of good versus evil. And I think the people that love you will cry if you cry. So please stop. I've always thought .... I mean, I think you're going to be great!" Steve was so humbled and he felt completely elevated from his physical self for a brief moment. He had grasped this little girl's true beauty. Something that would last forever in his mind. He told her she was right and thanked her profusely.

The last time he felt so comforted was when his mother was still alive. It felt exactly the same as his mother's warm words of encouragement when he was a child. It was so beautiful that it felt like they were in a bubble of serenity for an eternity, even though it was no more than a minute. She helped him more than perhaps she even realised. He asked her name, she said "I am Temyana and I can't wait to see you win this tournament!" Steve was genuinely pleased to meet this little angel. He said goodbye and started heading back. He turned around looking for little Temyana and she was already gone. He went to his father, sensei and teammates and they welcomed him warmly. They told him how amazing his kick was and they had never seen him show so much ferocity. Steve felt so grateful to that little girl and kept turning around to find her in the audience but could never spot her.

The Cherry Blossoms were either winning or cheating (or both) and they were the ones to fear on a number of levels. Cherry 1 had won two more fights with nothing more than a punch in each of them. Steve had never seen such a display of power like that before.

Steve and Max completed a couple more fights each against some other Karate clubs from interstate and managed to win easily. They were not wasteful with their techniques and didn't receive any injuries. Sensei Mike looked much more pleased with his students.

Later in the afternoon, it was Max's turn again. This time he had to face a Cherry Blossom. Cherry Blossom 5 had been technically fighting within the rules but he wasn't doing it within the spirit of the event. None of the Cherry Blossoms were likeable but Cherry 5 was particularly despicable. He would aim at the joints of his opponents and try to break them at every opportunity. The fight started and Max had the perfect reply to every one of Cherry 5's attacks. Max saw a chance and went in with a sweep to Cherry 5's leg. It was so powerful. Cherry 5 immediately shrieked and held his knee. He was hurt and it was a shame the round had finished because Max would have had a chance to really finish him off.

During the break between the rounds, Sensei Mike was rubbing Max's legs and keeping him motivated. He told Max what a great job he was doing and how he couldn't fault his fighting in this fight. Cherry 5 now had a weakness, his left leg was going to be a problem for him and Max knew he must take advantage of that.

Steve didn't take his eyes away from Cherry 5 and his trainer. The trainer looked like a bat flapping its wings around Cherry 5. He looked angry and it was obvious he wasn't encouraging his student at all. He was admonishing him and he even slapped him across the face. It was disgusting to watch and Steve *almost* felt sorry for Cherry 5. Steve noticed something quite odd. The trainer reached inside Cherry 5's Gi and it looked as though he gave him something. Steve ran over to Max and Sensei Mike and warned them. He wanted Max to know that his opponent might do something illegal and to be ready for anything!

Cherry 5 limped to his fighting mark and Max, the Crazy Polak, bounced to his mark. Round 2 started and Max immediately went for Cherry 5's injured leg. Cherry 5 sidestepped effectively and managed to hit Max with a few punches. But Max's skills were nothing short of sensational, he intercepted the strikes, performed a takedown of his opponent and then slammed him on the ground. Cherry 5 held on to him and Max was almost on top of him. The referee ordered a stop to the fight and went to separate Max from Cherry 5 and, at the same time, Max let out a scream. He stood up and his eyes were bleeding and his mouth was frothing. Steve saw Cherry 5 put his hand inside his Gi as though he was returning something there. Steve lost all his sensibilities and ran into the fighting area to protect his dojo brother and with a blind rage, he grabbed Cherry 5. He tried to reach inside Cherry 5's Gi to see what he used to make Max so violently ill. While this was happening he heard the same hissing in the old Okinawan as previously. Cherry 1 stepped forward and tried to grab Steve. Steve was much more ready this time and easily evaded Cherry 1's attempts to grab him.

Cherry 1 came back at Steve but Steve's father had already arrived. He grabbed Steve and pulled him back behind him. He glared at every Blossom with particular attention to the trainer and Cherry 1. Sensei Mike let the medics take over looking after Max and turned his attention to Steve's father. He knew that look, he knew what a strong and angry man was capable of doing and quickly stepped next to him ready for anything. The referee and a few other officials entered the area and quickly diffused the tension. The corner judges congregated and made their decision. Cherry 5 was disqualified, Max was awarded the win and Steve was issued a stern warning.

It was indeed a Pyrrhic victory for Max, he won the fight but would not be able to continue fighting. His vision was blurry and the poison he was given seemed to drain his energy. Sensei Mike thought it was best for Max to go to hospital. Even though he could barely see and he was slumped over his chair, he flatly refused "No way in the world am I leaving, Sensei. I'm not going anywhere while those sons of bitches are here," he said. It was abundantly clear Max was not going anywhere. It was less clear why the officials had not noticed the full extent of the Cherry team's skullduggery. It seemed the only ones who could grasp the magnitude of their mischief were the fighters and trainers who had faced the Cherry Blossoms.

In no time, there were only four competitors left and Steve was one them. He was eager to learn who he would be fighting. By that stage, everybody was a good fighter and had something unique that enabled them to reach the semi-finals. Cherry 1 was there, as expected, and so were two other competent fighters. One was from the Kung Fu Dragons and the other from a very unique Indonesian style called Pencak Silat. Every one of them were very good fighters and Steve knew he couldn't take any of these fighters lightly. They deserved his respect and he would need his best abilities to win.

Steve was up against the Kung Fu Dragon and the Blossom would be fighting the Silat guy. Everybody used to joke about the Kung Fu fighters. They would call them the Bean Curds! Bean Curd can look like polished stone, so solid and hard. But slapping it will cause it to disintegrate. Well, that was the case with many of the earlier fighters in the tournament, but this guy was different. He was so light on his feet and almost elegant in the way he won his fights. Sensei Mike was quick to instruct Steve about him. "This guy knows the soft way, but he can hit also, don't let him get you off balance."

Steve spent the previous two years thinking nothing was better than his style and, much to his genuine surprise, he saw other fighters who were actually quite amazing. Deep down Steve remained sure his style was the best, but the world seemed a little bigger than it had before the tournament.

Steve and the Dragon would be fighting first. Sensei Mike was pleased and reminded Steve he would have more time to recover for the grand final. Steve was happy with that information but then thought to himself, "Yeah, well, I still gotta win this fight first!"

The fight started and Steve didn't hesitate, he unleashed his frightening kiai and attempted a front kick against the Dragon. The Dragon barely moved but avoided the kick and, at the same time, managed to push Steve's hip and land a powerful punch to Steve's rib. He got him good! Steve was sore and a little shocked. He moved back to the starting position and managed to glance at both Sensei Mike and his father. He knew and they knew the Dragon had messed with his balance and won that contest. The fight started again and Steve went in for a punch, the Dragon just waved his hand around and managed to control Steve's arm and almost lift him off the ground at the same time. The Dragon then used both hands to bounce Steve out of the fighting area. Another point awarded to the Dragon! He could hear the Blossoms laughing at him. Steve was going crazy, he was not going to lose! Then it occurred to him Sensei Mike would often infuriate him in precisely the same way when they would spar. The more angry Steve became, the stiffer his body became and the easier it was for Sensei Mike to control him. Steve needed to go soft, not harder!

Steve made his way back to the starting position. He didn't dare look at his father or Sensei Mike. At the starting position, Steve took a moment to quickly perform a breathing movement and centre himself. The fight began again and Steve did not initiate an attack this time. He waited for the Dragon. The Dragon moved forward and Steve forced himself to relax. His feet were hanging on to the ground like an eagle holding its prey, but the rest of him was gentle and calm and ready to absorb and deflect. Dragon initiated a flurry of punches and Steve used a round movement with his hands to catch them all as though he was collecting fireflies in a net. He then punched back in combination with one of his powerful kiais. Dragon received the full force of it. He was an excellent fighter but was not ready for Steve's power. Steve kept going, punching and kicking and,

mindful of the boundaries of the fighting area, he made sure
he kept the Dragon within the boundary. He would even pull
him in sometimes so he wouldn't go outside the boundary. The
Dragon instructor threw a towel into the fight and the fight
stopped. Steve had won!

Steve admired the Dragon and went over and wished him well.
Dragon was very noble in defeat. He said "It was like you became a different fighter. You completely changed styles halfway
through the fight. You were better than me. I learned something
today and I thank you for this. Good luck!" Steve was humbled
by how gracious and polite his adversary was, he thanked him
and also thanked Dragon's trainer.

Steve was elated and quickly went back to his team. Sensei Mike
said he saw the change and was confident Steve would adapt to
defend against Dragon's style. Steve's father looked concerned,
he said "How is your rib?" Steve had forgotten about it right up
until then. He checked himself and "... ouch, it hurt," he thought
to himself. At the same time as he winced, he glanced over at
the Blossoms and they were all looking at him. "Oh brilliant,
now "FrankenBlossom" is gonna go straight for my injured rib!"
Steve said. Sensei Mike reminded Steve that Cherry 1 was going
to have to win his fight first.

Cherry 1 and the Pencak Silat guy quickly assembled in the
fighting area. The fight looked uneven, Silat was half the size of
Cherry 1. It was not going to be good! Silat went over to shake
Cherry 1's hand and Cherry 1 just pushed him away and snarled
at him. Silat just smiled and went back to his fighting position while everyone in the audience booed Cherry 1. The fight
started and Cherry 1 stepped forward and launched one of his
trademark punches that had been used so effectively up until
then. Silat was amazing, he literally jumped *towards* that punch
and held onto it while he launched both his feet into the midriff
of Cherry 1. He looked like an angry monkey and the only thing

better than that double kick was the look of shock on Cherry 1's face.

Silat landed gently on his feet crouched down looking like a cobra ready to spit its venom at Cherry 1. Cherry 1 was enraged, he tried to stomp his foot on top of Silat as if to squash a bug. But Silat jumped out of the way again and managed to steal some punches between those tree trunks (arms) of Cherry 1. He was incredible, so light and fast. Steve even began to think about the best strategy he would need to use if he was going to have to fight him! Silat initiated an attack this time, he sprung up from a coiled snake position and aimed his fists at Cherry 1's abdomen. Cherry 1 anticipated the attack. He swatted Silat in an upward motion and his open palm struck Silat to the chest and slid up to his face. Silat looked like he was electrocuted as he flew out of the fighting area. His face was covered in blood as he wearily stood up and made his way back to the start position.

Two corner judges held out their flags to disqualify Cherry 1 for an illegal hit to the face. The fighters waited at their start positions and the judges and referee met together to confer. The referee then advised everyone Cherry 1's hand appeared to slip up towards Silat's face due to the way Silat had moved and therefore it was not illegal. Cherry 1 was awarded the point. Silat looked a little shaky after that hit to the head. Cherry 1 was immensely strong and he usually only needed one good hit to win a fight. Silat was doing very well but Steve began to wonder what would happen after he took that knock. The medics cleaned him up a little and managed to stop his bleeding nose. They allowed the fight to continue as there were no other obvious injuries.

Silat luckily had a little time to recover before the fight recommenced. When the referee ordered the fight to start again, Silat was moving around very well. He managed to evade Cherry 1 every time he made a move towards him. But Silat seemed reluctant to initiate an attack. Perhaps he began to fear being hit like that again. He kept moving around and evading his opponent. Soon it became a game for him and the crowd was cheering his evasive abilities. Cherry 1 couldn't seem to get close enough. Finally, with Silat's confidence restored, he became the cobra again. Coiled up and hissing he was preparing for attack! This time Cherry 1 feigned another foot stomp. As soon as Cherry 1 raised his knee, Silat jumped upwards to spit his venom. Cherry 1 dropped his foot to the side and punched downwards with the most evil and guttural kiai. Silat's snakelike hands were no match for this massive display of power. Cherry 1's fist crashed through Silat's defenes and crushed through Silat's collarbone snapping it as though it was a piece of chalk. Silat was splayed on the ground in a mess. Everyone heard the crack as Silat was hit and it was clear he wasn't going to get up.

Impressively, Silat stood up immediately. He walked straight to his starting position and assumed a fighting stance. He went to raise his arms and only one arm went up. The referee seemed to be wondering if the fight could continue. Silat managed to stand upright a few more seconds before the adrenaline seemed to wear off. Then he just dropped to the ground and everybody in the stadium (except the Blossoms) sighed with a mixture of concern and disappointment. Cherry 1 had won and it was going to be Cherry 1 versus Steve in the grand final. The Blossoms all seemed to shriek at the same time and looked over at Steve. "They're such an ugly bunch of pricks!" Steve thought to himself, "Especially FrankenBlossom!"

The grand final would be held after the kata and weapon finals. Steve had developed excellent weapon skills under Sensei Mike and his kata were perfect. But the test for Steve was for fighting. He had no desire to compete in the other events.

The events were interesting to watch. Every style had their specialties and some were truly remarkable to watch. Steve couldn't focus on them. His mind remained focused on the impending fight. Cherry 1 was a fierce opponent and Steve was trying to think of what he could do to beat him. "You have an answer for anything he will try on you, you know that, right?" said Sensei Mike. Steve paused and seemed less than confident in that moment. "FrankenBlossom is a beast of a man. But I'll try my best. If I lose, I'll hopefully learn something and if I win, I'll have only you to thank Sensei Mike. In fact, I can't even believe I made it this far. Thank you Sensei Mike, you've changed my life forever. No matter what happens in the next fight, I am so grateful for everything you have done for me." Sensei Mike just patted him on the shoulder and said "Remember, this is just training. Another lesson for you. Losing can sometimes mean you win in the end."

Steve didn't even want to hear the "L" word! He didn't want to hear anyone mention losing again. Of course, Jake and Max were next to come up and congratulate Steve. "You did so well to make it to the final Steve. Don't worry if you lose, Franken-Blossom is a full grown man and you're only seventeen years old! You'd smash that ugly bastard by the time you're twenty-five! It wouldn't even be a competition," said Jake while Max wholeheartedly agreed. Steve was starting to get really annoyed.

Steve's father put one of his strong hands on his shoulder and it strangely seemed to energise him. "Don't forget, you're a lion and if you want to win, it's waiting for you," Steve's father said. They smiled at each other for a brief moment. So many years together and they could just look at each other and understand every word *not* said. Steve grasped all of his father's intent and wishes in that moment. He never wanted anything more than this in his life, he would give it his all.

Steve sat down and put his headphones on. Luckily he brought some extra batteries because he was getting his money's worth out of his Walkman during the tournament. On came Black Sabbath with the song "Sabbath bloody Sabbath". When the guitars came screaming through after a defiant Ozzie Osbourne vocally gave "the finger" to his oppressors in the song, Steve was ready to punch holes through walls .... Maybe even through time dimensions! Losing was not an option. Not at all. He threw off the headphones and started stretching and warming up. He was ready for anything.

The displays and katas had all finished and the fight area was ready. It was time! Sensei Mike asked Steve's Dad to come with him. Sensei Mike knew he had no choice, so he made Steve's dad carry some towels to look official. Steve walked ahead and had almost reached the fight area when he looked up and saw Cherry 1 and his trainer. Steve was horrified, the trainer had pulled down his hood and taken off his sunglasses and his eyes were just plain black and his face was hideous and his hands were long and they looked like claws and his teeth were sharp. He didn't even look human! Steve turned around to see if Sensei Mike and his dad had seen that hideous creature.

Sensei Mike sprinted towards Steve. Steve had never seen his Sensei look so agitated before. Sensei Mike said "Steve, listen to me carefully. I don't want you to fight. We must leave immediately. We must not, you must not fight. This isn't right. This can't ....." Then some wicked amalgam of thunder and whispers emanated from that hideous creature for all to hear. "Brother Mike, you don't want to play with your brother Hiro? Let us see who made the strongest fighter. Let us see who walks out of here." Steve understood immediately, this was Hiro, Sensei Mike's former training partner.

Sensei Mike was pale. He looked sick. Nothing normally phased him, but this wasn't nothing. This was horror personified. Sensei Mike's mind was racing. "Is this what my Sensei was talking about? He damaged Hiro when he summoned Luohan? What the hell has Hiro become? A demon?" ... as if his thoughts were interrupted, that hideous creature whispered again. "Yes, brother Mike, I have indeed changed. Maybe I still even have some human in me. I've missed you and I want you by my side, the same as before. Let us be together again, I promise you will enjoy it when I make you the same as me!" Sensei Mike grabbed Steve and said "We must go!"

Steve had so much adrenaline racing through him at this point. He wanted to fight and he begged Sensei Mike for the chance. Sensei Mike said "Steve, this is not training now. Please understand, you, all of us, will be fighting for our lives here. We need to get out and make plans ..." He was interrupted. "Son". Steve's dad had the most gentle smile as he looked upon Steve, "Son, you are a King with the heart of a lion. Show him who we are. Win the fight and together we will do whatever needs to be done after." Steve's dad never looked so huge to him before. He seemed to radiate power and confidence and Steve seemed to be nourished by it. He looked like a King! Even Sensei Mike seemed to calm down after Steve's dad talked. Steve turned to Sensei Mike and said "Sensei Mike, I've got to do this. You said I will learn about myself when I take away a win from someone else. I must do this for myself."

Steve turned and surged forward and stood on his fighting position. Cherry 1 thumped his hulking frame to his fighting position. Cherry 1 was a head taller than Steve and his body seemed twice as thick. The referee seemed oblivious to what was going on at each end of the fighting area. He asked his fighters to fight fair and they bowed in their own ways to him. Cherry 1 bowed like a disrespectful thug and Steve bowed in his traditional fashion. They both bowed to each other from a fighting stance this time. Steve didn't care about tradition at that point, "The thug doesn't deserve my respect and I'm not gonna give him even a microsecond of advantage!" he thought to himself.

The fight began and Cherry 1 pointed at Steve and told him he would kill him. Steve didn't waste any time. He summoned all of his power and kicked a sweep into Cherry 1's leg. This was usually the kind of attack that left an opponent limping around and would drain the opponent's desire to continue fighting. In classes, Steve's training partner's would hold three pads next to their legs and Steve would still make them limp away when he kicked them. Well, on this occasion Steve landed the perfect hit and it seemed as though time stood still for a moment. Then Cherry 1 merely took a step forward and roared as though nothing happened. The hideous demon Hiro squealed with delight and hissed and shrieked at the same time. Steve was demoralised. He didn't feel doubt, but he felt scared and he knew his job wasn't going to be easy.

Cherry 1 launched his fist at Steve and it sounded as though Demon Hiro's hisses were fuelling his attack. Steve's combination of adrenaline, speed, strength and, quite frankly, fear were the perfect mix. He managed to block the punches unleashed upon him and started to feel his confidence return as his well trained body and mind adapted to the monster in front of him. But he very quickly realised Cherry 1 would eventually get through if he didn't begin his own attack. Cherry 1 was big and had a longer reach than Steve. If Cherry 1 was in range to punch, Steve would need to find a way to move even closer before he could return a punch. In a split second he realised what he needed to do. He would kick, and when he finished one kick, he would kick again. He would not stop kicking until the fight was over and the fight was not going to be over until Steve won!

Steve didn't even give a moment's thought to the physicality required for this strategy. A single kick probably drained as much energy as four punches. He decided it was the best option. At worst, the kicks would keep that monster away from him and, at best, they would hurt him and give Steve the win he so desperately wanted.

At the same time as Steve launched his barrage of kicks, Cherry 1 was managing to make it through with his trademark savage punches. One of the punches hit Steve precisely in the injured rib from the previous fight and even Steve was expecting it to hurt. Curiously none of the punches hurt as much as Steve was anticipating. In fact, some simple physics was at play. Steve's kicks were hitting Cherry 1 at the same time as some of his punches were landing on Steve. They were negating each other. Steve was landing almost twice as many kicks as Cherry 1 was punching. Any observer would have logically thought Steve would tire soon. But he kept going and between the frenzy of kicks an occasional punch would thread its way through and send Steve back one metre only to have Steve charge back in with even more kicks. The timer sounded and it was the end of the first round.

Steve sat down and Sensei Mike was doing everything in his power to help Steve regain his breath. Steve looked over at that disgusting Demon who was furious at his protege. He was shrieking at him and hissing and weaving around Cherry 1 as if to imbue more of his evil into him. Steve turned to look at his father, he was leaning forward and smiling in a deep discussion with somebody. Who was that person? What? Temyana, the sweet little angel who humbled and encouraged him. This time she was wearing a golden half mask covering her burns. He thought to himself, "What the ...? They look like they know each other. This is crazy," as he focused his mind back on the war about to recommence.

Sensei Mike reminded Steve with a tap to his face. "Listen." He said, "That demon will not let his fighter lose. He will do anything for the win. You saw what they did to Max. They will try something, anything, whatever it takes for them to hurt you. Please be careful." Steve assured his Sensei that he understood the gravity of the situation and wouldn't let his guard down.

The fighters were called back for the second round. Steve was ready for anything but he wasn't ready for what he saw. Cherry 1 actually bowed properly to the referee AND to Steve. Steve bowed from his fighting stance and, for a moment, felt he was being disrespectful. But as his opponent rose from his traditional bow, he noticed something which horrified him. The hands he held to his side were changing as they raised into a fighting position. They darkened and, by the time they moved that short distance to their fighting position, transformed into hideous black claws. The referee seemed oblivious to this and the spectators didn't even seem to notice either. Steve was incredulous. That disgusting man/mountain was mutating before his eyes and nobody else seemed to be able to see it.

The fight started and Cherry 1 thundered towards Steve. His feet were thumping the ground and his talons were waving in front of him. One managed to reach Steve's blocking arm and ripped through his Gi and drew blood. Steve was acutely aware of everything around him. He could feel Sensei Mike's concern behind him and he swore he could hear that little girl behind him talking to his father. He thought to himself "Why are they still talking, can't they see I'm fighting for my bloody life against this filthy monster?!" Steve was kicking furiously again. He was trying to avoid the talons of that man/monster but sometimes his foot would be intercepted by those claws and his feet were becoming increasingly bloodied.

Cherry 1 wasn't even looking tired. He seemed to enjoy seeing Steve's blood and the hissing from the Demon Hiro seemed to be congratulating his protege. Steve refused to even think about losing. He was fighting for his life here! Cherry 1 managed to shoot forward at an uncharacteristic speed which shocked Steve. Cherry 1 grabbed him and pulled him close with those evil claws. Steve had excellent flexibility and, from such a close position, executed a perfect roundhouse to Cherry 1's head. Something peculiar occurred. Steve's feet were an absolute mess of blood due to those talons ripping them apart. His kick to Cherry 1's face left some blood on his face and eye and they started to emit a foul smoke. It clearly gave Cherry 1 some pain. He let go of Steve and stepped back and wiped his face with his claws. His face had deformed slightly but he regained his composure soon enough.

For the first time, Steve actually noticed his own breathing. He was a machine operating on pure adrenaline, but even that would run out eventually! He remembered an old trick he used once with success against Sensei Mike. Steve pretended to look tired. He lowered his hands from his regular fighting position and slumped his shoulders and sucked a whole lot more air in. All the tell-tale signs of someone reaching the end of their physical capacity.

Cherry 1 saw Steve's diminished condition and found himself some new vigour. He charged towards Steve with his claws ready to rip Steve's head off. Steve didn't waste a moment, he yelled his kiai and launched his sidekick. The kiai was even more impressive than the one he did in his first fight. It looked like he directed an earthquake straight at his opponent. The sound reverberated throughout the entire stadium like an explosion and the kick was a missile launch. Steve flew through the air and Cherry 1, with his wicked smile, was moving forward with his claws up and ready. But Steve unleashed a power that seemed beyond human, his foot was shredded as it crashed through the claws and landed on Cherry 1's upper chest and then slid up to his throat. Such was the power of the kick, Cherry 1's throat seemed to collapse and he was left gasping for air. He wrapped his claws around his throat to try to understand why he couldn't breathe. Steve kept going. He hit that man/monster with a barrage of kicks and punches until he was knocked out of the ring.

The fight was over and Steve had won. The judge awarded Steve the win and he was sure he jumped as high as the auditorium roof with his fist clenched in victory. He did win. He took away that win from that man/monster and he made his Sensei Mike and father proud of him. Most importantly, Steve was proud of himself.

Sensei Mike, Steve's father and Jake and Max came to congratulate him. It was completely surreal and Steve didn't hear a word they said to him. Among all that frenzied excitement, Steve asked his father if he actually knew that little girl he was talking to earlier and his reply was "I haven't seen her for a very long time, I've known her all my life." Steve was perplexed, but he didn't have time to think about it as they all lifted him in the air and pronounced him the winner to the auditorium. They paid particular attention to turning Steve around to face the Cherry Blossoms who were all hissing and scowling at him.

Sensei Mike still looked uncharacteristically agitated and quickly calmed the group. He said, "This is not over yet guys. Keep your wits about you because anything is possible. The trophy presentation is about to happen so stay close and be careful. We can celebrate later." With that message, the group made their way to the presentation area and sat down. Steve's dad wasn't even a step away from the group when Steve turned around and grabbed his old man and pulled him in for a hug. They were laughing and they walked the rest of the way with their arms draped over each other's shoulders.

Chapter 4 - The Presentation

All the competitors and trainers assembled in their groups for the presentation. Titles were to be awarded for best fighters, best katas, best weapons and best demonstration. After a few speeches and acknowledgements, it was time to award the best competitors.

Before the tournament, Steve didn't even realise so much diversity existed in martial arts. There were so many different ways to fight and so many weapons! Steve's competitor, the Kung Fu Dragon, had won the best weapons demonstration using his Chinese broadsword. "What a champ! Such a complete martial artist," Steve thought to himself. When Dragon was awarded his trophy, Steve cheered the loudest and his enthusiasm seemed to make everyone else in the stadium cheer louder for the elegant Kung Fu Dragon.

Soon it was Steve's turn to join the assembly for his presentation. Kung Fu Dragon was meant to fight Silat for the second runner up trophy, but Silat didn't recover from his fight with Cherry 1. He had to withdraw from the tournament. This left Kung Fu Dragon as second runner up and Cherry 1 as runner up. The three fighters made their way to the presentation area and lined up as Kung Fu Dragon was the first to accept his trophy. He was extremely gracious and smiled at Steve. Cherry 1 was next to accept his runner up trophy. He didn't even bow, he snatched the trophy out of the official's hand and threw it on the ground when he went back to line up with Steve and Dragon.

Finally it was Steve's turn. He would accept his reward and acknowledgement. He had lived and breathed his Gōjū-ryū every day and night for the last two years. He earned it because he was unequivocally sure that nobody wanted it more than he did. His name was called and the stadium erupted. Everybody was clearly pleased that Steve managed to trounce Cherry 1. Steve floated with a sense of accomplishment towards the official as he made his way to accept his accolade.

He accepted his trophy with a grin from ear to ear and held it in the air to a thunderous roar of approval from the entire stadium. Well, almost the entire stadium. As expected, the Cherry Blossoms were far from pleased and they made their disapproval known to everyone in the stadium.

Steve was congratulated warmly by his new brother-in-arms, Kung Fu Dragon, and he turned to his beloved family. His father was clearly very proud of his son. Jake and a much refreshed Max were jumping with delight for Steve. Sensei Mike seemed to have a cautious smile and then Steve noticed little Temyana standing next to his father. She was not smiling at all. In fact, she seemed to have a look of grave concern and seemed to be warning Steve as if in slow motion.

In a split second, everything changed. Kung Fu Dragon yelled and jumped in front of Steve. A spear coming from the direction of the Cherry Blossoms flew through the air and pierced his shoulder. If he didn't jump in front of Steve, that spear would have undoubtedly pierced Steve's heart. It felt like time stood still, Steve was pulling the spear out of his new brother Dragon at the same time as he was watching the Cherry Blossoms mutate. Dragon was contorted in agony on the ground. The Blossoms all looked even more hideous than before. All of their arms were talons now and their eyes had darkened the same as their demon master. They seemed to move like spiders and were crawling towards him while the Demon Hiro was gliding almost gracefully across the stadium towards Sensei Mike. Curiously, it seemed almost everyone else at the tournament was oblivious to what was unfolding.

Steve precisely understood the gravity of the situation unfolding. This was the battle Sensei Mike feared. Nine of those wicked monsters were coming for him and yet he only had concern for his father and dojo brothers and …. and his Sensei Mike against that Demon Hiro! "Nine of those monsters……." Steve said to himself as it suddenly occurred to him that one was right next to him!

Cherry 1, that man/mountain had transformed into something even more sinister and had already laid a talon on Steve's shoulder. The injured Dragon on the ground used his legs to reach at Cherry 1's legs and lock them up for a brief moment. Steve turned around and unleashed a fury he was not aware he was even capable of. If the tournament fights revealed Steve as a fierce competitor, then the madness of the situation propelled Steve to another level. With the assistance of the quick thinking Dragon, Steve managed to kick Cherry 1 and send him flat on his back, unconscious.

Steve saw all the other mutant Blossoms heading for him. They moved with a jerkiness not unlike spiders. They were hideous. "Even uglier than before!" he thought to himself. He guessed he would have been horrified at any other time but he didn't have time to think too much about that. There was a clear job ahead of him and it was clear in his mind it was a matter of life and death.

He saw Jake and Max running as they tried to intercept the mutant monsters and quickly wondered where his father was. As if to answer the question, Steve's father was already right next to him and said "I'm right here son. We've got a job to do." Steve was almost waiting for his father to remind him about hitting those abominations until he saw only the white of their eyes but it occurred to him that the filthy monsters had black eyes, and they would clearly have to play with a new rule book against them.

Jake was a strong man. He grabbed one of the black mutants and threw it at another one as they crashed onto the ground. They quickly regained their composure and ignored him as if he was a minor distraction. They were heading straight for Steve, and Jake was having none of it. He managed to intercept one of them again and axe kicked it with perfect precision. The mutant received the full brunt of the kick and, for a moment, lost its singular agenda for Steve. It turned to Jake and its sharp claws seemed to grow as they swiped towards Jake's throat. It was horrific, Jake's throat was split wide open and a pool of blood was already surrounding him when he fell to his death.

The spectators inexplicably did not appear to see the monsters in their hideous form. However, the death of Jake prompted a mass exodus from the stadium as people fled the war zone. It wasn't long before the entire stadium was evacuated and only the combatants were left.

Max was imposingly animated. He saw the threat to Sensei Mike and he saw those monsters heading for Steve. Like a true warrior, he launched himself towards the mass of mutants as they were inching closer to Steve and his father. He slid on the ground through them and bowled a few of them over as if they were skittles. He ended up on the other side of them and stole a sword that an Iado master was using in an earlier demonstration. He quickly put the blade to use and looked every bit the martial arts warrior as he stabbed one of the mutants. The mutant howled and shrieked and went straight for the blade with its talons. He ripped the sword out of Max's hands and went for his throat with those terrifying claws. Max was too fast, he'd seen enough of those claws for a lifetime and sidestepped his terrifying opponent. Max used a reverse knife hand

and managed to hit the monster in its throat. It was gasping for air while Max executed a perfect kick to its head. The mutant Cherry dropped to its knees. Max did not stop. He pummelled his enemy without mercy until it was a black pulp.

Max quickly turned around to look for his next opponent only to find the end of the very same sword that was taken out of his hands a moment earlier. One of the other monsters had grabbed the blade and pierced Max in the stomach with it. Max managed to maim that monster with a few powerful punches until the gravity of the injury began to take its toll on him. He dropped to the ground unable to fight. The monster stepped over Max and continued its increasingly apparent agenda towards Steve.

The monsters had almost reached Steve and his father. Meanwhile Demon Hiro was menacingly closing in on Sensei Mike who had armed himself with a Chinese styled demonstration sword. The kind of sword that wobbles around and looks impressive under bright lights but was of limited use in true battle.

Steve glanced at his father and couldn't help but notice how fearless he looked. What started with concern for his father ended up being a source of encouragement for Steve. They were shoulder to shoulder and steeled themselves for the imminent attack. Steve's father was a born leader. At stressful times, he always seemed to rise to the occasion and this time he seemed to glow with readiness and ferocity. He said to Steve, "Son, this has been your day, let's finish it well!" In no time the monsters had arrived.

The first monster launched itself at Steve and received a perfectly timed punch to its ugly head before bouncing backwards. Another launched only a moment later to meet the equally impressive fist of Steve's father. If Steve had time to digest the moment, he would have known the feeling inside him was that of pride when he saw his lifelong protector dole out that hit. But there was no time to ponder. Everything was happening at once and they were both already fighting their next opponents. It was a tangle of talons and powerful fists along with cyclonic kicks from Steve. It seemed relentless to Steve, there were so many of them. Steve's father was so violent. Whatever Steve was using had an element of refinement and his training helped him appear almost elegant in the way he was dealing with his adversaries. In contrast, Steve's father was terrifying and looked like a god of war as he seemed to gain more strength every time another of those monsters was ejected.

Steve and his father both noticed the monster which Max had beaten into a black pulp had also rejoined the fray. It seemed these creatures would not die. The fighting didn't let up. The monsters were continually being dealt with, but their wicked talons were getting closer and closer with every repeated attempt. It seemed only a matter of time before one, or both of them, would succumb to the relentless advances.

Temyana, with her golden half mask, seemed to appear out of thin air and yelled to Steve's father, "You know you can and now is the time. Pass it through your son." Steve's father seemed to understand immediately and, between breaths, he barked out instructions to his son. "Son, remember those screams you were making in your fights? You must do it when I direct mine through you. Aim at those black maggots. This is our Lion Energy, now roar!"

Steve understood immediately as his father went behind him. He placed his hands on Steve's shoulders and let out a roar the likes of which no normal man could ever repeat. Instead of surprising Steve, it summoned something deep inside him. He matched the roar and channelled the energy towards the disgusting mass of intertwined monstrous filth in front of him. Every other time Steve yelled his kiai in the tournament, it almost looked like a wave of energy. This time it was something different, this energy took a form. It took the shape of a lion and pounced on the monsters. In an instant, they were enveloped in that embodiment of rage. Most of them died. Steve was startled. He had no idea what was happening. The power surged through him. It wasn't foreign though, it felt so familiar to him, yet he had never seen it before.

Two monsters managed to survive the energy blast. Steve's father didn't hesitate as he rocketed himself towards them. His fearsome fists relentlessly pounded those monsters until they were lifeless. Steve didn't want these creatures to reanimate in the same way Max's had. He grabbed the spear that maimed Dragon and made sure their time on Earth was finished.

Demon Hiro was already engaged in battle with Sensei Mike and shrieked loudly when his minions were killed. It appeared as though the monsters were all connected to him in some fundamental way. He turned his widened black eyes to Steve and his father as if to notice an unfamiliar energy. He hissed something in the direction of Steve and his father, but the words were unintelligible.

Steve turned to his father who gave him a tired smile. At that moment, he saw the hideous monster that was once Cherry 1 swiftly rise behind his father. It was even bigger than before and it had grown another set of talons to match the equally menacing pair it already had. Its disgusting head offered a filthy smile to Steve.

The monster roared and the next thing Steve saw was its claws protrude from his father's chest. Steve's father looked into his son's eyes with a combination of determination and love. He reached up to grab that monster around its neck. In one powerful and heroic movement, he flipped the monster over himself in front of Steve and stomped on its throat with the last of his life-force. Steve was still holding the spear that impaled Dragon and powered it through the evil monster's head to its death. Steve's father held on to that spear and died standing up. He looked like a perfect Da Vinci stone sculpture depicting a great warrior standing over his defeated enemy.

Steve was overwhelmed with despair. His father was dead and life would never be the same. He cried and went to hug his father and experienced an inexplicable sensation. Similar to when his father placed his hands on his shoulders, yet different. His entire body felt as though it absorbed his father's energy. Temyana appeared again and quickly managed to draw Steve's attention. She said, "Good, the transference has happened. The enemy remains, you must leave!"

Steve could barely make sense of anything and could not see through his tears. As he was wiping his eyes, his ears took over to remind him this was not over. He heard the guttural hissing of Demon Hiro directed at Sensei Mike. He gently touched the human statue of his father and ignored the little girl's command and ran to Sensei Mike.

Sensei Mike was using the ridiculous sword in an unexpected way. The manner in which the pathetic blade was randomly flopping around was a source of frustration for Demon Hiro. Every time Demon Hiro tried to claw his way through to Sensei Mike, the sword would briefly lock up those poisonous talons. Sensei Mike used those moments to employ his powerful kicks to send Demon Hiro backwards. He succeeded time and time again and it was clear the Demon Hiro was growing increasingly annoyed.

Steve was making his way to Demon Hiro and saw his Sensei Mike fighting valiantly. But it was abundantly clear his opponent was not human. The monster was the most wicked thing Steve had ever seen. Demon Hiro seemed to be growing as his rage increased. He grew in size the last time Sensei Mike kicked him away. When Demon Hiro attacked Sensei Mike again, he made it through his defences. He kicked the blade out of Sensei Mike's hand, kicked him to the ground and then glided on top of Sensei Mike. Demon Hiro had wrapped one of his terrifying claws around Sensei Mike's throat. The other was pointing at him and he was screaming at Sensei Mike with that evil voice, "Now you will be my true brother again. I will give the power of darkness to you. Soon you will be my demon brother and the world will fear us. For the glory of Kumicho!" He pushed one of his wicked talons into Sensei Mike's temple and a dark haze enveloped them both.

Steve was within fighting range and immediately understood the monster before him was the apex of his group. Demon Hiro was the ruler of those other monsters and they were not easily overcome. Nothing worked except for that surprising roar. But his father was gone and he had no idea what he could possibly muster on his own. He decided there was simply no time and no other choice. He thought about his father, he could feel his father's hands on his shoulders and he summoned that roar. To Steve's surprise, the ball of energy took the form of the lion again and pierced that dark haze. Demon Hiro catapulted ten metres away from Sensei Mike, the energy pulse was phenomenal. Steve saw Demon Hiro shrink and take on a human form.

Steve ran to his Sensei Mike with grave concerns. Sensei Mike was screaming and convulsing. His rambling words didn't make sense. In a flash of clarity, he looked at Steve and said "Steve, I saw you. Such power. I was right about you. You have ascended. You will be a great man. You are a great man. You must kill me. Cut off my head or pierce my brain. Don't let me become a demon. Kill me and let me find my Chiasa. Please, listen to me and don't waste a moment thinking about it." Sensei Mike lifted his hands in a pleading gesture and they had already turned black. Steve could see them transforming before his very eyes.

The nails were growing into black claws and his Sensei's skin was becoming black and scaly.

Steve couldn't possibly consider killing his Sensei. He had just lost his father in a supernatural battle. His Sensei Mike was so important in his life. "How can I kill you, my Sensei?" he said to his teacher and role model in life. Sensei Mike was already unable to respond. Steve looked at his Sensei again, his face had blackened. His eyes were turning black and his head was elongating. It wouldn't be long before his Sensei would become a monster like Demon Hiro and probably even try to kill him! He knew what had to be done. His Sensei was already gone as Steve screamed his apology. He grabbed the nearby decorative sword and plunged it deeply through Sensei Mike's eye. Sensei Mike's suffering ended. He reverted back to his human form and found the peace he had craved in his tortured life. An endless flood of tears streamed down Steve's face. The gravity of his losses blanketed Steve. He lost all energy to his legs, fell to the ground and his broken heart and crushed soul merged to yield a most tragic and sorrowful cry.

Steve's mind was racing with competing thoughts. They all danced around in his mind's eye in a perpetual cycle of horror. The Demon Hiro quickly crashed his thoughts back to reality when he heard those evil whispers reverberating through the stadium. "We will meet again young Lion," hissed Demon Hiro.

Steve searched the entire stadium. He looked everywhere for the Demon Hiro. He was gone and so was the uncomplicated life he had known up until that day.

Chapter 5 - The Leaving

T he days after the presentation were a blur of terror and mourning for Steve. He wanted to hide from the world and not talk to anyone. His body was sore from the fighting, but that was completely shadowed by an immense feeling of loss. He couldn't find a way to ease his trauma. Sleeping was impossible. His thoughts flashed back to the award presentation time and time again. He had forgotten the elation of winning the title. It was all replaced with the horror of that day. The senseless deaths kept replaying in his mind and he had no internal mechanism to switch it off.

Each time an event from the fateful day replayed, Steve would be fighting again. If he was asleep, his legs would be kicking and his jaw would be clenched. Waking up would be his temporary release from his captive hell. And when he was awake, his hands would become fists and his body would ready itself for battle. He would see each moment and move another direction or construct sequences which may have produced a different result. Some alternative action which would have let his father live! Something that could have stopped Jake from losing his life. If only he killed Cherry 1 earlier! If only he helped Sensei Mike earlier, maybe he would have had someone to share his pain with. He had nobody and it was his fault, entirely.

The Australian Federal Police paid Steve a visit to discuss the murders at the tournament. Steve was the only witness who saw the entirety of the events leading to the deaths on that horrific day. He didn't admit to taking Sensei Mike's life and completely avoided discussing the supernatural events he experienced. Luckily for Steve, representatives from Interpol recognised the Cherry Blossoms and their leader as organised crime members from Japan. The murders were quickly attributed to the Japanese criminals and the line of investigation was placed in the hands of international law enforcement organisations.

Prior to the tournament, Steve had been anguishing about how he would ask his father to allow him to go to Japan to further his training. He knew the discussion about deferring his studies would not have been an easy one. After the tournament, he needed nobody's permission about anything. He had just turned eighteen, without celebration, and was an adult under Australian law. He didn't have time to think about his future. He had already buried Sensei Mike. It was a deeply moving farewell attended by a handful of people and it only reinforced Steve's sense of deep loss.

Jake's funeral was, in some ways, worse than Sensei Mike's. He saw Jake's wife and children crying and he felt guilty just being in their presence. It was Steve's fault that Jake was dead. His children and wife would suffer forever. The guilt was suffocating, Steve had to leave early.

Steve just wanted to escape all of the pain. Whatever the solution was, it evaded him. There was no solution availing itself. New complications and obligations were unfolding every moment. The burden of burying his father was weighing heavily upon him. Steve seemed to alternate between moments of denial and then obligation. He wished he took more notice of traditions and processes. Steve's father was a well known man in the Macedonian community and he wanted to make sure he honoured his father.

Funeral arrangements were made and he still didn't know entirely what he would need to do. He wanted to make a speech.

He didn't know what to say. He was hopeful some of the elders would help with some of the rituals associated with a Macedonian Orthodox burial.

It seemed as though time jumped forward in a flash. It was barely a blink of an eye and he was following the hearse carrying his father's body to the church. As they neared the church, Steve saw all the familiar faces from his local community. It normally gave him a sense of comfort to see them. He wanted to be reminded of uncomplicated times when he saw some of his relatives and friends there, but he simply couldn't escape the horror of that fateful day.

The usual faces were indeed there. The first to greet him was crazy old Baba Rada. "Baba" means grandmother and is also a respectful term to use for old women even if they were not related. Baba Rada was not a blood relative but she was from the same village back in Macedonia and knew Steve's family very well. As a very young child, Steve used to be scared of Baba Rada. She used crazy gestures all the time, had a cross tattooed on her forehead and she was so old! When he was quite young, Steve learned the significance of the cross tattoo. Baba Rada was indeed old. She was alive back when the Ottoman Turks were in control of Macedonia. The prettiest of the little girls were stolen and sold to rich Muslims in Istanbul. They would then spend the rest of their lives in someone's harem. In order to avoid having their child stolen, it was common to have the Christian cross tattooed on their foreheads. No Muslim would accept a girl so obviously branded as a Christian. Baba Rada was the last of her kind.

Baba Rada lived down the road from Steve. She would spend her days sitting at the front of her house. Many thought she was quite crazy. She would often just sit in her front porch area and just look at her garden and watch the people passing by. Other children would often mock the "crazy old woman" as they passed by. Once Steve understood the significance of the tattoo, he developed a sense of the tragedy of his people. He would always say hello to her. She would always greet him enthusiastically. She looked forward to seeing him and would always offer him treats and simply wouldn't take no for an answer. If Steve saw any other child mocking her, he would immediately come to her defence.

Baba Rada greeted Steve in her usual crazy manner. As always, she curtsied in front of him and performed her greeting. She would do the same for Steve's father every time she saw him. "Tvoe Velicheststvo" she would say. It meant "your Majesty" and she would always smile warmly at Steve when she said it but always in the most serious manner for Steve's father. Steve asked his father why she did it and he always dismissed her as being quite mad.

Steve thought Baba Rada's little inside joke was somewhat inappropriate on the day of his father's funeral. Nevertheless, he found it comforting to see her there. Steve and a select few carried the coffin into the church. Baba Rada was hovering nearby. She seemed to be conducting her own ritual. People would ignore her craziness because she more than compensated for it with her knowledge of the old ways. When it came to tradition and protocols, she was rarely questioned.

The coffin was placed near the altar and the lid was removed. As tradition would dictate, it was an open casket funeral and Steve saw his father once again. His father retained that fierce look of a warrior when he died on that terrible day. The priest was conducting his liturgy only to be rudely interrupted by Baba Rada. Few could understand her fully at the best of times. But she was even more difficult to understand on this occasion. Everyone tried to quieten her during this very solemn occasion. "Why is this crazy woman interrupting the priest? Shit!" Steve thought to himself as some of the community elders tried to stop her and move her away from the coffin. She pushed them away with remarkable strength and made her way to the coffin.

She reached in her bag and pulled out a mask painted in gold. It had a sixteen-pointed sun rosette etched into the forehead area. The rosette was well known to Steve, not because it was an official emblem associated with Macedonian royalty. It was simply always present in his life, whether it was on a doily or a tea towel or a religious painting in a relative's home.

She placed the mask on Steve's father's face. This was too much, even for Steve, as he rose to calm this clearly mad woman. The priest began to remonstrate with her. But she seemed to grow in stature and commanded attention from all that attended the service. Her voice rose and she glared at everyone in the entire church paying particular attention to the priest. She said "I have attended four funerals of the men in this line. Three in Macedonia and now this one here in Australia. Maybe I have lived too long and seen too much, but the men of this line have always been buried this way. If anyone thinks they know more than me about it, I'll sit down and let them do what's right. Otherwise, just shut up and stop interrupting me."

Steve stood up when Baba Rada placed the mask on his father. He had every intention of taking off that mask. But when he heard what she knew about the traditions of his family, he quickly realised how little he knew of these things. He yearned desperately for his father's return. He still needed to learn so much. He wondered why he didn't know more about his family's traditions. To add to the grief, he was completely disappointed in himself for not asking more questions when his father was alive.

The priest and Baba Rada maintained their nuanced battle for leadership in the proceedings while Steve motioned towards the coffin to see his father one more time. He looked at the mask and felt compelled to touch it. Perhaps to see if it was real gold. It wasn't, but Steve thought it still looked quite impressive. And he certainly did not want to break his family tradition, even though he had no idea of it prior to that day. He moved away from the coffin and sat down at the front of the congregation.

The smell of frankincense was almost suffocating. The priest was loading extra frankincense into his thurible and was directing the smoke near Baba Rada. He seemed hopeful she might faint and allow him to conduct his proceedings without interruption. She continued her deliberate movements and subdued chants without even looking at the priest. She took advantage of the smoke as she tried to wave it into the coffin. She demanded more and used the Macedonian word "temyan" for it. Steve was reminded of Temyana and had been wondering who she was and why she appeared when she did. He had so many questions for her, if he ever saw her again.

He looked up at the coffin surrounded by the smoke and there was the little girl. She was in her half gold mask and looked like she was part of the smoke. She would weave in and out of the smoke and was almost transparent on occasions. She seemed to appear and disappear. Steve noticed the mask she was wearing was quite similar to the mask on his father. It had the same emblem etched into it. Steve looked around and wondered if anyone could see what he could see. They all seemed oblivious, except for Baba Rada. She was looking straight at Temyana and her chants or instructions were clearly being directed at her. Baba Rada seemed to be directing her into the coffin, at one stage shouting at her to get in. Temyana was having none of it, she did seem to hover around the coffin but then looked up at Steve. She gestured towards Steve, said something to Baba Rada and she reluctantly complied with the little girl. Baba Rada retreated back to the congregation and let the priest conclude the funeral rites.

As the incense smoke subsided, Temyana's semi-transparent apparition disappeared. Steve had seen so many utterly inexplicable events in the last few days. He knew he needed to find Temyana again and he was absolutely determined to see Baba Rada as soon as possible after the funeral.

The sadness of that day didn't end with the burial. The feeling of loss and dejection permeated every cell of Steve's body and mind. People tried to visit him over the following days and he found excuses to avoid them all. He was trying to make sense of the impossible. He was mourning, and the relentless images of those fatal events continued to haunt him. He was not the same person as before the tournament. He wished he had never competed and that everything would simply return to the way it used to be.

He knew things would never be the same. He could still hear Demon Hiro's voice and he could still see what happened to Sensei Mike. Even if he wanted to hide his head in the sand and pretend none of it ever happened, he was sure that, when he least expected it, the Demon Hiro would find him. Steve was upset with the injustice of it all. Good men were killed for no reason and families were suffering. His competing emotions crippled him. On one hand, he wanted justice for the people he cared for. Yet on the other, his sorrow had depleted him. His energy was at its lowest ebb.

After a few days of misery in solitude, Steve was able to muster the spirit to leave his home and seek answers from Baba Rada. He bought her a cake, a jar of Turkish coffee and some chocolates. The same chocolates she would always try and force upon him every time he walked past her house as a young child. She was sitting at the front of her house and the moment she saw Steve, she mustered all her energy to curtsy and say "Tvoe Velichestvo (your majesty)". She didn't do it in a playful manner as she had always done in the past with a younger Steve. She did it as though she was still performing the rituals back in the church at the funeral. They went inside her small home and she immediately began preparing Turkish coffee for them.

Steve hated those coffees when he was younger. But as he grew older, the taste seemed to grow on him. That furry textured strong hit of caffeine was the only drug he would allow in his pristine body. He thought back to the times he would drink it with his father and yet another state of sorrow engulfed him as he tried to hide the tears welling up in his eyes.

Baba Rada noticed Steve's change in demeanour and promptly tried to lighten the mood by talking about her life in Macedonia. How many wars she managed to survive. How many languages she could speak and how many old Macedonian traditions were lost on the young people. She gave Steve his coffee and a slice of the cake he had brought. Steve wanted to talk about the church proceedings and Temyana and everything she knew that he didn't! But Baba Rada insisted on the coffee being finished first. She kept the conversation as jovial as possible. Sometimes she rambled a little and sounded like the crazy person most people thought she was. Other times the clarity was almost brutal in its precision.

Steve finished the coffee and Baba Rada quickly gave Steve instructions. He had to turn the coffee cup upside down and place it on top of the saucer. He had to swirl it three times, with intent, and let it settle for a few minutes.

Steve was well aware of her intentions. She would read the coffee cups of all the women in the neighbourhood and supposedly tell them their future. In fact, he was sure it was more of a technique for finding out everybody's business. Steve's father would often joke about her crafty ways. "A simple statement such as 'I see new money' would reveal someone's inheritance from a relative overseas. And 'I see a dark cloud, is someone unhappy?' guaranteed a limitless supply of neighbourhood gossip." he said.

Steve readied himself for the thinly veiled interrogation. He was willing to put up with the theatre of the process if he was going to learn a few things after that. She picked up his cup and saucer, before she even looked at it, said "You know, I read your father's cup many times. He had a very difficult life and the coffee grinds barely fell to the saucer. He kept his pain with him all his life. Such a pity. He would have been a powerful leader if he wasn't left alone from such a young age. I tried to help him sometimes in the village, but none of us had anything to give. And besides, he needed something much more important than food."

Steve interrupted her and asked "What did he need?" She said "He needed a teacher, or many teachers. People who could explain the ways of the world and how it all works. Just as Alexander the Great had Aristotle and his father, your father needed a great teacher or teachers. If a King lives as a slave, how can he rise? He missed his opportunity, he was too young and the war....."

She shook her head and stopped talking, then insisted on reading Steve's cup. She went to pick up the cup and it was stuck to the saucer. "A prophet's cup," she exclaimed. No sooner had she said that, the cup separated from the saucer and the saucer broke in half on the table. She paused for a moment and looked perplexed. She gazed carefully inside the cup. Steve's assessment of his cup was that it was simply "brown" inside. Baba Rada, in contrast, was mesmerised by its contents. Her eyes were wide open and sometimes she would ask and answer her own questions. "But the triangle is everywhere and so high with the sun at the top! And those lines so thick but broken, and the dots and that dark angry eye, I mean eyes, hideous, a knife, two moons near the handle." Then she looked at the saucer and nodded to herself as though she had her confirmation. Steve found himself curiously enthralled with the process. He started as a sceptic but quickly became eager to learn about his "coffee cup future".

"What does it all mean?" Steve asked. Baba Rada took a deep breath and hesitated for a moment. She looked at Steve and then the cup again as if to check that each were related to the other. She nodded to herself in answer to her own silent question, "Of course, King's blood." She then looked at Steve and said "The triangle dominates your cup. The sun at the top of your cup with the triangle means your power will grow and that power will be the change in you. There will be a dramatic change in your life. I have never seen such a dominant triangle so high. Your change will happen quickly but it will not cease. The lines show your path is strong but it will break, so there will be pain. That eye is evil, someone will always be looking for you with bad intentions. No, more than one. There are other eyes. The moon shows you will find love. But the knife tells me you will be in danger. I have never seen so much in one cup my dear King. It is too much for me. You carry the divine blood, so the scope is broad, of course."

Steve couldn't make sense of anything. He only remembered the change and the blood and the evil eye. He asked Baba Rada, "Why did you put a mask on my father at the funeral proceedings and how did you know that little girl?" Baba Rada stood up and pointed her finger randomly around the room, "That little girl is no little girl. Don't even get me started about her. She is a liar and she hides in the smoke. She should have helped your father more. Macedonian stories passed from my Baba to me about her. They say she was the highest Orphic Priestess the first time around and she learned how to ascend from the cycle of life. But she was bound to King Alexander who commanded her return. When he passed to the next world, she was meant to go with him as his guide. But for some reason she is trapped between both worlds. She lied to her King and was not allowed to pass with him. Now, she floats between the Heavens and Earth and hides in the incense smoke. Some call her Temyana, but she has had many names. Don't trust her! She will always look for you. She is bound to your line and has no choice. But she failed King Alexander and she will probably fail you when you need her most. Don't rely on that witch!"

Steve wasn't really understanding any of the discussion, "My line, she is bound to it? And you speak of King Alexander? You mean Alexander the Great of Macedonia? Am I to believe I come from his line?" Baba Rada quickly replied, "Do you think I am crazy? Why do you think I greeted you all your life as royalty? Did you think I was joking? You are the last living descendant of King Alexander. The last of your line, my King. If I was younger, I would do anything you commanded of me. Now I'm old and I don't have much time left. You must find your teachers. Your father didn't have his chance and his coffee cup showed it every time. Your cup is beyond my comprehension. Your future will be memorable, my divine King."

The more questions Steve asked, the more confusing and far fetched the notions became. Baba Rada could see Steve was overwhelmed with all of the information about his identity and bloodline. She said "Seek your teachers, your father gave you every chance to do what he couldn't. Honour him and honour your line!"

Steve simply didn't know what to believe but finally made the decision he was agonising over. He would go to Japan to pursue his path and seek his teacher. He hugged and kissed Baba Rada and thanked her for always being kind to his father and himself. She replied, "It has been an honour, my King."

As he was leaving, Baba Rada tried to return the chocolates

Steve brought for her. Steve smiled and didn't even put up a fight. He couldn't refuse her this last time. He knew he would most likely never see her again. He squeezed her hand gently and looked deep in her eyes as if to keep the memory of her strong in his mind. He caught a glimpse of the beauty that would have condemned her to a life in a harem had it not been for that tattoo on her forehead. She blushed as she smiled deeply and proudly at him. She pretended to spit at him three times for good luck and to ward off any evil spirits and sent her King on his way.

There was little to keep Steve in Australia. He would leave his old life behind. His father, his first teacher, who sacrificed so much for him. His second teacher, Sensei Mike, who started his path. And the world he knew. It was time to leave. He would go to Japan with Sensei Mike's letter to seek his teacher and begin his journey.

Book Two - Agari

The Japanese word for East is Higashi.

But the Ryūkyū of Okinawa, in their own language, call it Agari.

The word has cognate with Agaru in standard Japanese
and means "rise".

Just as the Sun rises in the East.

But everything rises in the East.

Including the sins of bloodlines which stain the world today.

Chapter 6 - Triangles

Steve had lost his uncomplicated life and was desperate to leave all his personal tragedy behind. He was lucky he had relatives who helped him settle his father's estate matters. Some of the matters would take more time. But he was lucky there was an income stream which would assist him while he was training in Japan.

He packed lightly. He was to be training after all. He spent more time narrowing down which of his taped music collection to bring than anything else. He had no idea what to expect but was strangely optimistic about Japan. He was hopeful the time away would allow him to focus on his training and help ease the pain of his losses.

The flight was uneventful, though Steve found it difficult to sleep. His mind kept returning to recent events. Nothing was normal about what he recently endured, and learned, and it relentlessly played on his mind. Sleeping seemed to bring out the worst of his memories and the noisy flight was not helping him relax.

Tokyo was to be the first destination. Steve was eager to see Japan's capital before he settled into what he hoped would be a dedicated and uncomplicated life of training in Okinawa. It wasn't long before he landed at the new Narita airport in Tokyo and was making his way to the train station for Shinjuku. The brightest lights and tallest buildings were there and Steve was eager to compare life in such a populous city with that of his quiet hometown of Adelaide in South Australia.

It was winter back in Australia and, although the winters were mild back home, it was nice to feel the warm climate of Japan in the summer of 1988.

The subway system gave him a gentle buffer before he reached the madness of Tokyo. Stepping out of the subway system into the heat of Shinjuku for the first time was a startling experience. The contrast with Steve's hometown was amazing. The feeling of space back home was replaced with dense crowds, bright lights and highrise buildings. There was a sense of urgency about the city that Steve had never seen before. He was overwhelmed and excited in equal measure.

Japan's economy had been thriving for decades and, by the late 1980s, it was a very expensive place to be. It wasn't easy for a foreigner in Japan. There was hardly any English to be seen and, although Steve had developed his conversational Japanese to a serviceable level, his knowledge of the writing systems was rudimental at best. Thankfully he did his research before he left home and he was sure his carefully marked map would help him find his hotel quickly. He wasn't going to stay there long and was hoping to stay in Tokyo for a few days before making his way to Okinawa.

The hotel was not far from the Shinjuku station. Steve calculated a ten minute walk from the station to an area within Shinjuku called Kabukichō. It was a warm afternoon and weaving through the swarms of people whilst holding his map and luggage was not easy. He couldn't seem to find a single spot where he wasn't in someone's way. He walked past some souvenir shops and saw the cute little Daruma dolls like the one Sensei Mike gave him for good luck. He considered buying some for friends back home but then thought to himself, "Who knows when I'll go back. Maybe never. The little dolls can wait." Finally the sweaty journey was over. He reached his hotel in just under forty five minutes. "Ten minute walk, my arse!" he thought to himself.

Steve had never stayed in a hotel before. He wondered if all hotel rooms were as tiny as his. It didn't matter, there was a bed and his exhaustion served him a dreamless sleep that was both welcome and invigorating. He woke a few hours later and quickly headed outside. He wasn't going to be in Tokyo for long, he needed to get out and see some of it!

It was late in the evening and a hot balmy night when Steve joined the hordes of people on the streets in Shinjuku. He passed a 7-Eleven convenience store and made a mental note of its location for later. Then he passed numerous other 7-Elevens and decided he could discard that memory safely, they were everywhere! Shinjuku and, in particular, Kabukichō was "party central" in Tokyo. People were clearly out for a good time. Drunk "salary men" and girls were out in force. Club promoters were trying to drag Steve into their clubs and he quickly developed a number of inoffensive responses to discourage their continued attention.

He had seen enough for one night and was heading back to the hotel when he decided to stop at a 7-Eleven for some water and a snack. He was walking through the Golden Gai precinct. Formerly known for its prostitution decades earlier, it had become a drinking area with numerous small establishments full of people drinking and laughing the night away. As he passed an alley, he heard some shouting and stopped to look at what was happening. Three men in suits were shouting at a short stocky man who looked extremely drunk and shaky on his feet. He looked to be in his forties and had his hair uncharacteristically fashioned in a ponytail. One of the men slapped the man and sent him sprawling to the ground. Then all three of the men in suits started to kick him repeatedly. Steve knew it was never wise to intervene in things he didn't understand, but he couldn't simply stand by and watch the man be kicked to death.

He quickly ran there and grabbed the nearest man and flung him away from the action. He kicked the second guy with a perfectly executed side kick and sent him away. The third man saw what happened and raised his hand almost apologetically to Steve, bowed his head and walked away from the scene as though nothing happened.

Steve found the response rather perplexing but quickly went to the aid of the man on the ground. He helped the man up and asked if he was ok. The man said he was fine and thanked Steve for helping him. His English was surprisingly quite good. He slurringly said to Steve, "Oh my Buddha. You kicked that man so well! Do you know Karate?" Steve wasn't sure what to answer. He didn't feel like telling anyone about himself or what he knew about martial arts. And he found it odd those perfectly respectable looking "gentlemen" in suits felt compelled to beat the man. "Shit, maybe this guy was the bad guy," Steve thought to himself. Steve told the man he had trained karate a little bit back home in Australia.

The man said, "Oh very excellent, I would love to hear every- thing about it. It would be very much my honour if you walk with me to my home so that I may practise my English a little longer." Steve didn't hear any alarm bells ringing in his mind and thought to himself, "Even if he is a criminal, he can't have a problem with me. I saved the poor bloke!"

Steve walked with the man to a building nearby and, to his surprise, noticed an English sign out front advertising Karate classes. He saw at the bottom of the advertisement a note saying "foreigners accepted". He noticed the actual Japanese writing and it was in fact Gōjū-ryū Karate that was being taught there. He thought he would love to visit that dojo the following day to see how the Japanese people trained. At that moment, the man coughed a little and gave a relieved sigh and said "Here is my home." Steve asked "Is this dojo where you live?" The drunk man looked a little embarrassed and slurred a little while he said, "Well, maybe I had another home before, but now I live inside my dojo where I teach my classes. It is very convenient and has a bathroom."

Steve perhaps looked a little too surprised and asked "Are you the Sensei here?" The man dusted himself off, tucked his shirt into his pants, bowed and said, "I am Sensei Oshiro Takeshi, it is a pleasure to have made your acquaintance. You can call me Taki." Steve instinctively bowed as he had learned from Sensei Mike. He introduced himself formally in Japanese and said "It would please me very much if you allowed me to attend one of your classes one day Sensei ummm, er Taki." Sensei Taki was taken aback with Steve's perfect self-introduction and said it would be his pleasure to have Steve attend. He asked Steve if he would like to come in for tea, but Steve politely declined saying it was very late and he should sleep. With that, they parted ways and Steve went straight back to his hotel. He forgot he was hungry earlier and went straight to sleep.

It was not a good sleep. Again Steve saw and heard the Demon Hiro and the terrible day was replayed over and over until he had to wake. He hadn't been exercising as frequently as before the tournament, but the dreams would see him wake up sweating profusely. He wondered if he was training harder than ever, in his sleep! He didn't want to think about the dreams a moment longer and he was starving. A visit to the nearby 7-Eleven soon opened up a world of delight for him. He found his amazing "triangles of joy", tuna and mayonnaise onigiri, small triangles of rice filled with tuna and mayonnaise wrapped in seaweed. Steve tried one, then bought two more. He ate one of them and kept another for later. He had never been so excited about triangles ever before in his life. They were, "Heaven wrapped up in a triangle of seaweed," he thought to himself.

He wanted to visit the nearby dojo but he was eager to visit Shibuya. There was something he needed to see. The famous Hachikō! A statue in Shibuya dedicated to the memory of an Akita dog whose fame came from his loyalty to his owner. When his owner died, Hachikō would wait at the station for his master for a total of nine years until his own death. He was finally laid to rest next to his master in 1935. The story captured Steve's imagination vividly and he remembered his beloved dog, Tsare (little king), and how much comfort he'd given Steve when his mother died. All the bittersweet childhood memories flooded back into his mind's eye. They quickly transformed into his more recent memories and Steve again refused to allow himself to think about them.

The statue was right next to the Shibuya station and Steve found it quickly. It was inspiring to see. The dog was immortalised for nothing more than its loyalty and fidelity. He immersed himself in the moment and tried to remember everything about his beloved Tsare running to school to escort him back home every day in his youth. Steve enjoyed that memory and decided this was a perfect time to eat his last tuna and mayonnaise onigiri. The unwrapping of the snack was an extremely technical process for Steve. The potential for the triangle of rice to collapse was ever present. He made a mess of his first attempt. His second was much better and he was completely committed to becoming a master in onigiri eating. He thought it would be nice to receive a black belt in onigiri eating. He would live a happy and uncomplicated life!

He had almost finished unravelling his onigiri from its wrapping when he was bumped. His little triangle from heaven had fallen from his hands and disintegrated on the ground. Steve was crestfallen. He didn't even look to see who bumped him. He just stared at the ground and his profound sadness was almost comical. A girl was apologising to him profusely and Steve was unable to drag his eyes away from his beloved fallen onigiri. The girl continued to apologise. She clearly saw Steve was a foreigner and proceeded to explain in English, "I am so sorry. I am carrying too many shopping bags and I am so late. I am rushing for the train. I am so sorry."

Steve finally looked up at her. She was strikingly beautiful. His "triangle from heaven" quickly became a distant and unimportant memory as Steve stumbled through an attempt at a response. He was hoping to sound relaxed about the incident and wanted to assure her that all was fine. Instead, he just pointed at the mess on the ground and murmured a few words with a starry-eyed look at her. He had never seen anyone so pretty in his life. "Those beautiful eyes!", he thought to himself. She was tall and slender and showing the deepest concern and empathy for Steve's loss.

Finally, the joy of language returned to Steve and he was able to string together a few coherent words. "No problem at all. Thank you very much," he said wondering why he thanked her. He bent over to quickly collect the mess on the ground. She joined him and helped clean up. They managed to find a bin and throw away that once much-loved onigiri and Steve asked her if she lived in Shibuya. She said, "No, I live in Shinjuku but better shopping is here in Shibuya." Steve quickly replied, "Oh, I am staying in Shinjuku, maybe we could ....". She interjected "Where are you staying in Shinjuku?" Steve told her the hotel name and she quickly replied, "I am so very sorry again, I am so late, must leave!" and she ran to the station entrance. Steve did not dare look away from her. He wanted to remember everything about her. If she turned around to look at him, even for the slightest moment, he swore he would search all of Shinjuku, and indeed Japan, to find her. He watched her shrink smaller and smaller into the mass of commuters and maintained his singular focus on her, the girl of his dreams. She was no more than a speck at that stage, but she did it! She turned around and looked right back at Steve and surrendered a tiny wave to him.

Perhaps she was still feeling remorseful about the accident, or maybe she was simply being polite. Steve was a rational young man, he accepted both scenarios were quite reasonable conclusions. But he much preferred the third option, that she was promptly as madly in love and attracted to him as he was to her! If only he knew her name!

Steve floated around Shibuya that afternoon. He didn't recall if his feet actually touched the ground for the rest of that day. He had been enchanted by that girl and, for a welcome moment, was relieved of his burdens. His spirits were lifted and he decided to visit Sensei Taki at his dojo. The train system was so efficient and logical. Steve quickly found his way back to Shinjuku and the dojo. He decided to simply attend and not train. He was concerned his skills might not be good enough and was under the perception that all training in Japan was surely superior to anything outside of Japan.

Even though Steve was confident nobody could be a better teacher than his Sensei Mike, he still had a belief that the birthplace of karate would somehow be able to offer more insight to a dedicated karateka. Steve managed to catch the tail end of a training session in the dojo under the supervision of Sensei Taki. He soon learned he had nothing to feel inferior about. He saw mostly Japanese students at various grade levels perform the Sanchin kata. He thought to himself, "Sensei Mike would have never allowed such wasted and thoughtless movement!"

Sensei Taki was delighted Steve visited his dojo. His class had concluded and he invited Steve for a drink at the back of the dojo. He warmed some sake and poured Steve a drink and shouted "kanpai" and encouraged Steve to drink. Out of politeness, Steve tasted it. He hated alcohol and, while the drink wasn't the worst thing he ever tasted, it most definitely wasn't anything he'd ever crave. Sensei Taki said "Sake is my weakness, I love it. I also love beer. And to tell you truth, whisky is also very favourable to me," as he poured himself and Steve another drink. Steve was already slightly drunk. He decided not to drink any more sake, but Sensei Taki was persuasive. He managed to coax Steve into yet another cup of sake.

Steve felt so relaxed and enjoyed the easy conversation. Sensei Taki asked what he did that day and Steve jokingly shouted "I fell in love today. I found my future wife in Shibuya. I don't know her name and I'm not sure I'll ever find her again, but I'm gonna try my best!" Sensei Taki's eyes widened, he enjoyed where the conversation was going and loved talking about girls. He said "There are so many beautiful girls in Japan. So pretty. But I love Wonder Woman, you know Lynda Carter?" Steve laughed, Wonder Woman was always on TV back home and he had an idea why Sensei Taki might have found her attractive. She was indeed a beautiful woman with large breasts and Sensei Taki confirmed his infatuation as he gestured with his hands in front of his own chest. Steve became serious. He looked Sensei Taki in the eyes and said, "She was quite tall, with beautiful eyes. She had a dimple when she smiled and her voice was like a sweet dream. She said she lives in Shinjuku. Do you know her?" Sensei Taki laughed and said, "I think I know her, Steve-san," Steve optimisitcally leaned in closer with eager enthusiasm. Sensei Taki continued, "She is everywhere you look in Tokyo!" Steve quickly reassured Sensei Taki there was only one girl like her in the world and he would find her, no matter what!

Sensei Taki then asked Steve what he thought of the training he saw earlier. Steve was indeed a little tipsy, but not stupid. He didn't want to upset his new friend. He said "The students seem motivated and eager to please their Sensei." Sensei Taki said "Ahhh, no. They want to play the Nintendo and they do not have the true spirit for fighting. I think maybe you are being too kind to me. I should be a better Sensei!" as he slapped his own thigh.

"Please come to the dojo and train with me tomorrow. I would like to see more of your skills Steve-san. I know you can kick like a horse. I look very forward to seeing more!" he said.

It was another long day for Steve. Soon he would leave for Okinawa. Somehow he would try to find the girl of his dreams in Shinjuku. It was time to go back to his hotel. He thanked Sensei Taki for his hospitality and said goodnight. Sensei Taki changed out of his training Gi and put on his shirt and trousers and said he would go to Golden Gai for a drink. Steve was astounded. He said "Aren't you afraid of crossing paths with those men in the suits again?" Sensei Taki said "They are low level Yakuza criminals, haha, I will never be afraid of such people!" as he walked with Steve and started singing the theme song to the Wonder Woman TV series. Steve hadn't heard the word "yakuza" since Sensei Mike talked about his history and crashed back to a reality he didn't want to hear about. He reminded Sensei Taki to be careful and stay out of the alleys. Steve worried about Sensei Taki all the way back to the hotel and finally managed to swing his thoughts back to the nameless girl of his dreams as he laid down to rest in bed!

Steve woke up with a thumping headache and decided that if there was ever a question, then sake was most definitely not the answer! He drank copious amounts of water and ate two of his beloved onigiri and some Japanese omelette at the local 7-Eleven. He would train in the morning and try to sweat out the sake of the previous night. He wore his Gi to the dojo but refrained from wearing his black belt. He thought it would be disrespectful to wear it. But he did bring his carefully-packed certificate and letter from Sensei Mike in order to learn whether Sensei Taki knew of Sensei Mike's teacher.

Sensei Taki looked no worse for wear in the morning. Steve thought to himself, "He looks as fresh as a daisy for crying out loud!" The class started and everything was surprisingly familiar to Steve. Other students kept looking over their shoulders at Steve's powerful movements. Sensei Taki asked Steve if he would like to perform his Sanchin kata. Steve had genuinely mastered the kata. He understood what it was like to dedicate an entire day to simply repeating the kata. It became a battle with oneself. And Steve had done it all before, many, many times.

He performed the kata with a ferocity and spirit that nobody in that class had ever seen before. It was almost a religious experience for them. The entire dojo descended into a hush as the students watched Steve move through the sequence of movements. The energy was intense. Steve finished and some students even clapped. Sensei Taki ordered the class to leave immediately. Steve thought perhaps he did something inappropriate in the class. He asked Sensei Taki if he did something wrong. But Sensei Taki reassured him that was not the case. He said he needed to talk with him urgently and did not have time to finish the class.

Steve sat with Sensei Taki in the same little room they were drinking in the night before. Sensei Taki's normal jovial demeanour had changed into one of intense seriousness. He said, "You can only be from one of two lines. Who is your Sensei? I demand you tell me!" Steve turned and reached for his bag. Sensei Taki was faster than Steve could have possibly anticipated and had already placed a firm and deliberate hand on Steve's shoulder and another hand on his elbow to ensure control of his movement. He asked "What are you reaching for young Steve-san?" Steve said. "I have a letter from my Sensei in Australia. I will show you." Steve sensed a danger that was non existent at any other time since he had met Sensei Taki. Steve said "I was hopeful you might know the Sensei I will be trying to locate in Okinawa. Here is the letter." Sensei Taki cautiously opened the envelope and looked at the letter. He read it. Looked up at Steve. Put it down. Read it again. He then carefully folded the letter and placed it back in the envelope. He handed the letter back to Steve.

He said, "Steve-san, I saw your true face when I saw your first movement. I saw your energy. Your presence dominated the dojo. I knew your line. I knew your teacher's teacher. I know you more than you do. I thought it could only be Mike or ...... Do not look at me now. I used to have what you have. I was successful here until the Yakuza burned me out of my home here. They hunt me all the way from Okinawa. I have not stopped drinking since then. Your Sensei Mike is my older brother. I would do anything for him. He proved his honour to our Sensei. You are family Steve-san. Whatever you need, I am here to assist you. I ask you to stay here with me before you seek our Sensei in Okinawa. The letter explains all I need to know about your skills. But there is much I can teach you about what your Sensei Mike left behind when he left us in Okinawa. I want to know all about Mike. I hope he is well. Please stay for a while. Leave the hotel, keep your money and stay with me."

Steve didn't have the heart to tell Sensei Taki about Sensei Mike. He decided it was best to learn more from and about Sensei Taki before telling him anything about what happened on that terrible day.

Steve could not believe how fate could have brought him to Sensei Taki. He thought about those "triangles from heaven", the onigiri, and realised he may have found an even better triangle. The triangle from Australia to Shinjuku which would guide him to Okinawa. He thought it would be wise to stay a little longer. He was eager to learn much about Sensei Mike from Sensei Taki and would have a little more time to find the nameless girl of his dreams. He thanked Sensei Taki and decided he would check out of his hotel the following morning.

Chapter 7 - Megumi

Steve arrived at the dojo the following morning. Sensei Taki welcomed him and showed him to a small room at the back of the dojo. It was even smaller than his former hotel room but it looked comfortable enough and would serve him well for a few days or even weeks.

Sensei Taki told Steve about the plans he had decided the night before. He said he went out drinking the previous evening and developed his final strategy in the second or third to last bar he visited. "You will find and teach the gaijin in my dojo! I know you have excellent Karate skills and you have strong positive energy. You will find many students and I will pay you to teach them."

Steve said "But Sensei Taki, I must go to Okinawa soon. I don't think I'll be here for very long. I'm not sure." Sensei Taki replied, "You can leave any time. It is your choice. But please let us try for a little. It is important for you to practise your teaching. You know? And I can teach you about Okinawa. There is much to know before you go there." Steve did know, he had been teaching back home in Australia under Sensei Mike's supervision. Teaching would not be difficult. The difficult part would be how he would extract himself from there!

Sensei Taki asked Steve if he brought his belt with him. Steve said "I do have it, but I did not want to wear it in your dojo." Sensei Taki said "If Sensei Mike calls you a black belt level, then you are probably almost the same level as me at third dan! I do not question your ability. You must wear it. You earned it under my great brother Sensei Mike!"

Steve was to take the first class. Sensei Taki introduced Steve to the class and said he would be assisting him. The mostly Japanese students looked surprised to be led by young Steve, a foreigner! As accustomed back home, Steve led the entire class in the Japanese language. He seemed to create a pulsing energy in the dojo. It was positively infectious. Everyone raised their level of energy. Steve demanded more from the students and they responded immediately. Sensei Taki looked on approvingly.

It was an excellent session, Steve thought. Some students thanked him for the class and promised Steve they would try harder next time. Others wanted to know more about him and practised their English with him. It was enjoyable. The students had left and Steve approached Sensei Taki to ask if he was pleased with how the class was conducted. Sensei Taki said, "You show great ability Steve-san. I have never seen a foreigner with your ability and I have not seen many Japanese with your ability either. You have made Sensei Mike very very proud. And you have embarrassed me. I feel ashamed. You have reminded me of who I once was and what I have now become." He bowed deeply to Steve in a very sincere and respectful way. "No way, no way a Sensei of his own school should bow to me that way," Steve thought to himself.

Steve wanted to swing the pendulum in Sensei Taki's favour and thought of a subdued way to return some respect, "I would like to prepare tea for you, Sensei Taki if you allow me," Steve said. Soon he performed a tea ceremony with the precision and mindfulness in the manner demanded by Sensei Mike. Sensei Taki seemed almost tearful in the way the ceremony was conducted. He said, "I look at you and only see the old ways. You are a true son of Gōjū-ryū."

He continued, "We will have lunch soon. I expect it to be delivered shortly. My niece never forgets her best uncle Taki." Steve was disappointed, he was thinking he could just sneak out and grab a few delightful onigiri and his life would be harmonious and full of the joy that only those tasty morsels could possibly bring. He thought, "The longer I am outside, the more chance I'll find that sweet love of my life!"

Nevertheless, Steve accepted his fate. He would buy some onigiri later and endure this lunch no matter how much less exciting the food was. Shortly thereafter he heard the front door open and footsteps coming towards the back room of the dojo. Sensei Taki started wiggling on the spot, he said "My niece always brings nice food for me. She has made me very fat! Well, maybe the beer has helped also! There you are my dear niece ... please meet my new assistant teacher ..." Steve turned around and exclaimed "It's you!" He was pointing at her with that starry eyed look again. He just kept pointing. The girl dropped one of the dishes and turned bright red. She was in just as much shock as Steve.

Sensei Taki quickly realised who she was in Steve's mind. Before his mouth could say anything, his body did the talking. He jumped up and stood between Steve and the nameless girl of his dreams as if to declare she was completely out of bounds. "This is my niece, Megumi, she is too young for a boyfriend or even looking at a boy. She is only eighteen!" he said.

Steve just heard the name "Megumi" .... he was immediately transported. He knew the word. In some contexts it meant "blessing", in other contexts it meant "love" and he just kept saying "Megumi ... blessing ... love ... Megumi" over and over as if in a trance. Sensei Taki quickly thanked his niece and ushered her out of the room. Megumi was taller than Sensei Taki and she poked her head over his shoulder and said "I asked your hotel about you and they said you were ....," by that stage Sensei Taki had almost thrown her out of the dojo. Steve had found her! And she was also looking for him! Destiny was smiling on Steve. It was his best day ever!

Days passed and Steve's absolute highlight was lunch time. Megumi would deliver the food and Sensei Taki seemed to regard each lunch as another challenge and triumph when he managed to keep Steve away from his precious niece! Sometimes Sensei Taki would try to limit interactions and meet Megumi at the front door and Steve would bounce around in the background. Steve thrived on Megumi's captivating smile. He tried every possible way to extract information from Sensei Taki about Megumi, but his responses were consistently rigid and dismissive. "There's no information to be had from this man!" Steve thought to himself.

The classes were growing. The young Japanese students had been talking about their cool new foreign "Sensei Steve" and a number of Japanese and foreigners had joined the classes. Additional sessions were added and Steve was extremely busy and would be making good money for an eighteen year old in a foreign city. But he wasn't going to have any chance to spend anything. He was quite simply too busy!

Sensei Taki had stopped visiting his favourite bars in Golden Gai. He would stay home and drink a little less than usual and play his favourite music to Steve. There would be endless rotations of Hako Yamasaki's music from the 1970s and Sensei Taki would try to play the chords on his beloved Kazuo Yairi acoustic guitar. In return, Steve would play the likes of Led Zeppelin and Black Sabbath to Sensei Taki who would always end up looking genuinely confused and ask "When does the music begin?" much to Steve's disappointment. Sensei Taki would then return to playing his beloved Hako Yamasaki tunes. The more drunk he became, the more he became convinced he matched her pitch perfectly. Steve didn't think so, but wouldn't dare say. Surprisingly he quite enjoyed listening to her soulful voice. Such an oddly pleasant departure from his normal diet of 1970s rock.

The attraction between Megumi and Steve was obvious. She would linger around the dojo stealing furtive glances through the windows at Steve. Steve was intoxicated by her. He couldn't understand what was happening with himself. He would forget how to perform simple tasks such as how to talk and breathe whenever she was near. If he managed to string together a few words to her, it was a major achievement because there were millions of other words, thoughts, wishes and desires competing for attention in his mind. He had never felt so frustrated, yet excited, in his life.

Finally, it was Sunday and Steve had a day off. He told Sensei Taki he would go out to explore Tokyo as he really hadn't seen much of it since his arrival. In fact, he waited around the corner for lunch time. Megumi would always leave her workplace and drop off the lunch dutifully to her uncle at 12:15 every day. This time Steve would catch her outside!

She was even more reliable than the Japanese rail system. There she was! Except she wasn't wearing her formal business suit. This time she was wearing an explosion of colours and her hair wasn't pulled back. It was down and she even had different coloured ribbons in her hair. "She was wearing the latest casual fashion and she still managed to look elegant, as always. She was already perfect, but "Today she is even more perfect!" he thought to himself. He startled her when he called her name and there was that blush of hers again. Megumi gestured for him to wait there while she took the food to her uncle. It seemed like an eternity before she came back. Megumi apologised saying "Uncle insisted we eat together. I brought food for both of you and he didn't want to waste it!" Steve asked Megumi where she was going and she said it was her day off, she was going shopping in Harajuku. He asked if it would be okay if he could accompany her. She covered her smile with her hand and ran on ahead. Steve just stood there until she waved him over and told him to hurry up!

It was a brilliant day. Steve was smitten and had a voracious appetite for information about her. He was entirely infatuated with Megumi and he learned so much about her on their first outing together. But there was so much to learn and he needed to know everything! They had many more outings together. Megumi worked in reception at a nearby hotel. She had such an elegant charm. Steve would sometimes wait for her in the hotel lobby and watch how she dealt with hotel guests and other staff. Anyone who was fortunate enough to interact with her were convinced they were the most important person in the world. But Megumi only had eyes for Steve and he felt precisely the same way about her. Steve and Megumi were inseparable. They would call each other "Baby Love". It was a lyric from Megumi's favorite artist, Anri. She would sing Anri's "Last Summer Whisper" to Steve and he would be dreamily bewitched. The intense attraction was mutual and it was only a matter of time before Sensei Taki realised what was going on and tried to put a stop to the relationship.

Megumi loved her uncle dearly. He was her mother's brother and her mother had died in a traumatic accident three years earlier. Her relationship with her father was strained and Uncle Taki had done everything in his power to care for his beloved niece. Though it seemed to Steve she did more to care for her uncle than the other way around. In any case, it was obvious there was a deep mutual affection and bond between Megumi and her beloved uncle.

Steve quickly adapted to the Japanese language and Sensei Taki preferred to speak Japanese on matters of importance. He pleaded with Steve, "Steve, you are a very good young man. I am proud to know you and I believe your future will be great. If Megumi was my daughter, I would welcome you into our family. But please know that there is more to know about Megumi than you realise. I am worried about both of your safety if you pursue this relationship with Megumi. You must understand that her father is a powerful and evil man. He will never accept a gaijin such as you for his daughter. This man is immoral. I hated how he treated my sister and I was powerless to intervene. I left Okinawa to get away from his evil tentacles there, only to find his influence here. To this day, I cannot even be sure my sister died accidentally. You should ask your Sensei Mike about him! He had to flee Okinawa to escape his wickedness."

Steve quickly, in an exclamation of disbelief, asked "Kumicho? The Yakuza leader who Sensei Mike was working for in Okinawa?" Sensei Taki looked shocked to hear "Kumicho" mentioned. He said "I am surprised Mike told you about him. It was not a good time in his life. His relationship with our sensei, and indeed all of us, suffered as a result. It seems Mike told you many things. The man truly suffered for his love. I really do hope he is better now."

Steve finally decided he must tell Sensei Taki about Sensei Mike. He explained the events of the terrible tournament. The death of Sensei Mike and his own father. How Demon Hiro had found Sensei Mike. Tears fell freely from Steve's face as he allowed himself to be immersed in that misery for the first time in a long time. Steve could not bring himself to reveal the extent of the power he himself unleashed that terrible day. Perhaps he still couldn't understand it himself or maybe he just didn't want to think about it.

Sensei Taki was visibly shaken by what he learned. His heart was broken for Sensei Mike and also for Steve and it was painfully clear he truly cared for them both. He became sombre and silent for an uncomfortable length of time. Finally, he said "I hope Mike found his beloved Chiasa. She was his only comfort. I am sorry for your losses Steve. I do not understand why your father was killed at the command of Demon Hiro. Hiro is no longer of this world. His life force comes from elsewhere now. I also do not understand how you managed to beat Demon Hiro's hench monsters. Many of them used to be my dojo brothers back in Okinawa before they followed the darkness. There is much to learn about you! But you must know it was Kumicho who burnt me out of my own home in Shinjuku. The hotel where Megumi now works stands in its place. He is the owner and he has done this all over Shinjuku and beyond as his power and influence grows unabated. I have never told Megumi who her real employer is. She would not stay there. She hates her father and also suspects he killed her mother. The only reason Kumicho's henchmen do not try to kill me is because he does not allow it. He still tries to bring his only child back to Okinawa. She would never return if she learned my death was at his command. If you saw Demon Hiro and the terrible power he summons, you must know that the Kumicho has much older and stronger power. He has the blood of an emperor, the heart of a vagrant thief and the soul of a demon. So you see, I am not only protecting Megumi. It is for all of our protection."

It was Steve's turn to digest the new information. He thought about how complex life had become. Only months earlier he had simple dreams and uncomplicated ideas. He looked at Sensei Taki and it was a look of resolve of a man many years older than he was. He said "Sensei Taki, thank you for explaining so much to me. Please know, what you're asking me is to never breathe again. I've lost everything that was dear to me back home in Australia. Megumi has been my cure. She washes my sadness with her smile and her love has cured the pain in my soul. To lose her is to lose my reason for living. I'm prepared to accept any consequences as a result of loving Megumi. I'm sorry if my actions will bring pain. But I have given myself to Megumi for this life. I can't turn away from her. I will defend her with my life. Just as I tried to save Sensei Mike from Demon Hiro when I made him human again. I'll use every power within me to fight the evil of Kumicho and his minions if they come for us. Please forgive me for being so bold, but my intentions are not for negotiation. If you can't accept this, I understand. With deep sorrow, I will make preparations to leave."

Sensei Taki understood the gravity of Steve's words and accepted the resignation in his heart. "Steve-san," he said "I can see I won't be able to change your mind. The path you have chosen will not be without consequence. It seems we have both dedicated our lives to our Megumi. A worthy recipient we both agree! Steve, I cannot stand in your way. Such deep love should be placed on a pedestal for all to praise, not be denied. You have my blessing and support for what it's worth."

Steve breathed a sigh of relief. He was grateful for the blessing and really wanted the approval from Sensei Taki who had become dear to him. He wanted to jump up and down with joy but Sensei Taki continued, "But please tell me, how did you manage to cast the demon out of Hiro? My Sensei has gone mad since he summoned the power to control Hiro and his gun. I believe he unleashed many demons unexpectedly that day and his spirit continues to fight them. A normal person would have been consumed by the demons but my Sensei has a strong spirit which refuses to be defeated by them. He suffers for this and has had no respite since that day. To be honest, I am not sure I can trust him fully anymore. Is it possible you have the power to restore my Sensei's spirit?"

"I don't know about this Sensei Taki, but I would do anything to help him. I know Sensei Mike loved and admired his Sensei dearly and I will honour Sensei Mike's memory in the best way I can," Steve said.

Sensei Taki said to Steve, "We will have much to do in the future, but I must insist on one thing! I would prefer you call me Uncle Taki. You are already family to me and your skills are beyond mine in many ways. I refuse to be acknowledged as a higher rank than you."

Steve said he was extremely uncomfortable with this. He respected Sensei Taki and his dojo. They eventually agreed he would continue to call Taki as Sensei in his dojo and Uncle outside of the dojo. They both bowed to each other formally and then hugged each other with great affection. Neither of them realised Megumi had arrived just a few moments earlier and was listening. She realised Uncle Taki had accepted her relationship with Steve and squealed with delight as she moved forwards and hugged both of them.

Megumi seemed to blossom with her uncle's acceptance of their relationship. She had already truly committed her heart and soul to Steve. But the blessing from her uncle gave her the freedom to express her devotion to Steve publicly. She even joined Steve's karate classes and displayed surprising skill with an incredible capacity to learn. Steve was extremely impressed with her progress. She was an excellent student and Steve taught her everything he knew. What she didn't have in strength, she had in resourcefulness and speed.

Steve certainly had an advantage when it came to Karate skills, but they were both blissfully unaware of matters in the art of lovemaking. Megumi's experience was limited to holding a boy's hand when she was fifteen. Steve was only a little more enlightened. There once was a night at a disco where a girl forced her tongue in his mouth and, after he recovered from the shock of the invasion, soon taught him how to kiss. Luckily Steve and Megumi required little assistance. They couldn't keep their hands away from each other and an unbridled passion was their guide.

It had only been a few months in Tokyo when Steve finally moved in with Megumi. Their life was idyllic. They were already discussing marriage and planning their future together. Megumi wanted to live in Australia with Steve. Steve didn't miss home one bit but would do anything for his "Baby Love". He felt obliged to go to Okinawa to fulfil Sensei Mike's hope for him to formalise his Gōjū-ryū qualifications. Every time he brought up the idea, Megumi quickly found something else more important to discuss.

It was clear she didn't want to be anywhere near her father from what Uncle Taki had said to him. "She was not well over there Steve-san. Her father's influence there was very strong and it made her very sick as a child," Uncle Taki said. But surely Steve could protect her from his attention. He pleaded with Megumi on numerous occasions. After repeated attempts over many months, he said "My baby, I don't have university qualifications. You can see I have dedicated myself to Gōjū-ryū. It makes sense for me to earn the highest qualifications possible in my art. Training in Okinawa will give me something we can use to make money in the future and provide for our family."

Megumi said, "My Steve, you do not know my life back in Okinawa. Everybody pretends to respect and admire my father there, but they all just fear him. He can take one look at a person and know what will be their downfall. He plays with them all. I have never known anyone to be a true friend there. Everyone was too scared to upset me for fear of retribution from my father. I am sure my mother did not die in an accident. I still believe my father did it and I refuse to be anywhere near that monster of a man. All my life, I have been haunted by him. His darkness terrorised me as a child and I was very sick when I was growing up. Don't look at me now, I have pushed him away from my life and my health has improved. I know I work in a hotel he owns. I dare not tell Uncle Taki. I know it was my father's criminals who burnt him out of his home to buy the land cheaper. If I go to work anywhere else, he will just buy it anyway. He is more than persuasive. He will leave you no choice. I even remember your Sensei Mike back when I was a young girl. He had no choice and I will never forget the sadness in his eyes. I cannot let you be caught up in my father's terrible web. He will take away your honour and replace it with evil. I will lose my Steve, my Baby Love, who I love with every part of my being."

It broke Steve's heart to see how much pain his beautiful Megumi had clearly suffered at the hands of her father. He couldn't understand how such evil intent was possible from a father to his child. He recalled the lifelong sacrifices his own father had made for him and then mournfully recalled his father's ultimate sacrifice at the presentation ceremony.

Steve was grateful Megumi had Uncle Taki in her life. He clearly loved his niece and had her best interests at heart. It surprised him to learn that Megumi knew her father owned the hotel where she was employed. Uncle Taki didn't dare tell her what she already knew. Steve resolved to never let his beautiful baby love suffer at the hands of that monster again. "I just can't understand how a man can be so evil to his own child," he said.

The discussion appeared to send Megumi back into her own private hell as she gently rocked herself and explained, "My bloodline is cursed. My ancestor was an emperor and his child was nothing more than a thief and a murderer. This is the curse of my family line. My father is the greatest thief. He is truly a demon my Steve, and nobody can stop him. Please Steve, we can find another way, far away from Japan. Far away from him! We can make a new life in Australia, or wherever you want."

Steve resigned himself to the fact that circumstances would have to dramatically change for them to go to Okinawa. He did however still feel that he should go there one day, even if it was to try and help Sensei Mike's teacher.

Steve never explained Temyana, or what Baba Rada had told him about his own bloodline. All of that seemed to be a distant memory for him and he started to doubt any of it. But he thought to himself, "Imagine if we had a child, the blood of a royal union!" He smiled at his beautiful Megumi and said "Whatever makes you happy, my sweet love," as he pulled her close and tasted her sweet lips again.

Chapter 8 - Vibrations

Time passed quickly. Steve had already been teaching Gōjū-ryū in Shinjuku for almost three years. He had learned his way around Tokyo as if he were a local. He spoke like a local and could even identify dialects in the region with an ability to slip into the Shitamachi dialect if he wanted to sound like an honest local working class man and the Yamanote dialect when he wanted to be more formal and sound more "educated". He had made many friends all over Tokyo. The most challenging aspect of his job was to try and accommodate all the invitations to social events organised by his students.

Occasionally, Uncle Taki would need to return to Okinawa. He had business matters and a property there which required attention. He would leave the dojo entirely under Steve's control and nobody ever doubted Steve's authority. Such was Steve's nature that the students looked up to him as if he were much older than his actual twenty one years. Students would come to him for advice and motivation. Sometimes they would talk about problems at their jobs or school and Steve would offer suggestions based on parallels he could relate to his training. One incident that made him laugh was when a student told Steve, "I hope I will be as confident and wise as you when I reach your age." In fact, the student was older than Steve but he didn't have the heart to tell him.

Even Uncle Taki couldn't help but be motivated by Steve's infectious ability to inspire his classes. Very soon after Steve had joined him, he had reduced his alcohol intake to weekends only and trained vigorously with Steve after the evening classes. His skills always surprised Steve. There were some unique traits he saw in Uncle Taki. Steve could see Uncle Taki was speaking the "language" of Gōjū-ryū but he still managed to introduce his own personality and flair to their martial art. While Sensei Mike was powerful and far reaching with his moves, Uncle Taki was shorter and used his low centre of gravity and body weight to move in very close and try to send Steve off balance. In fact, Steve was grateful to train with Uncle Taki. He gave him another insight into the broadness of their martial art and it only strengthened his desire to train under Sensei Mike and Uncle Taki's Sensei in Okinawa.

Megumi had also been training hard. What started as simply a desire to constantly be near Steve also soon became an addiction for her. She would look forward to training with Steve and with her new training partner, Tania. She was a beautiful American girl and had an ebullient personality which Megumi found utterly refreshing. Tania worked in any job she could find. She was desperate to stay in Japan and found herself working in one of the dance clubs in Kabukichō as a hostess. Both Megumi and Steve were worried about her. That kind of work placed her in a world where the yakuza are heavily involved and, once tangled in their webs, it was impossibly difficult to break free. Megumi was trying to teach her as much formal Japanese as possible so that she might find work outside of the seedy clubs. Tania didn't seem to mind either way. She was making money and she had debts to pay. It was expensive living in Japan and she found work where she would be paid to dance and sometimes she would earn even more just by sitting and talking with older Japanese men who frequented the clubs.

Meanwhile, Steve and Megumi's relationship had only strengthened over the years. Whatever they had missed out on in their youth, they found in each other. It was the deepest love, reliance and joy they shared. Steve had made his choice the first time he met her, Megumi would be his wife and it was only a matter of time before that became a reality. Both of them were deeply committed to each other and were eager to be married. There was little fanfare about the proposal, they both simply needed to express themselves as a single unit and being married formally was something they both wanted.

Steve would have liked to give Megumi his mother's engagement ring which was back home in Australia. When he left Australia, he didn't think he would find the love of his life and marry her in a foreign land. He thought he might train in Okinawa for a year and then return to study in Australia but instead, he found joy and a life he could never have imagined in Japan. His beautiful Megumi was the air that he breathed and needed.

Megumi explained to Steve that marriage in Japan was a relatively simple administrative process and they had all the paperwork needed to have their marriage formally registered. Steve found it a little peculiar, he was more accustomed to Macedonian Orthodox wedding ceremonies which were steeped in rituals and traditions. He wanted to honour his parents and have a marriage ceremony conducted under the Orthodox faith. But he was also mindful of Megumi's culture. He asked if she had any desire to consider a Shinto or Buddhist ceremony. She said "My father would die a million deaths if we married under Buddhist traditions and I am more than happy to follow your culture and beliefs. Besides, you know more about my culture than I know about yours, I would very much like to be married in your faith and tradition."

Steve wasn't particularly sure what his faith actually was. But he did want to honour the memory of his parents and was eager to preserve their traditions. There were no Macedonian churches to be found in Japan, but he learned the Russian Orthodox Church had maintained a presence in Japan over the last one hundred years and it was quite easy to find a parish nearby.

Steve went alone to the church to meet the priest and discuss arrangements for the wedding ceremony.

He walked in and a flood of memories came back to him. The candles everywhere, the architecture and the symbols immediately transported him back to his father's funeral. The icons on the walls with their Old Church Slavonic texts. Steve's father would correct him and call them Old Macedonian. He said the name was more appropriate, "After all, it was the Macedonian Saints, Kiril and Metodi, who created the written language!" he would always say.

Steve purchased three candles. He lit each one individually for a different purpose. The first candle was for his mother. He lit the candle and placed it in the lower receptacle where souls of the dead are prayed for. He prayed she was happy and at peace. He did the same for his father and tried to rid his mind of the very vivid events which led to his death. He finally lit a candle for himself and Megumi and placed it in the higher receptacle so they would be blessed. The flame extinguished and Steve had to persist to keep it alight. He thought to himself, "No way, nothing's gonna interfere with our flame!"

The priest was mid ceremony at the time. He was performing a liturgy and was a Japanese man with a Russian name performing rituals which were familiar to Steve. As odd as it all seemed, it was strangely comforting. Steve made the sign of the Orthodox cross with his right hand and then took a seat alone at the back of the church. He sat silently for a few minutes and then noticed someone sitting right next to him. It was an older Japanese woman. She looked extremely dignified and was dressed immaculately. Steve had been with Megumi long enough to finally be able to notice when a woman was wearing expensive clothing.

Steve was enjoying his solitude and felt a little annoyed the woman would choose to sit right next to him of all places. She then startled him as she spoke in Macedonian. She spoke in his own family's southern Macedonian dialect and asked, "Have you been to this church before?" Before Steve could even answer, the woman spoke in Japanese and said "I hope you haven't forgotten me already my King," as she turned to face Steve. He noticed her half mask and quickly realised the woman was Temyana. She wasn't that little girl who encouraged him at the tournament so long ago. She was now an elegant looking, middle aged Japanese woman!

"The temyan, the incense!" Steve thought to himself. "That's right my King" she said as if reading his mind. "It is easier to show myself to you where there is smoke, especially when it looks towards a god."

Steve said "I started to think you were in my imagination. Maybe you and I are in a dream, or perhaps even a nightmare right now!" She smiled and swiftly transformed into the little girl he remembered. "How could this little girl ever be a nightmare for you?" she joked. She then transformed back into the Japanese woman again and said, "My King, Australia was much safer than this country. This land is old and has worshipped many gods and been ruled by many demons. Surely you sense them. I have been watching you. Your power is growing and your enemies, those who fear the purity of your heart, are becoming aware of your presence. They cannot understand you. You are of a different world to them but they feel your energy and they abhor it. My King, please leave this place. Go back to Australia and give yourself time to grow. These are dangerous times. The world is realigning itself once more and I fear the darkness will ascend again."

Steve said "Temyana, I came to this church to make arrangements for my marriage to the woman I love." Temyana interrupted "Just like your ancestor Alexander when he married the

Bactrian Princess Roxana. Sure, he loved her desperately. Such a beautiful girl. Too smart for her own good. But Alexander knew the favourable politics that would follow. He liked his princesses! You also want to marry a princess I see. Does power excite my King? A dangerous decision, my King. Your ancestor the Great Alexander married Roxana and then died four years later after returning from India. Sure, he lost the desire for warring after India. When the great ten were asked the ten questions, he was forever changed. He had finally found a way to become a god, but he passed to the next world earlier than expected. Such a shame, I wanted to be on that part of the journey with him. A combination or a battle of the Divine always creates upheaval. It was lucky I helped his and Roxana's son, Alexander IV, escape or you wouldn't be alive today, my King."

Steve was catapulted back into the myths that Baba Rada had told him and now had them corroborated by Temyana. He said "I didn't choose a Princess. I chose the girl I love. That's all. There was no higher decision or agenda or attempt to make a new Kingdom or politics or whatever. And how do you even know about her anyway!" Temyana laughed, "You knew the moment you saw her. Didn't you? Something about her. She carries the Divinity. It is like an enigma for the masses. They either fear or worship what they cannot understand. But you, you were like a moth to a flame with her. You had no choice. Did you think you had a choice? Of course you had a choice my King. But I can see this is the path you have chosen and all I can do is offer suggestions. My suggestion is to leave Japan immediately. You are not ready for the gods or demons here. They are the same, but they are different. You will die in a foreign land and be forgotten, the same as many of your ancestors in faraway places. You don't have to do this my King.

"I shouldn't care, but I do. You are a special one. Every few generations one stands out and roughly every thousand years, someone amazing appears from your bloodline. The last one was the Priest King who forever changed Asia. I think you could be the next. Your powers came early. Perhaps it was your Karate that quickened you. Or maybe it was the vibrations of the next world at that tournament. Once your body feels them, it can never be the same.

"I have an ancient covenant with your bloodline. It is my duty to assist you, no matter how I feel or wish. But if you die without any children, my covenant ends. I will guide you in your death so you can finally understand the real truth in death and then, finally, we will both find our peace."

Steve waved her away as if smoke was getting in his eyes and she instantly disappeared. It was too much to digest. Did he really choose Megumi? Or was it some higher force propelling him towards her? He decided there was no higher force than love and that was the only thing guiding him. "Plain and simple!" he said out loud, just as the priest had walked over to greet him. The priest asked him "I am sorry my son, what is plain and simple?" Steve smiled and said "Plain and simple is how love is the answer" and introduced himself to the priest.

The priest introduced himself as Father Dmitry. He warmed to Steve immediately and agreed emphatically with his statement about love. He was a short and slight Japanese man of remarkable intelligence. He spoke perfect Russian, and could even read Old Macedonian. They chatted about their histories with the Orthodox church and both enjoyed the exchange. Steve was surprised the priest even knew about Macedonians. Thanks to his father, Steve was always proud of his ancestry, and was extremely happy to hear the priest talk about the famous Macedonian brothers Kiril and Metodi. The saints who created the Glagolitic alphabet, the precursor to the Cyrillic alphabet which is most commonly associated with the Russians. Steve thought to himself, "Dad would have loved this!" They finally turned their attention to the wedding ceremony and the significance of the rituals. How the crowns they planned to wear would symbolise the glory of sharing the Kingship with God and also to acknowledge the sacrifice of giving one's life to the other and together to Christ. Father Dmitry became lost in his own discussion. He then proceeded into esoteric discussions about "Theosis" where man can become God or god-like through a process of purification, illumination and sainthood. "It isn't easy, but it is real and it is our purpose!" he said. He then discussed the importance of Hesychasm and the Ladder of Divine ascent and Steve's eyes seemed to glaze over. "Too much!" said a smiling Father Dmitry. "I am sorry my son, I became a little excited and remembered my days on Mt Athos or Sveta Gora, as we would call it. My monastic life there was so fulfilling. I plan to go back there."

"Heavy stuff, but so interesting! Thank you very much for the discussion, Father" Steve said. He was indeed surprised by how fascinating the discussion had been. The notion of going through a number of processes to become God or God-like was such a bizarre and fanciful concept to grasp. Finally a time was set for a wedding ceremony the following week and they parted ways as though they had been friends forever.

Steve was well aware he would need a best man for the wedding. A very important person in the Orthodox faith. Someone who would make sure Megumi and any of their children were safe if anything happened to him. There really was no better choice than Uncle Taki and it was a delight to see how he received the request. He was ecstatic and told Steve it would be his deepest honour. He wanted to learn everything about the ceremony in advance. But Steve assured him the priest would give instructions where necessary. Steve said "Just don't drop the crowns at the wedding ceremony!" Uncle Taki laughed and said, "Oh I see, a royal wedding no less!" Steve laughed and thought to himself, "Well, they mean a whole lot of other things in the orthodox church but I can't say he's wrong."

Megumi promptly decided she would ask Tania to be her maid of honour. Their relationship was full of fun. Tania's outgoing personality was such a pleasant departure from the girls she grew up with. She wasn't the least bit constrained by the Japanese cultural traditions developed over centuries and she had such a magnetic and positive energy. Though it occurred to Megumi she seemed to be less effervescent than usual in recent times.

Megumi asked Tania if she would like to be her maid of honour at the wedding and she was ecstatic. "Absofuckinglutely" Tania said. Megumi laughed and blushed. She was still not used to hearing people swear, it always felt a little jarring, and she would always overreact when trying to make it look as though she wasn't shocked. Tania just laughed even louder, gave Megumi another hug and danced with her. She looked to be back to her old self and it pleased Megumi to no end.

Megumi asked Tania, "My sweet crazy friend, please tell me, is everything okay with you?" Tania's smile faded quickly and in an exasperated look, she said "A man keeps coming to the club. He is a rough and nasty guy. He calls himself Osamu, but everyone calls him Sami Black Eyes. He threatens anyone who wants to come near me and keeps talking about taking me away with him back to his home in Okinawa. He's repulsive and nobody will dare say a word to him. They all fear him. He is covered in tattoos and missing some fingers. I don't know what to do about him."

Megumi said, "Please, just leave your work. I can get you a job at the hotel I work at. Let's go there now. I will take you to meet my boss. Come with me now, Tania!" Tania replied, "It's impossible babe, I owe them too much money. They paid for my modelling portfolio and they paid off my gambling debts. Now I owe them and they own me! I don't think I'll ever make enough money to pay them back. They'll never let me go."

Megumi was well aware of the practices of the animals in those clubs. Her father owned more than enough of the clubs and the people inside the clubs. She remembered seeing those evil men grovelling to her father as a child. They were the people who would lie, cheat and steal as naturally as breathing. It was normal practice to indebt someone in any way possible. What may have started as a simple exercise in learning how to play mahjong could easily turn into a gambling debt of life ending proportions. Nothing was ever fair or left to chance about the process and everything was stacked in the criminals' favour. Victims were nothing more than hosts and the evil men were the cancer feeding on them until there was no more money, or use, for them. "And my father is the worst of them!" she thought to herself as she trembled in contemplation.

Tania said "Don't worry babe, this will pass! Anyway, we gotta make plans for your wedding! Oh my god, it's less than a week away." Megumi remained worried about her dear friend. Megumi decided she and Steve would find a way to help Tania out of that wicked mess after they returned from their honeymoon in Kyoto.

The days passed quickly as last minute details were being attended to. Megumi had much to do and Steve was taking his students through some gradings. It was a busy time for everyone, but they were both very much looking forward to the coming Saturday. The night before the wedding, Tania came crashing into the dojo. She was disoriented and crying and her mouth was bleeding. She was calling for Megumi. She wasn't there, but Steve had just finished his evening class and quickly came to her attention. Tania was clearly in pain and a state of shock. Steve flung a coat around her and tried to calm her. She wasn't making sense and was too distressed to talk. Steve decided to take her back to his apartment to see if Megumi could help settle her.

Megumi was shocked and upset seeing her best friend in such a state. She immediately cleaned Tania's face and tried everything in her power to soothe her. Tania said Sami Black Eyes grabbed her when she was talking to other club guests. He said "Enough talking to them, soon you will come to stay with me in Okinawa. You will pay back your debts to me!" She told him he was being rude and he grabbed her by the throat and proceeded to choke her. Then slapped her so hard that she fell unconscious to the ground. "After I came to, that bastard Sami Black Eyes and all his men were laughing at me. I ran out of there and came straight here to find you, my sweet friend," Tania said.

Steve had heard enough and was livid. Steve's sense of justice and chivalry could not accept such behaviour. He didn't even bother to change out of his karate clothing. He charged out of the apartment and headed straight for Tania's club in Kabukichō. Tania and Megumi begged him not to go but he was already out the door.

Uncle Taki had quickly ushered the remaining students out of the dojo and was rushing to Steve and Megumi's nearby apartment. By the time he reached the apartment, Steve was already heading out. Uncle Taki quickly followed. It was obvious where Steve was going and he was at pains to arrive at the best course of action. On one hand, Tania was their student and friend and she shouldn't have been treated this way. On the other, she entered a world where this treatment is normal practice and a confrontation would invite consequences after the inevitable loss of face. Uncle Taki was double stepping to keep up with Steve's pace. He said, "Steve, I know I cannot stop you from going, but please let me talk to them first." Uncle Taki thought he heard Steve say "okay" but he wasn't completely sure.

They reached the club in no time and a security man attempted to halt Steve and Uncle Taki as they walked towards the entrance. Steve averted the man's attempt to grab him and flung him away as though he was flicking some trash away. They entered the darkness of the club. Music was playing loudly and girls were on the stage dancing and parading around while men were drinking and ogling at them. Steve found a young lad collecting glasses and asked him to point out Sami Black Eyes. Before the lad could even respond, they were surrounded by three men in suits who clearly were not there to welcome Steve and Uncle Taki. Steve could sense the danger. The vibrations Temyana was talking about in the church had grown markedly since they entered the club.

Uncle Taki tried to diffuse the tension. He asked politely if it was possible to speak with Sami Black Eyes. The men just glared at him and then one started to laugh at Steve. He was pointing at his Karate Gi and laughing about the "karate boy" among his associates. They were all laughing and one went to grab Steve's jacket. Steve intercepted his hand, twisted it and, at the same time, swept away his feet from under him. As the man was falling, Steve grabbed him and picked him up, as though he was a sack of rice, and slammed him on top of the bar. The sound of smashing glasses and bottles attracted everyone's attention. The other two advanced to attack Steve but Uncle Taki moved forward in an exquisite and powerful move which managed to render one of them completely off balance and he, in turn, fell on the other associate in such a way which also sent him off balance. Both were on the ground attempting to regain their composure when Steve felt the vibrations intensify.

A man had joined them, he had managed to stay out of the spotlights in the club, and appeared as little more than a shadow when he said "Lucky me, my little karateka friends are looking for me." He spoke to Uncle Taki in a raspy voice, "Taki-chan, why do you come here with your karate boy to make trouble?" Steve found no joy in being called a boy at all and started moving towards the shadow. Uncle Taki stepped in front of

Steve and interjected "It appears we have a friend who works here. Maybe she was mistreated by someone you know?" Steve added, "There is no maybe, it was you. Leave her alone. She is not yours to treat like a dog!" Uncle Taki was doing his best to keep Steve behind him and also trying to look calm. He was failing miserably.

Sami Black Eyes stepped out of the shadows, he was as tall as Steve with a similar sized frame. He looked like a 1950s rock and roller with his slicked-back hairstyle and long sideburns. His face was pock marked and he was wearing sunglasses even in the darkness of the club. He looked at Steve and smiled with a toothpick in his mouth. "You must be Steve-san, we know all about you. Isn't it time you go back to your little kangaroo land? Don't make a mistake and make me angry now. Fuck off out of here." Steve was agitated and his body seemed to sense the danger in this man. The vibrations were strangely familiar to him. The last time he experienced them was when he fought that terrible monster who killed his father. Steve could feel his body involuntarily activate. Perhaps it was the adrenaline. He wasn't sure, but he was ready to fight him.

Sami Black Eyes leaned forward at Steve and lowered his sunglasses when he was only a few centimetres away from him. His eyes were all too familiar. They were indeed black. He didn't have black rings around his eyes, he had black eyeballs. He had seen them before. This was a monster or demon and Steve knew all too well what kind of opponent he found in this creature. Sami Black Eyes said "The girl is mine, I own her. She can be free of me when she has paid what she owes me."

Uncle Taki tried to diffuse the tension and asked, "If I may, please let me know how much she owes you. Perhaps we may be able to come to an arrangement?" Sami Black Eyes turned his gaze towards Uncle Taki and said "You will not have the seven million yen she owes me. You still live in your dojo. Why would you pay for her when you still don't have a real home? So sad how your previous home burned down." Steve abruptly interrupted the discussion, "You've cheated her out of money and now you want her to be your slave. It's not going to happen!"

Sami Black Eyes said "Listen karate boy, your friend was a willing participant. There are always consequences and she will pay, one way or another. If you want to pay, it will be my pleasure to take your money. Do you need two girlfriends, Karate boy? Is your Megumi not enough for you?" he disappeared into the shadows as Steve's rage peaked. Then Sami's voice reverberated out of the club DJ's music system, "Just bring me the money karate boy, and you can have her," as his wicked laughs echoed throughout the club.

Uncle Taki managed to calm Steve and escort him out of the club. He said to Steve, "It was best for all that the confrontation did not escalate into a fight. We did not need this trouble the night before your wedding." Steve begrudgingly agreed as they were heading back to his apartment. Steve said, "The man was evil. You could feel it, right? There's no morality in monsters like that."

They arrived at the apartment to the relief of Tania and Megumi. They both looked relieved after seeing Steve and Uncle Taki were unharmed. Steve told Tania that Sami Black Eyes was looking for seven million yen in order to release her. He asked if this was correct. Tania was adamant it was three million yen and that some of that debt had been repaid with her time in the club. She was even more upset and it was clear to everyone that there would be no solution found that evening.

Steve promised Tania they would find a way to resolve the problem and urged the girls to get some rest. Uncle Taki bid everyone goodnight and returned to his dojo. Megumi and Steve insisted Tania stay with them that evening and she slept on the couch. Steve spent all night thinking about that monster, Sami Black Eyes, and how he was going to deal with him.

The next day Tania was back to her chirpy self. She woke up Steve and Megumi to advise them her duties as maid of honour had already begun and she had made pancakes for the soon-to-be newlyweds! Steve wasn't completely prepared when Megumi had changed into her wedding dress. She was wearing a beautiful white dress which looked halfway between a traditional kimono and a western-styled wedding dress. He had never seen anything like it before and was mesmerised with his soon-to-be wife, again.

Once everyone was ready, it was time for the bride, the groom and maid of honour to make their way to the church, together with Uncle Taki. Upon entering the church, everyone except Steve looked as wide eyed as he did when he first arrived in Japan. It was all completely foreign to them. They had never seen anything like it. Some of the icons were so graphic. One showed a man with a glowing halo spearing a king and another with a halo was killing a dragon. Uncle Taki was clapping his hands and said "I like this, these heroes are fighting like true warriors!" Uncle Taki had bought a new camera specifically for the wedding and was furiously snapping away at all the icons and, of course, Megumi and Steve.

Father Dmitry greeted them all warmly and welcomed them to his church. He proceeded to give them instructions and, with little fanfare, he advised the ceremony was about to begin. He lit some frankincense in his thurible, and commenced the blessing of the rings. Temyana appeared in the smoke. "Thankfully she was wearing the half mask," Steve thought to himself as he looked at the tall blond woman only twenty centimetres away from Megumi. She was inspecting her as though she was at the fish markets looking to buy the best tuna! She gave Megumi a wink and he could have sworn Megumi smiled towards her direction. Temyana then smiled at Steve and gave him an approving nod. Steve had long given up wondering why she was invisible to almost everyone but him. But he began to wonder if Megumi could see her also.

Soon enough, the crowning ceremony commenced. Father Dmitry placed the joined crowns upon the heads of Steve and Megumi. Immediately, Steve felt an energy rush of powerful vibrations through him. Megumi also seemed slightly overwhelmed as she corrected her standing position. Temyana immediately appeared next to Steve. She said, "Did you feel that? Oh my Orpheus! You are linked with your princess my King. Something very old joins your bloodlines. It's impossibly energetic! I cannot understand this. But I feel it. Old souls call out to this bond. Perhaps the Priest King, Daruma. I don't know what to make of this, but it is powerful my King, so powerful."

Father Dmitry instructed Uncle Taki. He was clearly proud to be involved in such an important part of the ritual. He was swapping the crowns three times as a witness to the sealing of the union. Steve and Megumi drank wine from the common cup, then they were led around the altar three times and finally the crowns were removed with the traditional blessings from Father Dmitry.

Steve and Megumi looked at each other wondering at which point they were actually married. Perhaps they still weren't! Father Dmitry made it very clear they were most definitely married under the eyes of God and suggested a kiss between the bride and groom was not unreasonable at that point. They kissed and Tania and Uncle Taki were clapping and ran in to hug them. It was a joyous moment.

Meanwhile, Steve noticed Temyana, looking utterly perplexed, lying down on one of the pews and talking to herself or the ceiling. He gave up trying to understand her and decided it was time to celebrate! He and his Baby Love were finally married!

They went to the Shinjuku Gyo-en national gardens and took photographs and danced in the parklands. Later it was dinner at an extremely expensive restaurant where Steve, half jokingly, asked for tuna and mayonnaise onigiri! They laughed all night and enjoyed Uncle Taki's impersonations of famous movie stars. It was the perfect day and Steve and Megumi were deliriously happy.

The next day, the couple were headed to Kyoto for a short honeymoon. Tania's problem was not yet resolved and it wasn't easy leaving her alone to fend for herself. Steve and Megumi insisted she stay in their apartment and implored Uncle Taki to check on her frequently. Tania assured them she would be fine and said she wouldn't step out of the apartment until they returned. Uncle Taki promised he'd bring food to Tania and make sure she was safe. Steve and Megumi were finally comfortable enough with the arrangements to leave for Kyoto.

Chapter 9 - Shisa

Steve and Megumi stayed in the Higashiyama district of Kyoto. It was the ancient capital of Japan and the historical buildings fascinated Steve. They visited many temples and Steve was eager to learn about the symbolism of many of the statues. Some depicted a peaceful Buddha while others portrayed utterly frightening characters. He particularly liked the pairs of statues called Niō or Kongōrikishi, one always with its mouth open and the other with its mouth closed. One carrying a thunderbolt, the other carrying a sabre. They were fierce-looking warriors or kings or even gods whose job was to protect Buddha and, even though Buddha was a pacifist, these mythical creatures were apparently justified to help guard against evil and protect cherished values.

Steve remembered Megumi saying her father would have died a million deaths if she married under the Buddhist faith. He asked her what his problem was with the religion. Megumi said, "I don't know the full story and maybe I never will. But my father blames Buddhism for his suffering. I don't know what he is suffering from. He is extremely wealthy and has whatever he wants. I really don't know, but I was always told as a child the Buddhists caused our family to suffer great loss and that Buddhism was a curse to our family line. It means nothing to me and I couldn't care less, I still take comfort in praying to Buddha. I feel sick talking about him though, enough about him please!" Steve noticed Megumi physically reacting to the mere mention of her father. She would sometimes rock herself slightly to cover the trembling. Steve found it very distressing to see his wife like that. He hugged his sweet love tightly and thought to himself, "That bastard made my poor baby a wreck. Anyway, how can a religion be the enemy of a man? I can understand why people can become enemies using religion as an excuse, but how on Earth could a religion be the man's personal enemy? Too strange!"

Their honeymoon was over and it was time to return to Tokyo. Steve was already thinking about how they might resolve Tania's problem. Megumi thought they might negotiate with that animal, Sami Black Eyes, and try to reduce Tania's debt to a more reasonable amount. Steve was of the opinion that a monster like him wouldn't negotiate one bit and that trouble would be imminent.

They used the new fast train to reach Tokyo in record time and reached their apartment in only a few hours. Something was wrong, the door lock was broken and it was wide open. There were signs of struggle and Tania was clearly gone. Megumi checked with neighbours and nobody saw, or admitted to seeing, anything. Steve went straight to Uncle Taki's dojo. Steve was naturally very worried about Tania. But as he was running to the dojo, he began to wonder if anything had also happened to Uncle Taki. To his relief, Uncle Taki was fine. He was teaching a class and his delight upon seeing Steve quickly faded when he observed the concerned expression on his face.

Steve told Uncle Taki what their apartment looked like and they both quickly came to the same conclusion. They were sure that Sami Black Eyes had taken her. Uncle Taki had checked on her the previous evening and she looked well rested and happy. He was extremely upset with himself and he had been due to go back to the apartment after his karate class.

It was afternoon and too early to go to the club. Uncle Taki said he knew one of the young lads from the club where Tania worked. He had been a student of Uncle Taki's when he was younger and always showed honour to his former Sensei. He would find him and try to find where Sami Black Eyes lived. Steve was grateful and went back to the apartment to see if Megumi had learned anything.

Steve found Megumi extremely emotional and crying in the apartment. She said "We shouldn't have left her alone. Did you find out anything? Please tell me, is Uncle Taki okay?" Steve consoled her and told her that Uncle Taki was fine and had gone to see one of his former students who worked at the club. Megumi told Steve, "You don't understand my Baby Love, that man is under my father's control. If he has taken Tania to Okinawa, then she will never return."

Uncle Taki eventually arrived at the apartment. "I am going back to Okinawa," he said. "He is already there with Tania. They are in my home city. I will fix this. You must stay here. Megumi, you remember what you were like back home. Stay away from your father. You must not return!" Megumi replied "Uncle Taki, you must not go alone. I'm better now. You know my father does not hurt you here because I am in your care. If you go there, we cannot be sure. I must come with you. Steve, my love, please stay here. You do not want to meet my father. Trust me!" Steve spoke with emotion, "My Baby Love, you are my wife and our life is one. If I don't go with you and something happens, I will never recover. There's no choice for me, if you must go, then we all must go. Hurry, there's no time to waste." Steve's unshakeable resolve made it clear there was going to be no room for negotiation.

Steve and Megumi already had their toiletries packed from their honeymoon. They replaced a few clothes in their luggage and Steve took, what seemed to be a distant memory for him, the letter from Sensei Mike to his own Sensei. Later that afternoon, the three of them were on a flight to Naha, Okinawa. Steve was surprised how far away Okinawa was from Tokyo. It was in the middle of the East China Sea and looked almost as close to China as it was to "mainland" or "Naichi" Japan where Tokyo is situated. The weather in Tokyo had begun to cool down and Steve was surprised to feel the abrupt change into a much warmer climate upon their arrival.

Uncle Taki still had a small home in Naha. It was just down the road from his Sensei's dojo and would be a good place to leave their luggage while they looked for Tania. They grabbed a cab and made their way to Uncle Taki's home. Steve noticed a number of small stone tablets or monuments with characters carved on them. They were curiously located at the end of forked roads or T-intersections. Upon asking Megumi about their significance, the cab driver interrupted the conversation saying, "They are the Ishiganto, they are named after a heroic Chinese general in the service of a God who was able to catch and remove evil spirits. They are placed in those locations because it is known the evil spirits can only attack in straight lines. The Ishiganto stones will either kill the evil spirits or at least deflect them. You will see them everywhere here. They are our evil spirit defence system," he said. Megumi and Uncle Taki just nodded in confirmation as though to confirm another very normal aspect of life in Okinawa. After what Steve had already witnessed in his life, he decided it would be wise to learn as much as possible about how the Okinawans dealt with matters pertaining to supernatural forces.

Megumi was not feeling well so Steve suggested she take a rest. It was a stressful day and neither of them had had a single moment to collect their thoughts. Uncle Taki wanted to check on his Sensei as he was aware his health had been deteriorating and there was also a chance he might know more about Sami Black Eyes' movements in Okinawa. Steve asked Uncle Taki if it was okay to go with him. Uncle Taki said, "I was hoping you would want to come with me. But please remember, Sensei has not been himself for a long time. Do not judge him now. He was once a great man and the greatest Sensei."

The dojo was only a short walk from Uncle Taki's home. The building looked quite historic and flanking the gated entrance were two statues resembling lions. One with its mouth open and the other closed. Steve noticed the similarity with the Niō statues he saw in Kyoto. The mouth formations and the location near the entrance was a recurring theme. He asked Uncle Taki what they were. He said, "They are the Shisa. Lion dog creatures who fight evil spirits away and help keep good spirits in. You will see them everywhere in Okinawa. Our legends say the Gana-mui woods were created when a tiny Shisa roared at a dragon and a boulder fell from the heavens to kill it. The smallest Shisa can kill the greatest enemy. Do not confuse Okinawa with other places in Japan. Our history is unique and our influences and relationships with neighbouring countries are long and enduring. We are Ryūkyū, we are Japanese but we also know China very well." As Steve passed the Shisa, he could have sworn they moved. He was a little weary after a full day of travelling all over Japan and decided his mind was playing tricks with him. He liked the lions and decided to himself the Shisa would have to be friends with a Macedonian.

Uncle Taki said "This is not how the dojo from my youth looked, it used to be so clean and tranquil here. It is a mess!" They both bowed as they entered the dojo and it was immediately obvious nobody had trained there in a long time. The floor was dusty and training equipment was strewn all over the space. Uncle Taki called out to ask if anyone was there. Steve remained near the entrance while Uncle Taki looked for his Sensei. They heard some shouting at the back of the dojo and both went out to investigate. It was Sensei. He was submerged in the unruly gardens and shouting. He looked as though he was pushing away invisible adversaries. Uncle Taki called out his name and he did not respond. He shouted louder the second time, "Nakandari-sensei, your loyal student Oshiro Takeshi has returned to see you." Finally he looked up. Uncle Taki appeared thankful he had managed to attract Sensei's attention. "He is so old," Steve thought. Sensei was a short and stout old man. He looked weary and had unkempt hair and filthy clothing. His movements seemed unstable and he was mumbling some incomprehensible words. Steve felt embarrassed to see Sensei Mike's great Sensei in such a dishevelled state. He bowed his head deeply to express a greeting but, more importantly, to suggest he had not seen the man's obvious shortcomings. By the time Steve had raised his head, with uncanny dexterity, the Sensei was right next to him clutching his arm.

Uncle Taki tried to conduct a formal greeting, but the Sensei quickly interrupted "Ahhh, Taki, who is this shining light? Who have you brought to me? I can feel him. So good!" Uncle Taki said "Nakandari Kiyoshi, Nakandari-sensei, please allow me to introduce Steve Nedelkin, a true son of Gōjū-ryū and former student of honourable Mike Fergusson. I can attest to..." Nakandari-sensei interrupted him with surprising clarity and calm, "Steve Nedelkin, it is my honour to meet you. Please excuse the mess in and around my dojo. I have not been quite myself for a number of years now. Your presence is deeply comforting to me. You have a way with demons, you have fought them and won. I feel it. Such a sweet energy about you. Please tell me more about you, Steve Nedelkin. I am blessed to be in your presence."

Steve was speechless. He used the Okinawan dialect to greet the Sensei, "Honourable Nakandari-sensei, I am not the man you think I am. It is my hope to learn from you! Sensei Mike praised you every day of my instruction with him. And Uncle, I mean, Sensei Taki, also has praised you as a teacher and a great man. It would be an honour if you allowed me to be a student of yours one day."

Nakandari-sensei said "Nonsense, you have more to teach me

than I can teach you. Your presence has overwhelmed the evil which is presently torturing my spirit. I need to spend time with you and learn from you." Uncle Taki was flabbergasted. He hadn't seen Sensei with such clarity for many years and had certainly never observed him display such a degree of deference to anyone before, much less a young aspiring student such as Steve. Sensei turned to Uncle Taki and said "Thank you Taki-san, you have always been a faithful student and teacher, now you have brought hope to me in my darkest of times." Uncle Taki was utterly confused. Perhaps he wasn't seeing something which was perfectly obvious to his Sensei. Or perhaps his Sensei was even more crazy than when he left him a few years ago. "But he had remarkable clarity," Uncle Taki thought to himself.

Uncle Taki went on to explain the main reason why they had arrived in Okinawa. How they had to find Sami Black Eyes and rescue their friend Tania. Sensei said "Oh yes, they brought you here then. Why did they want Steve here?" Uncle Taki thought his Sensei misunderstood, "No, we came to help a girl who was kidnapped. Steve's wife Megumi is her closest friend," he said.

Sensei Kiyoshi exclaimed, "Your Megumi? That monster's Megumi? Oh Taki, you were brought to him at the click of his fingers! How willingly you have returned to the spider's web!"

Uncle Taki was instantly ashamed of his naivety, "Of course Sensei, how could I have been so foolish? It has nothing to do with the girl. He wanted Megumi here." Steve interjected, "Who wanted her here?" Sensei and Uncle Taki responded in unison, "Kumicho." Steve apologised to them both for the inconvenience of the entire situation and said he needed to go and warn Megumi. Sensei asked Steve, "Must you go? I have enjoyed your presence immensely. Please return as soon as you can." Steve sprinted out of the dojo and instinctively gave one of the Shisa a little pat on the way out. He could have sworn the statue felt more like a real creature than a piece of stone.

As soon as Steve left, Sensei's thoughts seemed to wander and he became less coherent. Uncle Taki swept the dojo and left soon after. As he was leaving, he could hear his Sensei laughing maniacally and talking to what looked like invisible assailants, "You will see, back to your darkness you will go. Not a moment too soon!" His unsettling laugh reverberated through the dojo.

Steve arrived back at Uncle Taki's apartment and was pleased to see Megumi looked much better. She told him she had thrown up earlier but now felt much improved. Megumi seemed to think it may have been the food they had bought at the airport. She prepared a pot of tea for them and Steve told her about the possibility of her father manufacturing the entire situation in order to make her return to Okinawa. Megumi said, "Of course, I knew it was likely. It is why I didn't want you to come. And I couldn't leave Uncle Taki alone. And it still doesn't help Tania. We still need to get her away from these people. I fear I might have to face my father if we can't get to Tania quickly. I don't want to ask him for anything, he'll demand too much in return."

It had been a long day and Steve was exhausted so decided to rest. He asked Megumi to wake him if Uncle Taki returned. It was a terrible sleep. He kept hearing whispers and movements as though they were just outside his door. He woke to hear Megumi and Uncle Taki quarrelling. Uncle Taki was eager for Megumi and Steve to return to Tokyo and Megumi was not prepared to leave without Tania. They were at an obvious stalemate when Steve went to calm them down.

The next morning, Steve woke up early so he and Uncle Taki could visit the dojo. Steve walked past the Shisa and made a point of touching the statue he hadn't touched the previous evening. Again his sensation of touch belied what his eyes were telling him about the stone statues. He knew what stone felt like and the Shisa felt nothing like it, even though that was precisely what they were!

Steve and Uncle Taki had developed some routines together which helped them warm up and centre their energy. They went through some two-man training kata and Sensei entered the dojo clapping. He was utterly delighted to see Steve again. He said, "Wonderful, Sensei Steve has arrived!"

Steve was embarrassed and reluctant to accept such a title. He politely insisted this was inappropriate and asked if he could show him the letter from Sensei Mike. Sensei read the letter and began to cry. He said "Your Sensei Mike was my greatest failure and greatest success. He was one of my best students but his spirit was damaged in his war. When I tried to save myself from Hiro's gun, I mistakenly summoned Mike's past evils. His beloved Chiasa could not wash away those sins completely and I made the greatest sin of all. I summoned that power to save myself. And now those lowly demons taunt me. They do not own my spirit yet, but my resolve has been weakening, until you arrived young Steve-san. My mind is much more clear when you are near me. They refuse to taunt me in your presence. They are with me, but they do not understand you and they fear you. I believe they can be banished with your energy. Tell me Steve, what is your power? We, I mean, I want to know. No, no, forget it, do not tell me. You must never tell me."

Uncle Taki glanced at Steve and, while Steve did not return the glance, he felt it. How was Steve to know if this was indeed Nakandari-sensei or, in fact, the demons looking for information? Steve said, "Sensei, I have nothing to tell. I am not aware of any power. I had a great Sensei and he had the best in you as his Sensei. I was lucky to find such people in my life. If I may Sensei, I would be honoured if you would allow me to perform a kata for you." Sensei said, "I am most eager to see what my student taught you. Please show me." as he clapped his hands with the joy of an eager child.

Steve cast a glance at Uncle Taki. They had developed an understanding between each other over the years of training together. One look was often enough to tell an entire story and it was clear Steve was up to something. "Nakandari-sensei, please, I asked my wife to look through the window to watch me perform my kata for you. Would you mind watching my demonstration from near the entrance gates? She will be able to see also. I know it is a silly request, but this is one of the proudest days in my life and I want to share this with my bride." Sensei waved in the general direction of Uncle Taki's home and assured Steve it was fine. Steve called Uncle Taki to join him and said, "If I may, I would like him near me so we can also demonstrate our two-man kata." Sensei waved Steve on to proceed.

Steve had mastered every kata within his fighting style. He decided to perform "Tensho - Turning Palms", a highly-advanced kata which resembled the Sanchin kata but was completely different. It was uniquely Okinawan and represented an evolution in the application of breathing. The way of internalising the breath was transformative and, if done correctly, was immediately obvious to a master. Steve bowed to his Sensei and began the kata. His technique was superb and even Uncle Taki had a sense of pride watching Steve perform it to perfection. Halfway through the kata, Steve stomped his foot on the ground and summoned his roar. He hadn't done it for a few years but it was something he could never forget. His body vibrated and he visualised the energy deep inside himself. Out it came, the lion leapt forward and pounced on Sensei's tortured spirit.

Sensei was knocked over by the energy and then what appeared to be black serpentine mists shot out of him. Uncle Taki ran towards his Sensei but Steve told him to wait and stay close. Then they both watched the legend become reality as the two nearby Shisa roared and came to life. One launched itself at the black serpents and devoured them all. The other ran to Sensei and fiercely stood guard so none could find their way back inside him. Their job was done, they turned towards Steve and bowed their heads before returning to their locations next to the gate.

Steve and Uncle Taki helped Sensei up. His face had changed. There was a lightness in his eyes and his spirit was liberated. He looked at Steve and said, "You summoned the Shisa. I have only read about this in the ancient texts. But you did it. I sensed your power but I could never have imagined what you were capable of. Thank you, my son, you have rescued me. My spirit is cleansed and I now truly understand the great shame of my past. I am deeply indebted to you".

Uncle Taki was amazed and confused. He asked Steve, "How could you have possibly believed the Shisa would help you and what on earth was that lion that shot out of you!" Steve smiled, walked over to touch one of them and said, "I knew the Shisa would help the moment I touched them. They believed in me and I believed in them. You need more faith in your Okinawan protectors, Uncle Taki! As for my lion energy, I fear I will never truly understand it."

Nakandari-sensei said, "It is your gift and you used it to help me. I am grateful and have learned much about myself and the ways of the world during my period of torture and during my salvation. Thank you again young Steve-san. Now please tell me everything, I am ready to learn again."

Steve explained the series of events which led him to Japan. He talked about his bloodline and Sensei Mike, Demon Hiro and the monsters. Sensei was astounded that Steve had managed to expel the demon out of Hiro. He said the demon that entered Hiro was far more powerful than the lowly demon "spies" that fought for his own spirit. When Steve heard the word "spies" he asked Sensei, "Who were they spying for?" Sensei said "Here in Japan, they all answer to one, your father-in-law. He already feels you Steve-san, I know this."

Sensei was a wealth of knowledge. His years of resistance against the demons gave him a knowledge most humans would never learn. Steve learned there was a hierarchy of demons and the notion that all demons were evil was folly. That even prophets could be understood to be demons in the right context. They are merely familiar conduits through which the gods interact with Earth unobtrusively. Their power corrupts them almost every time and most cannot control their greed for the delights of the mortal world. He learned Kumicho is one of The Few. Destined for greatness and one of the highest level demons on Earth. They can even play the gods against each other. Sensei said, "He lies to the gods and they still trust him. Such is his way. The moment he bends your will, you are already in his servitude. Your first concession is fuel for the darkness and they are the worst virus. They will consume most men in an instant."

Steve said, "You talk about gods, I was brought up to believe in one God. Which is it?" Sensei replied, "Who are we to understand gods or God? Whoever He, It or They are is beyond the comprehension of us mortals. How they or it chooses to resonate with mortals is entirely up to the mortal's relationship with them, or it or him. A single God can have innumerable thoughts. Each thought can be a god. It doesn't matter to most mortals, Steve-san. You can fill your stomach with ramen or rice. Whichever tastes better to you is fine, the job will be done. God or gods will be the same and can nourish your spirit if you allow yourself. Just, please, do not eat junk food."

Steve was quite overwhelmed with that answer but had so many more questions, he asked, "Megumi said her father carries a sin in his bloodline which had made him evil. But how can evil remain in a bloodline? Megumi has never had an evil thought!" Sensei said, "There is indeed a stain on their bloodline. Megumi has been wise to stay away from her father. Her physical resistance is a manifestation of her own choice to avoid the darkness. In the beginning and end, Steve-san, it is always a choice between good and evil."

"But how can I do what I do with that lion energy?" Steve asked. Sensei explained, "You told me of your royal bloodline, you carry the celestial blood, you also are a conduit for the gods. If you choose to receive them and favour good over evil, you can be a positive force in this world. But it can also corrupt you. With nothing more than a single temptation, you could abandon good and embrace evil. It is a dangerous path for someone with your power potential. Just as you harnessed the Shisa with the purity of your heart, you will be able to do more as you grow to understand your path. You must look beyond this world and embrace the celestial cities. It will come for someone as powerful as you. But you will need to make a great choice one day. It will not be without sacrifice."

Steve thanked Nakandari-sensei for his insight, even though it was difficult to grasp. Uncle Taki was completely out of his league with much of the discussion but was clearly pleased with Sensei's dramatic recovery. He said, "Sensei, you look twenty years younger and the light has returned to your eyes. Steve has been a blessing to both of us. Will you teach me again?" Sensei replied, "My faithful Taki, my time as a teacher has ended. I am ready to leave. I want to go to Fujian, China and seek to restore balance in my spirit. I tried to help people and ended up creating terror. It weighs heavily upon me. I will find those who understand the old ways of the Five Ancestors. It is the only way I will find my peace. It has often been the path of Okinawan Gōjū-ryū masters."

Sensei looked at Uncle Taki and noticed how fit he looked, he smiled and said, "Taki, you have not looked so strong and fit since you were a young man. It would please me if you could demonstrate your kata." Uncle Taki was honoured. He performed like the true master he was and Sensei nodded and smiled. He asked them both to return the following morning as he wanted to present them with a few items. Soon he would embark on his journey.

Chapter 10 - The Cave

Steve was elated. He helped Nakandari-sensei banish his demons and also learned a great deal about them. He managed to raise the Shisa and, for the first time, truly began to believe he may have a greater purpose in life. He rushed back to find Megumi retching in the bathroom. She emerged looking unwell and Steve insisted on taking her to the local hospital. She assured Steve she was fine and said, "It's stressful being back in my home city. And with Tania being somewhere with that monster, I just can't rest." Megumi looked pale and anxious and Steve was sure she seemed to be rocking herself more since she had arrived in her hometown. She eventually said she was feeling a little better and she would perhaps visit an aunt later in the afternoon.

Steve explained to Megumi everything which had happened that morning. She was both amazed and concerned and said, "I saw my father do some outrageous things when I was a little girl. All of my life I have associated those supernatural abilities with evil. So it is strange to learn how you helped Nakandari-sensei with yours. I am proud of you, but I worry what might happen to you if your power grows. My Baby Love, I only have bad memories here. Please find Tania and let us leave as soon as possible." Steve had noticed a growing tension within Megumi since she arrived and began to worry about the decision to bring her closer to her father. Steve gave his wife a comforting kiss and asked if she would be okay alone. She assured him she was fine and he reluctantly left to go with Uncle Taki to find Tania.

Steve went back to the dojo to find Sensei clearing his gardens outside. He asked if Uncle Taki was still there and Sensei said he had already left and was looking for Sami Black Eyes. Steve was disappointed and angry to learn Uncle Taki had left without him and implored Sensei to tell him anything which might help find Taki. Sensei said, "I sensed a new disturbance, when the demons were still with me, ten kilometres south of here near the Gyokusendo Cave. It happened at the time Taki believed Sami Black Eyes arrived with your friend. Steve-san, my heart tells me to go with you, but my mind reminds me the demons know me too well. I am not yet whole again. I am still vulnerable in their presence. I should not go until I am remedied. Otherwise I could just as quickly become another enemy inside the caves. It pains me not to assist you after all you have done for me. Please know that Kumicho, your father-in-law, rules the darkness in the souls of his people. If Taki is deep inside the caves with Sami Black Eyes, the danger will not be of this Earth. You must be aware and search deep within yourself for your answers. Your powers are yours to command."

Steve was grateful for the advice and realised he only had a few hours of daylight left so immediately left and hailed a taxi for the Gyokusendo Cave. The taxi driver had a wealth of information about the cave and surrounding area. The cave was five kilometres deep and less than a kilometre was open to the public. People had gone missing near there for as long as history had been documented and the driver said he never enjoyed going anywhere near the region. He touched the Daruma doll hanging from his taxi's mirror for good luck. Steve wondered if he should ask the taxi driver to stay and wait for him, but the driver looked extremely eager to leave as soon as they arrived at the cave. He departed soon after Steve paid the fare.

Steve surveyed the perimeter of the cave which was surrounded by a beautiful, lush green landscape. The climate bordered on being tropical. The region shared its latitude with Hawaii and the thick vegetation could have been from anywhere in the world on the same latitude. But the vibrations Steve began to feel reminded him precisely where he was. His body reacted involuntarily to the sensation. His body's core tightened and his shoulders rolled forward slightly as his breathing began to focus through his diaphragm. He was a trained fighter and he could sense a looming threat.

The vibrations seemed to be most powerful from inside the cave and Steve abandoned the thought of more thoroughly examining the thick forests outside of the cave. It was near closing time and Steve was only allowed in after using every bit of his charm. His limited knowledge of native Okinawan helped his cause.

The cave was quite stunning. Beautifully lit with innumerable stalactites and stalagmites and waterfalls and pools of water. It would have been nice to enjoy the scenery but Steve's head was increasingly throbbing with vibrations as he ventured deeper inside the cave. He reached the end of the tourist-permitted area and deftly jumped over the rails.

The cave was almost pitch black in the non-tourist designated area. Thanks to the taxi driver, Steve realised there might be four kilometres of cave paths to traverse. He was completely unprepared. "Yeah, I go deep inside a cave without a torch. Brilliant, I must be a genius," Steve thought to himself. He walked for about twenty minutes and came across what looked to be Uncle Taki's new camera broken in pieces on the ground. If the vibrations weren't enough, then the camera was certainly the catalyst for Steve to quicken his pace.

He soon saw a faint light up ahead and heard some muffled and reverberating voices. His senses were overloaded as he tried to decipher what was being said. The path soon opened up into a large cavern which was brightly lit and his eyes took a moment to adjust to the view. Steve then discerned Uncle Taki to the left and Sami Black Eyes with Tania to the right. Sami Black Eyes was holding a sobbing Tania by the throat and shouting at Uncle Taki. He said "You think I care about this foreign trash? I will kill her now and I will enjoy the sound of her last breath. It will be even better knowing you are here to see it. But I don't care, I am waiting for your little Karate Boy and I know he is close now."

Steve ran into the cavern and screamed, "Let her go immediately!" At precisely the same time, a cyclone of foul-smelling black smoke entered the area and blocked Steve's view for a moment. When the smoke subsided, Sami Black Eyes had changed into a monster with the same talons which Steve vividly recalled from the tournament. But there was another creature in the room. And the vibrations and wicked laugh were terrifyingly familiar. The foul black smoke had formed itself into Demon Hiro. Steve noticed the look of shock and disbelief on Uncle Taki's face. Steve fleetingly thought of a time in his own life when he was completely unaware of such evil. He had seen all of this before.

Demon Hiro said, "It was a good plan Sami, we have our little Karate Boy here now. You will be rewarded well by Kumicho! Karate Boy, you come to my world and you think it will be easy for you here? You will be my best demon soon! And Taki, you have annoyed Kumicho for too long. It is your time to die."

Just as Demon Hiro turned his focus on Steve, Taki furiously charged at Monster Sami who was holding Tania by the throat. She tried to break free but the monster merely tightened his grip around her throat and cracked her neck. He dumped her on the ground. Steve ran to Tania and managed to slide a hand under her head as she fell. Steve was sure one wrong movement of her neck and she would be dead. He quickly packed the soil on the ground to provide Tania's neck some support and comforted her while pleading with her not to move.

Monster Sami ran at Taki with his talons ready. Taki's response was masterful. He went low and used his low centre of gravity to his advantage as he charged at the monster's hips. He managed to knock him to the ground but Monster Sami quickly thrust a talon into Taki's thigh, releasing a stream of blood. The blood seemed to empower the wicked creature. He roared and jumped back up. Before the monster could regain his footing, Uncle Taki had already pounded his fists into its abomination of a face. Monster Sami was struggling against Taki's fierce attack. Finally, Monster Sami gained a solid footing and aimed a talon at Taki's face. But the stout, pony-tailed warrior was again too clever. He dived to the ground, grabbed some sand and threw it at Monster Sami's eyes. He blocked a talon strike and hand chopped Monster Sami in the throat, then kicked him in the ribs. Uncle Taki had overwhelmed and surprised his evil enemy.

Steve was conflicted, how could he tend to Tania while such mortal risk was present. He pleaded with her one last time, "Please Tania, don't move your head the slightest bit. A single movement and we could lose you. I beg you!" He stood and turned to Demon Hiro and readied himself for his lion roar. He unleashed his energy and the lion's forelegs were almost upon Demon Hiro when he vanished into black smoke. As the lion energy dissipated, Steve turned to look at Uncle Taki only to see Demon Hiro reanimate immediately behind Taki.

Steve ran to Uncle Taki and screamed "Behind you!" Uncle Taki's response was sublime. He dropped himself to the ground and rapidly shot himself backwards between the legs of Demon Hiro. The movement was such a surprise to Demon Hiro who had already commenced his deathly attacking movement. His talon shot forward, missing Uncle Taki and instead piercing Monster Sami's chest. Monster Sami shrieked and fell to the ground as a human with his demonic traits absorbed by Demon Hiro. He was no more.

Steve was summoning his lion again but quickly became concerned for Uncle Taki who was right next to Demon Hiro. Demon Hiro could disappear at any time leaving Uncle Taki to take the full force of Steve's fighting energy. In the last moment, just before the lion launched, Steve pulled the energy back into his fists. His fists glowed a bright orange as he punched Demon Hiro. He knocked the demon five metres out of him with his first punch and kept hitting him until he fell to the ground. He was only human and Steve was confident he would finish him. At that moment, he noticed Hiro's demon spirit spring forward trying to find its way back inside Hiro. Instead it found Uncle Taki and the dark clouded mass of evil had enveloped him. Steve feared he would lose his much-loved uncle to the dark world. He kicked Hiro into the black cloud and the darkness immediately descended into Hiro instead of Uncle Taki. Hiro's eyes became black again and then he vanished into that foul black smoke and flew out of the cavern.

Steve and Uncle Taki were overwhelmed by the events that transpired and also with each other's abilities. It was a remarkable effort from both of them. But Steve was genuinely astounded with Uncle Taki's power and resourcefulness. Steve said, "Uncle Taki, what you did today is only possible from a true master. I learned so much from you. I've got to remember to sink my body lower when in battle sometimes. I saw your true warrior spirit and I'll never forget this!" Uncle Taki said, "I wouldn't be alive if you didn't come looking for me. And I wouldn't be alive if you didn't use your powers. I am in awe of you Steve-san, I am blessed to be in the presence of someone so remarkable. I believe you may be the reincarnation of Ishiganto himself!" Steve didn't agree with the idea he was a reincarnation of a famous Chinese general, but they looked warmly at each other, what they had experienced was both real and unreal. They quickly turned their attention to Tania and went to her. Fortunately she hadn't moved although she was clearly frightened and in a state of shock. Tears were streaming from her eyes but she could only whimper instead of talk. Her eyes were saying way too much to Steve and Uncle Taki. She was pleading for their care. They needed to find a way to safely transport her to a hospital. Without a brace around her neck, Tania would surely not survive the journey to the cave exit.

Steve learned something about his powers earlier and wondered if the pulling in of his roar could be used in a different manner. He told Tania "I did something today that I've never done before. I think I might be able to create some kind of protecting energy around your neck. I'm scared it may hurt you, I really don't know whether it's the right thing to do." Tania managed to whisper to them, "Both of you are my heroes. You were willing to give up your lives for me. I don't deserve it. If I die, I'll die knowing people cared about me for the first time in my life. I trust you Steve and I know you only want to help me. Please try. And tell Megumi I love her so much. I love you all."

Steve looked at his hands and focused his energy, his Ki. He placed them next to Tania's neck. He summoned his roar in a different way. He roared deep within his mind's eye, relaxed his arms, and let the energy slowly trickle out of his hands. He created a small ball of orange energy around Tania's neck and she was instantly calmed. Steve was able to pick her up and carry her while the energy seemed to provide a safe, reinforcing cushion around her.

Uncle Taki's leg was bleeding still and he was looking a little weary as they made their way out of the cave. It was a long and exhausting walk. As they neared the tourist-designated area, Steve felt those vibrations again. Uncharacteristically cold wind swept through the cave. Steve yelled out to Uncle Taki and warned him something wasn't right. As soon as he sounded the warning, the ominous black smoke had circled them. Uncle Taki yelled "watch out!" as he ran in front of Steve and Tania. A huge stalactite was launched from the cave ceiling, flew through the air directly towards them and pierced through Uncle Taki's chest. Steve placed Tania on the ground next to Uncle Taki and started summoning his roar when he heard that demonic voice, "I told Taki he would die today. I will come for you another time Steve Nedelkin and you will be my greatest slave soul," and with that threat, the dark smoke flew out of the cave.

Steve quickly turned to Uncle Taki. He was holding Tania's hand and looking at Steve intently, as a true warrior with no fear, when he took his last breath. Steve had lost his beloved uncle. He recalled every bit of emotional pain he previously experienced such a long time ago at the tournament. He touched Uncle Taki's face and felt his warrior spirit pass through his body as it moved on to the next world. Steve had no time to grieve, Tania's life could still be saved. He ran outside and found a caretaker of the cave facilities and organised an ambulance to take Tania to the hospital.

Steve's next task was to tell his beloved Megumi about their Uncle Taki. How could he tell her when even he was struggling to cope with the cruel reality of their loss? After making sure Tania was safe in hospital, he finally made it home. He walked in, covered in Uncle Taki's blood, and was in a daze. He looked at Megumi and just couldn't say the words. His mouth was moving but nothing was coming out. Megumi saw his pain, ran to him and fell on her knees begging Steve to tell her what she already feared was true. Part of her knew just from the look of Steve's eyes, but she needed to hear it. Steve was unable to look his wife in the eye as he stoically stood tall and falteringly whispered, "Oshiro Takeshi-sensei, Uncle Taki, died this evening as a great warrior. He saved my life and also Tania's. He is a true master, a true uncle, a true father, a true brother and a true friend." Megumi was already wailing for her beloved Uncle, the only man, before Steve, who loved her unconditionally and had never let her down. Megumi was sobbing and holding on to Steve's leg. He gently picked her up and held her tightly as he allowed his emotions to escape him.

Steve told Megumi about Tania. How she may not live, or if she did, it was likely she probably would never walk again. They both descended into their darkest and most painful places and memories. There was no talk of reprisal, nothing about who, what, why or where. They were simply hurting and bewildered. They held each other tightly and cried into each other's arms. They eventually drifted into a sleep replete with sequences of cascading nightmares, each one worse than the one it replaced. They awoke early the following morning and both searchingly looked into each other's eyes as if to confirm whether the events of the previous night actually happened. The looks they shared confirmed it was heartbreakingly true.

They needed to go to the hospital to see Tania. But Steve told Megumi he had to let Sensei know what had happened to Uncle Taki and then he would quickly return so they could go to the hospital. On arrival, Sensei saw the look on Steve's face and immediately understood the news was grave. "Taki?" he asked. Steve just looked at Sensei, rubbed the back of his head and looking downwards said, "Demon Hiro killed him". Sensei was visibly crushed to learn of Taki's death. He tried to remain calm but his stoic facade quickly faded when he learned it was Demon Hiro who killed him.

The burden of guilt weighed heavily upon Sensei. He explained to Steve, "When I summoned the power of Luohan, the technique my master learned from his Five Ancestors master, I didn't fully comprehend the powers in the room. Hiro was already almost completely evil, but he still loved his sister and I was confident his last remaining goodness would redeem him. But Mike, he carried a demon of war inside him. I didn't realise until the summoning. His Vietnam war experience was unjust.

It haunted him and he suffered much guilt and pain. I am to blame for Hiro, Mike and Taki, and countless others, and I will carry this burden for the rest of my life. Steve-san, are you sure Taki is dead? Is there any doubt? I fear his spirit may be condemned to darkness. Did Demon Hiro touch him when he was dying?"

Steve explained precisely the events which led to Uncle Taki's death and took some comfort in learning that it appeared Uncle Taki would rest in peace. Sensei warned Steve again, "They know you and they know your power, Steve. Kumicho is hideous and fierce beyond your power. If Demon Hiro is unable to destroy you, Kumicho surely will take the matter in his own hands. You must leave immediately. Take your wife away from this place. Leave Japan and find a harmonious life elsewhere." He looked Steve in the eyes and grabbed him by the shoulders with surprising strength. It was only at this time did Steve see Sensei's knuckles were scarred and callused, the obvious markings of a trained fighter. "This master has trained all of his life here and fears the power of Kumicho. We should leave here and go far away as soon as possible." Steve thought to himself. He left Sensei in the dojo and went to collect Megumi.

Megumi hadn't been well lately, she hated being in her home town and the recent trauma only compounded her feelings of despair. She told Steve, "We will go to the hospital, we will pay for Tania to be transferred to a hospital in Tokyo and I will care for her there." Steve agreed and they went to the hospital. Steve could see Megumi was not at her radiant best, but she was still impossibly beautiful and he noticed everyone looking at her and whispering among themselves. He initially thought his mind was playing tricks on him. But it was indeed everyone looking at her and, as Megumi was asking at the reception lobby about Tania's location, the chief hospital administrator came to officially welcome Megumi to the hospital.

He said "Dear Miss Megumi, we are honoured by your visit to our hospital. It would be my pleasure to personally assist you. How may we be of service to you?" Megumi was gracious with the nervous-looking gentleman and asked about Tania's location. The administrator promptly found out all he could about Tania and returned to Megumi and Steve, "Oh yes, the American girl. Very dangerous situation for her. I presume this man is her boyfriend and you are helping them. So kind of you, Miss Megumi." Megumi curtly replied, "This man is my husband, and the girl is a friend of ours. We need to know everything about her condition and we must see her immediately." Everyone nearby looked shocked and whispers were abound in every direction. One doctor walking past had the audacity to approach Steve and look quizzically at him as if to question his worthiness as a husband to Megumi. The administrator stepped in front of the doctor and bowed to Steve and welcomed him to the hospital in English. Steve replied in perfect Japanese, "Thank you, we would be most appreciative if we can go to our friend immediately."

They were escorted to the intensive care unit and Megumi insisted the attending doctor advise her immediately about Tania's condition. Everyone in the ward immediately fell silent when Megumi arrived. They all bowed to her and didn't even move or say a word until the doctor arrived. He was a pleasant man who appeared somewhat nervous when addressing Megumi. He assured her that Tania was receiving his best care and he was doing everything possible to keep her alive. He explained Tania had been placed in an induced coma. She had suffered a broken neck and a partially damaged spinal cord. "It would need many months to recover from this ordeal and it is possible she may never walk again," the doctor said.

Megumi insisted Tania be transferred to the best hospital in Tokyo and the doctor said "She was extremely lucky her neck didn't move one millimetre by the time we retrieved her. It would be impossible to move her for many months without causing irreparable damage. Please Miss Megumi, it is best we care for your friend here. We will give her the best care possible and are most thankful to your father for his donations of world-class testing and monitoring equipment. Please be sure to let him know how truly grateful we are for his benevolence."

Megumi resolutely ignored the doctor's request and asked if it was possible to move Tania to a private ward. The doctor assured her he would facilitate the move as soon as it was wise to do so. "We will prepare a room now and move furniture for you and this girl's boyfriend ..." Megumi exasperatedly addressed the doctor, "This is MY husband, she is our dearest friend and I expect nothing less than the best attention for her. When I return, I will look forward to your update and am eager to learn all the best practices for her rehabilitation." The doctor bowed to both of them and apologised profusely for any offence given and assured Megumi of his best intentions.

Megumi left the hospital with Steve and both were extremely upset. Megumi said, "I wanted to avoid all of this attention here, and now I am right in the middle of it. The longer we are here, the more likely it is that my father will construct a way to enter my life. He is the ugliest man in the world my love, I do not want us to be anywhere near him." Megumi wanted to go to a temple to pray for Uncle Taki and Steve went with her. She purchased some osenko (incense) and lit it, waved the flame out and began praying for Uncle Taki's soul. Steve did the same and then noticed the elegant, older Japanese Temyana sitting at the back of the temple.

Steve reassuringly touched Megumi's shoulder and retreated back to Temyana. Before he even reached her, Temyana was pointing her finger at him, "I warned you. The gods are numerous and old and the demons are powerful here. Taki was a good man. He loved you dearly, my King. But you are on your path, what must be, must be. Your Queen is truly beautiful, my King. She has rejected the darkness and has a strength I have not seen for many centuries."

She then looked around and said "I haven't been inside a Buddhist temple, or Japan for that matter, since the other great one, the Priest King." she said. Steve had nothing to say and he held his head, looking utterly forlorn. A moment later, something clicked in Steve's mind and he said, "The Priest King?" as he turned to Temyana. Temyana had already vanished.

Megumi finished her prayer and came back to Steve looking extremely anxious. "My Steve, I am worried about Uncle Taki. I can't be sure he is safe. We must see a yuta, Yuta Hinako, and she will be able to tell us. Please let us go now!" said Megumi. Steve said "What is a yuta? I have been in Japan for a long time now and never even heard of this before." Megumi replied, "This is older than Japan, the Ryūkyū have always consulted with the yuta in matters of concern like this. Maybe you would call them witches, I'm not sure how to say it in English. Please, let us go now."

They grabbed a cab and soon arrived at the yuta's apartment building. She was located on the third floor and Megumi surprised Steve with how tired she became from walking up the stairs. She would normally leap up flights of stairs. They knocked and the woman opened the door. She was middle aged with slightly greying wavy hair and was wearing white robes. She was clearly pleased to see Megumi and ushered her and Steve inside her apartment. Megumi introduced her husband. "So many people! I only have a small apartment. Sit down please. Megumi, you look so well. Your life away from here must be good for you, or maybe your husband has given you peace. Maybe both! You look so good now." she said. Steve thought to himself, "She looks unwell right now, I wonder how she used to be when she lived here."

Megumi did not waste a moment, she told her she was there for Uncle Taki who had died the previous night. "Taki was always naughty, I always fancied him when I was little, but he always seemed too busy running around looking after his little sister, your beautiful mother! Let me try to find him," she said. She raised her head, burped loudly and looked around the room and concentrated on the corner where nobody could be seen. "Too many people! You are with him? Why are you here?" She was nodding and there were pauses. After a lengthy time she finally turned her attention to Steve, "I am truly honoured to be in your presence. Daruma's very own guide told me who you are. She is the oldest yuta I have ever met. One of the powerful ones who was there when the worlds changed. Today I have learned more than I could learn in many lives. The bond with your wife, your Queen, creates many possibilities. Some will improve the worlds again, others will force the darkness to grow, to overcome."

Megumi said, "Auntie Hinako, I know who you speak of, she has come to me also. The one with the half mask. She has warned me many times about our path. She didn't want us to come to Okinawa and expose ourselves to my father." Steve looked at his wife incredulously, "She speaks to you?" he said. Megumi replied, "I saw you speaking with her in the temple earlier today and we have talked before. She has a job to do, my baby. I used to have a spirit yuta guide when I was younger. My father found her and banished or destroyed her. She has never returned to me. His way is to kill everything you love. Your guide is also scared of his power. She says she cannot understand why she thinks she knows me. Something binds our royal lines. But none of it makes sense to her or me." Megumi began to rock herself slightly and it didn't go unnoticed by Yuta Hinako as she seemed to wave something bad away from her.

Yuta Hinako said, "Listen to me, Taki is fine. His soul is pure and he is free of this world and elevated. You have nothing to worry about him. He loves you both dearly and he need not be of concern to you. Megumi, if you remain, your father will either turn Steve to darkness or, even worse, he will kill him and poison the mind of your son growing in your womb right now. In any case, he will win and his evil will only grow. You know it! The warnings from Steve's guide are clear. This evil is not even fully formed yet, but is already one of the strongest forces of darkness in the world."

Steve's eyes widened as he searchingly looked at both Yuta Himako and Megumi, "Wait, what? We're having a baby?" He looked at Megumi and she looked up at him. With a tear falling from her eye, she said, "My body has changed recently. I began to wonder if I might be pregnant. This is a terrible place to raise a child. It's not just morning sickness here. My dreams have been dreadful since we arrived and I can feel my father reaching to me. I am scared for our child. If I am surrounded by this evil, it will affect our baby. It affected me all my life until I managed to get away. It was only when I met you that I felt cured. That I could even have a chance to be normal. But now I feel it in every part of me. The darkness. The whispers. But how can we leave while Tania is still here?" Megumi said. Steve said, "Your and our baby's health is too important. We must leave earlier. After Uncle Taki's funeral tomorrow, we will go back to the hospital and find a solution for Tania's situation again." Megumi just shook her head, "I cannot leave her here alone. I will not do that to her!"

Megumi insisted Yuta Hinako take some money, which she accepted after much protestation. Yuta Hinako said, "I should pay you for the privilege of being of assistance to you. And to meet the high priestess on this day, I will never forget it! Thank you!" Steve and Megumi left with mixed emotions. They were having a baby and they were all in danger. The next day would be a funeral for their beloved Uncle Taki and new plans needed to be made.

Steve looked intently at Megumi with his heart ready to explode. "Nobody said every day of our lives was going to be easy. Every time I wake up and see you, I'm the happiest man in the world. We're now having a baby, made from the deepest love ever known. And I'll do everything I can to keep you and him safe. If I can give my life now and be sure of your and our baby's safety, I'd do it without hesitation." Megumi said, "I know my love, but if you are gone, my life will be over and our son will be stolen by my father and our baby will only ever know evil. I cannot lose you. So you see, if I lose you, I lose everything!"

Chapter 11 - Ishiganto

It was yet another uncomfortable night for Steve and Megumi. Megumi seemed to be getting worse with each progressive night. Her tortured sleeps were all-night marathons. She was running away from invisible enemies and calling for her mother and Uncle Taki. They had already experienced too much horror since coming to Okinawa. Steve began to really notice the effect it was having on Megumi and was becoming increasingly concerned about her health, both physically and mentally. He was feeling helpless watching his Baby Love in such a state.

Megumi managed to finally doze off to a dreamless sleep in the morning. The pregnancy was clearly affecting her but Steve wasn't confident that was all that was making her unwell. It seemed as though coming back home had amplified her negative thoughts and fears. Even the way she moved, and her demeanour, had changed since she arrived. Steve was feeling an increasingly-concerning dilemma. His concerns for Megumi and his unborn child were directly in conflict with staying in Okinawa and ensuring Tania's safe recovery. "The longer we stay here, the more at risk Megumi and our baby are," Steve thought to himself. He took some comfort in seeing Megumi sleeping less fitfully and hesitantly left her to try and rest a little more before this particularly stressful day would start.

He went to see Nakandari-sensei. He was in his pristine dojo dressed in formal clothing in anticipation of the funeral. Sensei was visibly affected by the loss of Uncle Taki. He gestured to Steve to follow him into his office space. He said, "Steve-san,

Taki loved you like a son and Megumi like a daughter. He has no-body and I do not know who else to present this to. Before I was even aware of his passing, it was my intention to award him his godan, his fifth dan. He was always talented and, perhaps I didn't recognise his brilliance when Mike and Hiro were training in my dojo alongside him. But he persisted and, in many ways, sur-passed all of them. Time rewards a focused mind, Steve-san. It would have pleased him very much to receive this. Please ac-cept this on his behalf," as he handed a certificate and belt to Steve.

Steve bowed deeply and solemnly accepted them on Uncle Taki's behalf. "This is very dear to me personally and I thank you deeply for his most worthy award," Steve said. He was well aware Uncle Taki was a third dan and had jumped two grades, which was not normal, "But nothing has been normal lately, and he truly deserves it anyway!" he thought to himself.

Sensei said to Steve, "You know, many people loved Taki. I expect a few may attend the funeral to pay their respects to him. Those who loved him here are the ones who continue to resist Kumicho. Some have also learned you were the one who expelled my demons. They agree with me and are calling you Ishiganto's reincarnation. You give them hope." Steve didn't even know how to respond. He was uncomfortable being com-pared to a mythical Chinese general who banished evil spirits. In truth, he had expelled demons, but he was still unsure of the limits of his abilities and his potential. And, to complicate mat-ters, his sense of destiny evaporated the moment he learned his Megumi was pregnant. He returned to Megumi thinking of noth-ing more than how he wanted to make sure his family was safe and happy.

Steve, Megumi and Sensei, all in black, arrived at the family tomb. It was a serene location situated on a hill in front of a dense forest of trees. Uncle Taki's body would be interred in the central chamber of the traditional Okinawan turtle or womb-shaped tomb. In years to come, after the body fully decomposed, the bones would be washed and placed in a separate chamber, their final resting place. It upset Megumi to even visit the tomb as her mother's body was not allowed to be placed with her own family. Despite Megumi's protestations at the time, there had been no room for negotiations with her father.

Yuta Hinako was already there and was kind enough to clean the tomb and surrounding area. Megumi was both pleased and grateful and thanked her deeply. The funeral was to be a very private affair. The trauma of the death and fear of the evil spirits had affected Megumi and Steve so much that they dispensed with a wake. They wanted to conduct the appropriate ritual with a Buddhist priest as soon as possible to ensure Uncle Taki's safe transition to his afterlife.

The Buddhist priest arrived and immediately attended to his duties, rituals and processes and it gave Steve some sense of relief to see how calm Megumi looked. After a short while, Steve noticed a few people arrived and remained in the distance behind them. The small group gradually increased and, in a short time, it seemed as if there were hundreds of attendees. Sensei whispered to Steve, "It appears some of Taki's supporters have arrived." They didn't say a word, but Steve could feel the positive energy from the people who gathered. Every face looked supportive and concerned for them.

As the ceremony neared completion, a large black limousine arrived. Some of the supporters at the back linked their arms and attempted to obstruct the vehicle's advance. But it simply powered forward, paying no attention to the people in its way. The weather had even changed with the car's arrival. Steve wrapped himself around Megumi as if to shield her from the cold. Sensei and Yuta Hinako also instinctively huddled closer to her. Megumi shuddered and looked downwards. She whispered to Steve, "He is here. I know it. I can feel him." Steve suspected the same thing, he turned around to try and see Kumicho but the windows were heavily tinted and nothing could be discerned. At the completion of the ceremony, the limousine reversed and drove away.

Megumi's tension reduced as soon as the car left. She gave Steve's hand a reassuring squeeze to let him know she was fine. Some of the supporters came forward to offer condolences. All were familiar to each other. They handed Megumi "okoden", condolence envelopes with money inside. They all knew Sensei and most seemed to know Yuta Hinako also, but it was more than apparent they all wanted to look at Steve up close. One older gentleman, who appeared to be the leader of the group, was the first to motion towards Steve. He bowed deeply and quietly said "Ishiganto" and pointed his right index finger and touched the inside of his open left palm. Others soon followed and it wasn't long before the entire group repeated the actions of the first gentleman. They also greeted Megumi warmly and reminded her how loved and admired her mother was. Megumi was touched and shocked by the warmth of the people from her community. She had always been distanced from these people in her youth and felt slightly awkward in her interactions with them.

Steve was confused and embarrassed by the attention. He asked Sensei what the hand signal meant as he had never seen it before. Sensei said he'd also never seen it but knew precisely what it meant. "They are calling you 'Ishiganto', the pointed finger is the evil spirit and the open hand is you stopping the evil." Sensei continued, "Please understand Steve, the pain for our people on these islands is still very real. Our own wars and the strong presence of old evil here has forced us to be almost militant against the threat of dark forces. You have seen the Ishiganto monuments everywhere, and you must know how important the "mabui", the essence of yourself, is to people who are afraid of being possessed by the evil spirits. You have given rise to hope in these people."

Steve, grieving and confused with the attention, met with the others who approached him. He was cordial and tried to be self effacing. The group of supporters were extremely polite but the earnest and sanguine looks clearly indicated they were all desperately looking for someone to believe in. The supporters were all deeply respectful and were mindful not to intrude too heavily on Steve and Megumi in their time of grieving. They all soon left and Steve, Megumi, Sensei and Yuta Hinako remained. Hinako was talking with Sensei about the state of the islands and how things had deteriorated in recent times. How people used to see Hinako just to check on their parents in the afterlife or to help find something that was lost. "But now, they fear for their own souls and come to me to look for ways to expel demons from family members or protect them," she said. Sensei nodded and explained how his life had become a blur over the last few years with his demon possession and how his recent clarity had given him newfound hope. They both turned and looked at Steve at the same time and then looked at each other and shrugged their shoulders saying "Ishiganto".

Steve and Megumi made their own way back to Uncle Taki's home. Megumi seemed much improved. "My baby seems different. Relaxed, like her old self," Steve thought to himself as all the sweetest memories of her came flooding back into his mind. He pulled her in close and kissed her head and reminded her how much he loved her. Megumi said "I really do feel much better. I hated being here all my life because people feared my father so much and, for the same reason, feared me. Nobody was completely honest with me because they couldn't be sure if I was going to tell my father or, worse yet, become as bad as my father in the future. But seeing all those people embrace us and feeling their hope when they greeted me showed they don't see me as a threat or a curse to their lives. I think it was beautiful and Uncle Taki would be proud of us today."

Steve said, "Do you really think I can help these people? I don't really know what I'm doing or what I can do. But I could see how much they believed in me. How can they believe in me when I can't even be sure about myself?"

Megumi said, "Everything I have ever loved or cherished has been taken away from me by my father. In a way, I have become selfish and secretive about the things I cherish. It has been my way to deal with the life I was forced to live here. I am now selfish for you and our baby but I don't want to obsess about it any more. If we can help these people, maybe this will help cure me. The people looked at me differently today for the first time. It really was lovely and it encouraged me."

They reached Uncle Taki's home and found a mountain of flowers in front of the entrance. There were little notes on all of them. Beautiful and thoughtful words from people that Uncle Taki had touched in one way or another. It was overwhelming for Megumi and Steve. Steve hadn't quite grasped how many people Uncle Taki had helped in his lifetime. Steve only knew him for a few years, but he was family to him in every sense. It didn't really occur to him that Uncle Taki had lived such a full life before Steve met him. "He touched the hearts of so many people. An amazing man," he thought to himself as the sadness of his loss resonated just as deeply as all his losses over the years.

Steve and Megumi quickly collected the flowers, changed their clothes and headed to the hospital to check on Tania. As soon as they arrived, the hospital staff looked almost fearful as they pounced on Steve and Megumi and tried to be of assistance. The chief hospital administrator arrived within moments to greet them. A small, older woman, a hospital cleaner, was walking behind the administrator and smiled warmly at Steve and Megumi. She discreetly bowed and made the Ishiganto sign whilst looking at Steve and then said to Megumi, "My sweet Megumi, you look just like your mother did at your age. I used to babysit her. She would be so proud of you." Megumi awkwardly responded, "Thank you so much. Lately I am learning there are so many people here who cared about my mother." The woman replied, "Your side of the family has always been loved, my dear girl."

The administrator was clearly annoyed with the cleaner's intrusion and was preparing himself for an announcement before the interruption. He urged the cleaner to move along. With a barely-concealed sense of theatre, he explained to Megumi, "Your father was kind enough to donate new, state of-the-art equipment, to assist in Tania's recovery. He said he was most upset to learn of her unfortunate accident and wanted to assist his daughter's friend in any way possible." Megumi was agitated by the mention of her father and was quick to end any further flattery of him. She was eager to see Tania.

The administrator led Steve and Megumi to Tania. She was still in her induced coma and nestled among an array of cables connected to a number of monitoring devices. They were both hoping for any sign of positive progress, but she looked no better than the day earlier. Megumi and Steve met the doctor attending to Tania. He said, "The equipment donated by your father has been extremely helpful to us, we are now very sure our treatment strategy is optimal." Megumi was becoming increasingly annoyed with the mention of her father. "We want to move her to Tokyo as soon as possible. She needs the best care!" she said. The doctor responded, "We have the best West German equipment here. In fact, thanks to your father's worldwide connections, we were able to have this equipment supplied overnight. There is absolutely no better place for your friend to be receiving treatment and she will remain extremely frail for a very long time. I do not advise her to be moved at any time in the foreseeable future."

Steve gently pulled Megumi to the side and said, "My baby, we can't move her, that's totally clear, so maybe we should go back to Tokyo so I can look after you the best I can." Megumi shook her head, "No, it's fine, we must stay here. It's best for Tania and I'm also starting to think it's best for me. I am not a little girl anymore. I think I need to be here right now and make peace with this part of my life. I can't have my father interfere and haunt me anymore. I believe in you, my Steve. I think you are greater than any evil, including my father, and I think the people here need their Ishiganto."

Steve found it difficult to reconcile Megumi's positivity to the almost manic tendencies she had displayed in recent times. But he was overjoyed to see her in such a positive state of mind. It gave him the confidence to want to stay and ensure Tania was supported in her recovery. They both talked to Tania and included her in conversations to try to engage her subconscious mind. It was something they would repeat for many weeks.

Steve had been filling his time over the ensuing weeks with helping Megumi, particularly as her pregnancy progressed. Together they were visiting Tania and he was also training with Sensei. With regard to the training, initially there was a review of all of Steve's martial abilities, including his kata and fighting skills. But later, much more time was spent understanding Ki and meridians and understanding "chinkuchi". Chinkuchi was an interesting concept, particularly as it related to Steve. Conceptually, it was a transference of all the fighter's energy into his opponent. It would almost feel like a shockwave if done correctly. However, Steve's chinkuchi was metaphysical. It was beyond the comprehension of men, including Sensei. It wasn't a shockwave, his "lion energy" was very far from intangible. It was visible and had proven to do far more than simply shock an opponent.

On one occasion, one of the "supporters" who came to Uncle Taki's funeral brought his son to the dojo with him. He pleaded with Sensei for "Ishiganto" to help the teenage son who was not studying well and being disrespectful to his parents. Sensei admonished the man for wasting their time and ordered them away, but when he took a closer look at the boy, he noticed the youth was indeed troubled. Sensei called Steve to observe the boy and Steve sensed the familiar vibrations. Sensei discussed the "case" at length with Steve. His years of being possessed gave him an insight which few men had. He did his best to describe the vibrations to Steve and how to measure or sense them in a meaningful way. This was obviously a small and relatively innocuous demon but had the potential to steer this boy to a lifetime of bad choices. These bad choices would be nothing more than invitations to greater demons.

Steve grabbed the boy by the shoulders. The petulant youth tried to fight Steve and did his best to break free, but Steve was a powerful man. The boy was not going to be freed until Steve wanted it so. Steve summoned his lion energy and pulsed it through the boy. What appeared to be a small black-winged snake was released from the boy's body. Steve summoned his chinkuchi into his foot as he stomped on the winged snake. It hissed before splattering on the dojo floor. The vibrations had gone and the boy, visibly lighter, ran and hugged his father. It was a joyous moment and yet another affirmation of the new legend of Ishiganto incarnate.

The exorcisms were repeated numerous times over the following months. Steve was able to gauge the vibrations. He still recalled the totality of Demon Hiro's vibrations and used that as the highest reference for measuring the level of evil trapped inside the human victims. In most cases, Steve was expelling lowly demons. They were simply purposeless souls who gravitated to evil. Others were much more intense, they were clearly soldiers of evil with clear mandates. On those occasions, Steve noticed Sensei moving in unison with him. Somehow it seemed to assist or intensify Steve's energy pulses. Sensei was definitely on his own path of discovery during the process. Steve, with the aid of Sensei, had fully tuned himself to the presence of demons and their power. He was also able to summon his lion energy and channel it wherever necessary. It could be used offensively and defensively. His skills had developed substantially.

Tania was taken out of her induced coma after a few weeks and it took a long time before any positive signs were evident. Initially, she had no feeling in her feet and had lost the ability to talk. But the excellent care she received at the hospital, and the devoted attention from Megumi, ensured her continued recovery.

After six months, Tania was talking effortlessly and undergoing rehabilitation to teach her how to walk again. She was doing very well. Megumi's slender body had remained the same from all angles, except from the front. The signs of the baby were amply evident, it looked like she had stuffed a basketball under her clothing. Tania took great delight in discussing everything they would need to do to make sure the baby was perfectly welcomed into the world. The impending birth was the best therapy for her. Steve encouraged Tania by telling her how important her role was under the Macedonian tradition. "If anything happens to us, it is your duty as a godparent to look after our child. So hurry up and get better!" he said.

The chief hospital administrator had come to see Tania, Megumi and Steve with some news he was eager to share. "A prominent national news broadcaster wants to deliver a piece about the incredible work we have done in our hospital. Particularly in helping you, Tania. They would like to come here and film you all with this equipment and it would be a wonderful family event to see you with your father, Megumi" he said.

It had been over six months and Megumi had successfully managed to avoid her father. Aside from relatively-frequent recurring nightmares, Megumi was coping quite well. It was as though Steve's increasing strength and influence as Ishiganto had given her strength and a resistance from the ever-present sphere of evil emanating from her father. Megumi's father had made numerous attempts to contact her. He sent gifts for the baby before most even knew she was pregnant. He sent new cars to her and even keys to another residence in the expensive part of town. All were rejected immediately. It was abundantly evident she wanted absolutely nothing to do with her father. Yet her rejections only seemed to motivate him even further. Megumi didn't put it past her father to have organised the media event. He most likely owned the news broadcaster through some hidden entities with puppet owners off-shore. It was all within the realms of possibility for such an impossibly-wealthy man.

Tania felt extremely grateful for the treatment she had received. She was willing to support any endeavour which promoted the hospital, but she was mindful of Megumi's strained relationship with her father. She left the decision entirely to Megumi. Much to Tania's surprise, Megumi agreed to a short segment to be filmed at the hospital. Megumi explained to Tania how she needed to rise above her personal trauma and try to be of benefit to the people of Okinawa. So many people had embraced Megumi over the seven months since she had returned and she wanted to do more for them. She also thought this might be a way to help normalise the tensions which had existed within her community all her life.

Steve, in the meantime, had been refining his skills with the assistance of Sensei. His ability to channel his energy was at a level where he could use it with precision both in relation to power and location. Previously, he would unleash the lion energy and it would just explode forward, glowing bright orange. The changes through training and application also led to a profound understanding of the nature of the energy. Steve's intent was everything. Anger created a different energy pulse from that of a desire to heal. Even the colour would change depending on the intent. Anger was always bright orange and an attempt to heal would be much a more subdued warm yellow glow.

Sensei was truly in awe of Steve's abilities. He did his best to try to distinguish what appeared to be superhuman from that which was man. He encouraged Steve to develop his energies, but he also helped with the gaps in Steve's knowledge of Gōjū-ryū. He said, "Gifts such as yours can be a blessing from the gods or even a punishment. In any case, they may disappear one day. You must still persevere with your natural human abilities and ensure you can rely on yourself in every circumstance." Steve understood this and, despite his increasingly full agenda of expelling demons, he trained very hard with Sensei and elevated his Gōjū-ryū knowledge to such an esoteric level that only Sensei and few others could truly comprehend.

Sensei intended to leave many months earlier but he had changed his own path in order to fulfill a duty to his community. By helping Steve, he was helping his own people so he viewed the process as cathartic for both himself and his community. He felt it would be selfish to leave now while they were doing such good work together.

Steve would sometimes feel contemplative about his years of training and the events which had occurred in the last few years. Training with Sensei always left a tinge of sadness for him. He was always reminded of Sensei Mike and Uncle Taki and, of course, his father on that fateful day. Everything had always happened so fast, it occurred to him that he had never grieved each death properly. He continually busied himself to avoid thinking about some of the raw emotions which sometimes would creep up on him.

On one occasion, after a particularly gruelling exorcism, Sensei expressed his desire to formally acknowledge Steve's abilities. He instructed Steve to prepare tea and they both sat together while Sensei made a very formal presentation. He said, "A true teacher is always willing to learn. I have made it my life's purpose to share what I have learned. You have been my greatest student because you have forced me to reassess everything I have learned. I have learned from you and shared all I reasonably can with you. Today, I wish to acknowledge your level within our style and also to thank you for saving my life and the lives of others in my community. I present you with two belts. The first, jūdan, your tenth dan black belt for your Gōjū-ryū abilities and your honour, and also to acknowledge this path has fully travelled its distance. The second belt, a white one, to remind you that your path as Ishiganto has only just commenced. You must seek more knowledge about your purpose. Perhaps you could find a master in Fujian, China. Or perhaps you may find the reason for your gift or your purpose in Macedonia. I cannot know. When you are ready, I believe it will come to you. And finally, I give you this necklace with the two shisa, blessed by one of our most eminent monks, to remind you of your great gift and purpose.

As I've mentioned to you before, I intended to leave much earlier. But now I truly feel I have been part of something remarkable here with you. I remain forever grateful for this. But I still suffer guilt from what I did to Hiro. I would like to believe, one day, we together could banish the demon from Hiro. I learned much about what I did wrong when I summoned Luohan. Seeing your energy and understanding the way of the demons that used to be inside me has given me an insight few people have. It would give me great comfort to try this before I leave. And you must know, I want to leave. I lost my "mabui", my essence of myself, for too long. Even though I am old, I need to follow my path, nurture my essence and clear my way for my next life."

Steve felt surprised and elated when he replied, "I genuinely did not expect such praise and acknowledgement from you, Sensei. In truth, the events over the last six months have given me a focus beyond my Gōjū-ryū. The work we have done together to help create harmony on the island has given me so much joy. Before I arrived here, all I could dream about was being able to learn from you. Learn everything from Sensei Mike's Sensei! To be a jūdan, a tenth dan, is a phenomenal achievement. An accolade many aspirants will never achieve and I do not think I deserve this, but I treasure it deeply. I feel an immense sense of responsibility for both belts you have given me. Thank you very much, Sensei!" Steve put the necklace on immediately. It looked like a coin on a black rope. The small medallion had both shisa, one mouth open and one closed, on both sides and Steve joked, "I might need their help one day!" Sensei said, "I believe anything is possible with you Steve-san. I think there will come a time when you can summon more than shisa if you open yourself to your path and full potential."

Steve was eager to tell Megumi and found her at home looking somewhat anxious. She told Steve how she had agreed to the news segment in the company of her father at the hospital. Steve was absolutely incredulous. He could not believe Megumi would agree to such a request. She had feared and hated her father the entire time Steve had known her. He was incensed, "And now you're willing to feign filial piety to please that evil man. He did it, he won. He finally found a way to get to you," Steve said, instantly regretting his anger at the predicament.

Megumi began to cry, "I don't know! I just don't want him hanging over me every minute of my life. I don't want that fear and hatred inside of me. When I let him get inside my mind, you see how I become. I have become so much stronger with you by my side. And the more you have helped the community as Ish-iganto, the more the love and humanity which binds us all here has grown and grown. Being here has helped me face my fears. I want my father to see that my life is my own now and that I will never be like him. We will film that news segment in two weeks' time and then we will leave. I will help with Tania's rehabilitation back in Tokyo and then I can look forward to her company and help with our baby."

Steve hugged his wife and kissed her. He said, "I understand my sweet love, I just want you to be happy. If you need to do this, then I'll be right next to you." He placed his new belts next to their bed and Megumi noticed them immediately. She could see the level on the black belt was jūdan and seemed to be more excited than Steve about it. He was lying on the bed and she jumped on him shouting, "What? Now I can beat up tenth dan black belts! I am so strong!" as they wrestled and laughed together.

Chapter 12 - Kumicho

S teve was eager to consult with Temyana about the upcoming meeting with Kumicho. He went to a nearby Buddhist temple and lit some incense to summon her. He was
thankful the fearsome samurai warrior next to him was wearing a half mask, otherwise he would not have realised it was
Temyana. Steve pleaded with her, "Can you at least be one of
the people I've seen before? I'm not sure if I should talk to you
or fight you!" Temyana promptly reverted back to the elegant
older Japanese woman whom Steve had met before. She said,
"I'm sorry, I've been having too much fun learning about what
has been happening in Japan since the last time I was here. It has
been well over a millennium, you know."

Steve asked, "You were here over one thousand years ago? I
thought you only assisted my ancestors. Surely none of my
ancestors found their way this far?" Temyana replied, "Much
more than a thousand years ago. I told you before, I was with
the Priest King. Another of the Great Ones. Here they call him
Daruma, but he started as Skandar. And I have learned who
Megumi's people are. The Priest King knew Megumi's Emperor
ancestor very well. They had many wonderful discussions and
a very meaningful intellectual relationship. Now I understand
much more about your connection to her. Promises were made
between the Priest King and Megumi's emperor ancestor. It was
truly a meeting of great minds. Such a pity the emperor didn't
realise his dream. None of that matters now and it isn't necessary to concern you with the details."

Steve thought about Temyana's information and said, "Wait,

you said Daruma, isn't Daruma the name of those little dolls in every Japanese souvenir shop?" Temyana looked at Steve as though he were a backward child, she said "Daruma, Bodhidharma, Da Mo, Skandar, so many names for the Priest King. Yes, he was the founder of Zen Buddhism here in Japan. You really should try to learn some history one day. As I said, he was one of the great ones in your line. But look at you, "Ishiganto", I think you will also have many names. But you must know, a new name means you will lose a part of your former self. It can happen by choice or it can be taken from you. A curse and a blessing!"

Steve asked, "We will meet with Kumicho, Megumi's father. Is there any advice you can give me about him? I have heard so many times about how powerful he is. Surely my gift can help me if he tries anything?" Temyana replied, "Your gift can beat the man. But the demon is another matter. Stronger than you can possibly imagine and, you must understand, completely foreign to you. He is one of The Few, the evil he carries is multigenerational and is as old as the Infinite. He carries the sins of his fathers as a badge of pride and he will confound you with his every breath. Make no mistake, there are forces at play here that even I do not fully understand. But I can see now - this meeting is inevitable."

Steve was deep in thought. He knew nothing would be uncomplicated about the encounter. He was almost asking himself as he replied to Temyana, "But if he tries anything, surely I can expel that demon ..." Temyana interrupted Steve, "You think expelling his demon is a good idea even if it's possible? To free that evil from the constraints of his human body so that it can roam freely? What if the evil chooses you? Where does the man end and the demon begin? I don't think you understand, this demon is so powerful he even bewitches the gods. When you see major disasters around the world, look to one of The Few like him. They are merely creating opportunities for themselves. Listen to me Steve, you must resist this man's deceptions, he would love to own you and he owns easily. Do not assume your power will work against him. Oh, and I would recommend you take your Sensei with you if you ever meet him. I have seen how he helps your power. If anything happens with Kumicho, it would be wise to have him near. Your line has never been at more risk than now. I have warned you enough times but you are in his sphere of evil and I now understand this is your destiny. You must understand my essence has been preserved for thousands of years now, I know all the worlds and I can tell you things nobody on Earth can. The illusions and deceptions humans use to justify their existence are all just part of a process beyond their scope. Some will rise above their days and nights and break their cycles. I can't help you break your cycle, but I can tell you that a turn towards evil is only rewarded by evil and that cycle is perpetual. It is the simplest yet most difficult decision you will ever have to make." Temyana faded into the smoke and left Steve to reflect on her advice.

Steve always concluded his meetings with Temyana thinking he had learned something extremely important, but he was never quite sure if any one part was more important than the other. "Don't be evil," seemed to stick out in his mind, which seemed reasonable enough. At least he learned about Daruma and also how Sensei might be essential if anything was to happen. He decided to discuss the matter with Sensei.

Steve found Sensei training in his dojo. He admired the toughness of the old man and the obvious power stemming from his connection to the ground. He still found it amazing he was the same person whom he met a little over six months ago. "So much power in the man," he thought to himself. Sensei was doing kata Steve was unfamiliar with. When he asked about the techniques, Sensei said, "These are movements of the Luohan style, I have been trying to merge my essence, my mabui, into these movements. I believe I know more now than when I created Demon Hiro. But in truth, I know enough now to say death is better than spreading the evil I created. I was wrong to try to summon the Luohan when I had so little understanding of the energies at play."

"I think I will need your help Sensei," Steve said. "We have done some amazing work together when expelling demons. I have felt the way my energy multiplies when you work with me and I feel your gift is every bit as important as mine. Megumi has agreed to a meeting with her father. I'm sure we all agree he is not to be trusted, but she feels it might help her finally be rid of him. I am not sure it is a good decision, but I understand why she wants to do this." Sensei was not surprised at all, "She is a lovely girl. Her mother's side were healers on this island for as long as anyone can remember. If there is any way I can help, then it is my honour and hopefully my redemption."

Steve and Sensei discussed potential scenarios and thought about Demon Hiro's relationship with Kumicho, who wields his power with such undisputed authority. Sensei spent many years steering away his best students from the impossibly-addictive yet evil allure of Kumicho.

Steve had often wondered what Kumicho might be like. He was quite sure the man would be someone resembling a cross between a smarmy politician and a gangster thug. Yet so many men had given up their "mabui" to serve him. Steve wondered how and why such strong and capable people such as Sensei Mike, Uncle Taki and Nakandari-sensei feared Kumicho's power so much. He also couldn't fathom how so many people seemed oblivious to his evil nature.

Megumi had reached twenty-nine weeks into her pregnancy and was both physically uncomfortable and extremely nervous about seeing her father. It had been six years since they had last been in the same room together. Before she left, there were heated discussions and accusations made against her father. She was questioning the nature of her mother's death. Her father dismissed her questions and accusations as though he were talking to a little child who didn't know any better. But Megumi knew her mother and was aware that she had been trying to divorce her father at the time. She had told Megumi how she could no longer remain with such an evil man and had made plans to relocate abroad with her daughter. Megumi had always harboured nagging doubts about the story of how her mother fell while jogging near the Shuri Castle. Nothing had ever been resolved and Megumi remained forever traumatised about her death.

The day had arrived. Steve and Megumi had bought some new clothes for the event and Sensei had even dressed well for the cameras. They arrived at the hospital ahead of time and Tania was grateful. She was lying in bed and said, "I can't stop thinking about this. Megumi, we don't have to do this. After all you've done and sacrificed for me, the last thing I'd want is to do anything which would upset you." Megumi smiled warmly as she responded, "Tania, you have been a wonderful friend to me. We're so happy to have you in our lives. It would be nice to give the hospital some acknowledgement for their amazing work. And if I must face my father, I have decided it's a good thing to do. Please don't even think about it."

Steve asked Tania how close she felt to being her old self. She replied, "Talking isn't a problem now. My legs sometimes still seem to have a mind of their own and still ache with a terrible pins and needles feeling in them. It freaks me out. Every time I stop thinking when I'm doing my walking exercises, I fall over straight away. It's been pretty tough, but I am so lucky to have you guys around all this time. I owe you my life." Sensei leaned in and whispered into Steve's ear and Steve replied to Sensei, "I had been thinking the same thing." Steve glanced at Megumi and then turned to Tania and said, "I'd like to try something which might help you. It's similar to what I did to protect your neck that night, but I have learned a little more since then and only now am comfortable enough to try it on you."

Tania pleaded with Steve, "Please, if you can do anything to help. You don't have to ask. You already saved my life once. Anything you can do is more than welcome, I trust you completely!" With that, Steve positioned his hands on Tania's knees and summoned his energy. In a similar way to when he protected her neck, he retained the lion energy and allowed it to radiate around her legs. But this time, Steve breathed into the energy which seemed to oxygenate it. The warm glow subsided after a few seconds. Steve smiled and stepped back away from her. He looked for any sign of change. Nothing seemed immediately apparent until Tania squealed with delight, "Oh my God, the pins and needles are gone and my legs feel brand new!" Tania moved herself and swung her legs over the bed and stood up. "This is the easiest thing I have done with my legs in over six months. I can't believe it!" she said. Just at that time, she faltered slightly and Steve caught her and helped her back in bed. Steve said, "I unblocked your energy paths, but I think your muscles will need some time to catch up!"

Soon after, they all heard a commotion outside the room. The news crew had arrived. Steve saw the crew just outside the door, assembling lighting equipment and checking their cameras. There were four people in total including the journalist who entered the room. He introduced himself professionally and immediately began rearranging the space for better lighting and angles. He called the others to help and they were ready. Sensei stepped out of the room and shortly after, a very corporate-looking middle-aged woman hustled into the room and surveyed the environment. She looked very similar to Temyana's elegant Asian woman persona, but seemed to have a bitterness about her which was quite repelling. She had a stern face and was extremely abrupt with everyone, until she saw Megumi. She turned to Megumi and said, "Oh Megumi, it has been so long since I last saw you. You look beautiful, and with a blessed event on the way," as she pointed to Megumi's obvious pregnant state. Her smile and gestures could only be described as feeble attempts at sincerity. It looked as though she was unable to even convince herself that she was being genuine.

Steve could see Megumi did not enjoy the company of this woman. Megumi curtly replied, "Hello Nakano, I see you're still working for my father. Is he here?" Nakano replied, "Oh the chief hospital administrator wanted to greet him and thank him formally for all the good work he has done for the hospital. They also had a little business to discuss. But he is on his way, he is most eager to see you." Megumi was less than impressed with Nakano's reply. All her life she had heard how her father was doing something extremely important and it was of absolutely zero interest to her. Her anxiety was peaking as she reached for her husband's hand and she couldn't help but notice Steve's powerful grip. He was just as anxious as her. Megumi did her best to avoid obsessing about what she would say to her father - but rapid and abstract memories and thoughts continued to race in her mind.

"Nakandari-sensei" a voice boomed in the hospital hallway. Steve looked at Megumi and there was no room for doubt about who the voice belonged to. "You look like a young man, Kiyoshi-san. Perhaps you might teach Karate to some of my men?" he said in a questioning way which seemed rhetorical. "I remember how you used to punish me in your classes," bellowed Kumicho. Sensei quietly replied, "Agari Shin, Agari-san, I recall you were a very capable fighter with great potential in my classes. I am confident you have already taught your men a great deal." The voice boomed again, "Haha, indeed, indeed."

Kumicho entered the room. Steve was sure the room had shrunk. The man who walked in seemed to fill the entire room. He acknowledged everyone upon his entry and headed straight towards Megumi. His smile didn't quite reach his eyes as he raised his outstretched arms and said, "You look positively radiant today, my daughter," as though he had seen Megumi every day since she had returned to Okinawa. Megumi replied, "You have not changed one bit, father." He then picked up Tania's hand and looked deeply into her eyes asking in perfect English "I hope they have looked after you here, my dear girl. I wanted to make sure you are fine. Is there anything I can arrange for you?" Tania blushed and replied, "Ummm, no, thank you. I have had the best treatment and am very grateful for your help."

He turned to Steve and said, "Steve Nedelkin, the Macedonian lion from Australia! I have heard so many interesting things about you. Such an interesting young man. Some are even calling you Ishiganto lately. What a handsome husband my Megumi has chosen." He shook Steve's hand and grinned while looking penetratively into his eyes. Steve was shocked, "This is no thug or smarmy politician. Refined and distinguished. Regal in fact. How old is he? He looks thirty, or is it sixty years old? It's impossible to tell. Megumi is taller than him, but he fills up the room. So charming. I don't feel any vibrations. So charismatic! Who the hell is this guy?" Steve thought to himself. Steve finally replied as if slapped into reality, "A pleasure to meet you Mr …..ummm, Agari," it occurred to Steve he only heard this man's given name, Shin, a few moments ago for the first time. Kumicho was the only name he ever used for him. "Otosan, please or father. Whatever makes you feel comfortable, we are family after all," said Kumicho. Steve would never call another man "father" and promptly decided he would avoid calling him anything at all.

The news crew filmed their segment and assured Kumicho it would be a wonderful piece highlighting the efforts the Agari family have undertaken to help an unfortunate American friend. Kumicho was pleased and spoke to Megumi and Steve, "What a lovely day, I insist you all come to my residence for dinner tonight. I would very much like to welcome you. I will not take no for an answer. I will send a car for you at 7pm". He turned to Sensei and said, "Kiyoshi-san, I will expect you there also. It is time we caught up."

As quickly as Kumicho swept into the room, he had gone. His voice reverberated throughout the hospital as he called for the chief hospital administrator. Megumi was livid. "He pretended as though the six years was six minutes. And he didn't even wait for our reply when he invited us for dinner. He just expected it! As if we are all his servants!" She continued venting with Tania about her father while Sensei approached Steve, "What did you feel when you were near him?" he asked. Steve said, "I didn't feel the vibrations like I normally do. I felt ..... I felt ... amazing, great! What a charismatic man."

Sensei smiled and explained, "Drug addicts don't take drugs because they are terrible. They love the feeling and become addicted to it. Kumicho's vibrations are very different indeed. He is the best and worst drug. His vibrations are precisely what you described. You must recalibrate! Whatever you ranked Demon Hiro on your scale, you must now understand Kumicho represents your highest score now. Keep that in mind tonight and listen to yourself."

Steve began to second guess himself, "Maybe I was captivated by Kumicho's charm. Did I miss any clues about the evil nature of this man? Why couldn't I feel his vibrations? Normally my body instinctively reacts to demons. Who is he? What is he?" Steve couldn't stop thinking about Kumicho. He felt so inadequate and ignorant compared to a man of such culture. "How could someone from a family of peasants expect to match himself against someone of such culture and refinement?" he asked himself.

Megumi looked tired from the ordeal and asked Steve if they

could leave. She was hungry and most definitely eating for two people. She was craving a McDonalds burger and Steve knew better than to deny his pregnant wife's cravings. They made the journey to Makiminato a few kilometres away and discussed the morning's events. Megumi asked Steve what he thought of her father. Steve replied, "I had such different expectations about him. He was so worldly and charming. He seemed larger than life."

Megumi rolled her eyes at Steve and said, "That is the outside layer, peel away the charming exterior and you see the nasty man. He looks like he has learned to conceal it even better nowadays. Don't let him fool you. He has been cruel to me all his life. I don't know what he thought he would do with me. I was always made to feel like I disappointed him because I would never find happiness in his cruelty. He tested me every day of my life. Always made impossible bargains and created situations which rewarded cruelty. To be honest, I've been so worried for our baby. What if the baby carries some of his evil? I can't believe someone would try so hard, for so long, to encourage his child to become evil. If it wasn't for my sweet mother, I would probably be some evil demon-witch hanging off the ceiling ready to eat you!" as she poked at Steve.

Megumi was increasingly tired and uncomfortable as the pregnancy progressed and asked Steve, "Please take me home so I can rest and find the energy to deal with my father tonight. And tomorrow we will start making arrangements to go back to Tokyo. It's time we get our lives back to normal." Steve agreed. "It is definitely time to start making some real money so I can feed and house my family properly!" he thought to himself. The issue of financial security for his family had been weighing heavily upon Steve. He wanted the best for his wife and his soon-to-arrive baby and yet he only had the small income stream from Australia. He wanted to prove to both himself, and his family, that he could be a good provider and be successful in his own right. He always thought he could do anything, but in truth, he had nothing to show for it.

Chapter 13 - The Castle

It was precisely 7pm when the limousine arrived. "Just like the bloody train system in Tokyo, not a moment sooner or later," Steve thought to himself. Sensei had joined them earlier and they all arrived at the entrance to the residence within twenty minutes. Megumi seemed surprised with all the security equipment installed. "The walls and security gates and cameras are all new, how long have they been here?" Megumi asked the driver. He replied, "Well over two years now. Some people used to come and try to bother Kumicho."

Passing through the outer gate, Steve noticed two plinths which would typically have been the perfect locations for Shisa statues. In fact, it looked like they were there previously. They had patently been destroyed, yet parts of their lion paws still remained. They crossed over a moat and proceeded to weave around the complex until passing through two more secured gates. Finally they reached the residence. It was a majestic castle. A combination of intricately carved timber and stonework in the Japanese style with an incredible five storey tower in the middle. Steve looked at Megumi and asked, "You lived here? You poor girl, such a tough life!" Megumi replied, "I would have preferred living with my mother in Uncle Taki's little home to any of this!"

Kumicho's assistant, Nakano, was waiting at the front of the residence. Megumi was holding Steve's hand and her fingernails dug into him when she saw Nakano. "I have despised that witch my entire life." Steve didn't dare ask any questions about her. Nakano feigned her pleasantries and welcomed them inside.

She said, "Your father has been looking forward to this all day, he is waiting for you in the lounge. Please walk with me."

The lobby was bigger than any house Steve had ever been inside. It was a huge white space and elegantly simple with large white marble flooring and impossibly high white walls. After traversing the distance of a normal-size block of residential land back in Australia, they finally entered the lounge. Kumicho welcomed them all with his booming voice. He looked like a king. His suit was impeccably tailored and every movement and gesture he made was perfect. Steve again began to feel inadequate in his rather poorly-fitting suit as he adjusted his collar. The room was incredibly impressive. It looked like a museum with beautiful paintings adorning the walls and carved traditional Japanese furniture in addition to the most modern "magazine style" furniture pieces from Italy and Germany.

Steve had begun to bow to greet Kumicho as the others did, but Kumicho walked towards him and said, "No, allow me to welcome you to my home your way." He went to shake Steve's hand. Steve looked at Kumicho's outstretched hand. He could have sworn a tattoo of a serpent or dragon peeked its head out from under the cuff of his shirt and then disappeared from view. They shook hands and Steve tried to sense the vibrations in Kumicho. The deeper he searched, the stronger there seemed to be a resistance. "Like pushing into a pillow up against a wall," he thought to himself. It was something he had never experienced before. Kumicho was smiling and looking at Steve intently. He invited them all to look at some of his antique collectable items. He described a few, but Steve was drawn to the collection of swords like a moth to a flame. "Ahhh, the jūdan likes his swords. I have many special swords in my collection. Some are more valuable than others, but others are more sentimental to me," said Kumicho.

Steve couldn't contain his awe. He was quite sure he was looking at a collection of some of the finest swords in the world. The blades were exquisite and showed the highest level of craftsmanship. The way different metals were used to create the perfect combination of strength, hardness and sharpness. The ornate handles. But there was one sword, unlike all the others. Steve was immediately drawn to it. In comparison to the others, it was inelegant. It was almost in the shape of a Chinese broadsword, a little less broad perhaps, certainly not as beautifully proportioned as some of the other katanas in the collection. Yet it had the symbol on the blade, near the handle. The sixteen-pointed sun shaped rosette Steve had seen all his life. And on the pommel, a lion's head. The blade's attraction to him was magnetic.

"You like this one? A special one indeed. This is the sword of Daruma. It has remained in my family for centuries. The charlatan Daruma gave it to one of my ancestors. It is indeed a powerful sword. Some blades carry a spirit and this one carries the spirit of my family's royal blood. We will look at it together later, but let us eat first!" said Kumicho.

Steve could not stop thinking about the sword. It would have meant nothing had he not seen the symbol and the lion on it. It seemed to corroborate everything Temyana had told him about his own lineage. "If Daruma carried the sword with Macedonian symbols on it, perhaps he did have some connection to Macedonia. But how? And why would a Priest King carry a sword anyway?!" he thought to himself.

They moved to the dining room and Steve was positive the dining table was larger than Uncle Taki's entire apartment. It began to dawn in Steve's mind that Megumi really did abandon a life of great privilege when she went to live in Tokyo. His disconcerting thoughts about being able to provide a future for her and their baby returned to trouble him again. Kumicho insisted they all sit close to each other at one end of the table. Nakano had taken the seat to Kumicho's right and Steve to his left, then Megumi and Sensei.

Kumicho said to Steve, "I personally went to my cellar to find something to remind you of home and found some wine from your hometown. Let us enjoy this 1960 Penfolds Grange Hermitage with our meal. They say it is a very good vintage." Glasses were poured and dinner was served by competent house staff. Steve had still not acquired the taste for wine. He knew the Grange Hermitage was the most expensive Australian wine money could buy. Especially older vintages such as the one they were drinking. Yet he could barely discern the difference between a $3 bottle and a $500 bottle. He was embarrassed about his lack of knowledge and refinement and recalled his father's chip on his shoulder about his peasant background.

The food looked like a menu from an expensive restaurant in Tokyo with expensive Japanese items such as wagyu beef, fugu fish and matsutake mushrooms in combination with various French cuisine food. It was all a little rich for Steve and Sensei. Megumi, in contrast, looked comfortable around all the exotic foods, and even knew which cutlery to use. She avoided the fugo or pufferfish due to her pregnancy. More lethal than cyanide, only a fully trained and licensed chef is able to prepare the fish so no lethal doses of Tetrodotoxin remain present to paralyse and kill the unsuspecting diner. Steve didn't bother with sampling the delicacy, however he noticed Sensei did - only after Kumicho ate the delicacy.

Kumicho proposed a toast to the small gathering. "To the good fortunes that reunited my family today. To my lovely daughter and her husband and the wonderful gift of my new grandchild on the way. May your child never disappoint you."

Megumi had impressed Steve all evening with her restraint. She didn't take the bait with other comments her father had made as the night progressed. She didn't want anything to inflame the already tainted relationship between her and her father. She had no intention of reconciliation, but she was certainly hopeful for a way to coexist without being in constant fear of his impositions. However, the toast was received in the worst possible way.

Megumi could now no longer contain her anger and replied, "There were no good fortunes which brought us here. It was one of your little criminal thugs who wanted my friend to be his full time sex slave. The same one who broke her neck and then another of your slaves who killed Uncle Taki. I have no idea how that could be understood to be 'good fortune'. It was not good fortune, it was just a good example of the way you see the world through your selfish eyes. I hope my child disappoints you as much as I have disappointed you. It will mean my child will reject everything you believe to be important!

"I wanted to find if there was a way I could look at you and not question how mother died and not blame you for Uncle Taki's death. I wanted to find a way we could have a normal relationship. To be honest I wanted to think, in spite of every evil thing you have done, somehow you could change and be a good man!" Megumi was trembling with rage. It was as though she finally let out all her internalised pain and anger. All of it was directed at her father. Steve had never seen Megumi in such a state. He could see she needed to tell her father precisely how she felt. But he could feel the tension in the room and was worried about how she was coping. He helped Megumi sit down and tried his best to comfort her. His movements were awkward, he felt uneasy but Steve tried his best not to let his thoughts and concerns betray his actions. Nothing was more important than ensuring his wife was comforted and safe.

Nakano had been very quiet up until Megumi's outburst. She was sitting next to Kumicho and tsked at Megumi, rolling her eyes. She said to Megumi, "Have you no shame? Talking to your father like that? After all he has done for you! Disgusting." Megumi seemed to be unravelling in the toxic environment. She replied to Nakano, "You call me 'disgusting', wearing my mother's jewellery and wearing my mother's husband, before she even died! Why are you even sitting at this table? Servants should sit elsewhere!"

Sensei made an attempt to de-escalate the tension. He said, "Yes Agari-san, Steve has been a wonderful influence in our lives. A calm and good man. A very special young man. Surely you can sense this Agari-san?"

Kumicho had done well to conceal his emotions. He almost maintained his smile during the entire time of Megumi's outburst. However Sensei seemed to have inadvertently hit a raw nerve. Kumicho's mood quickly soured as he replied, "A good man?" He raised his voice as he slammed his fist on the table. "A good man? And what does it mean to be a good man? My gardener is a good man. I can't even remember his name! What does a good man know of the world? Is it noble or honourable to be oblivious of the world's challenges and complexities? To not crave the sweetest nectar? Is a good man tested often, or does he merely avoid the challenge? How can a good man judge others if he has never fought for, or savoured the taste of success? I don't believe in good men. They are just men who dare not dream to reach for the fruit at the top of the tree. They have no temptation because they know that deep in their hearts, they don't deserve it! They lay in bed at the end of the night paralysed with the fear of what the next day will bring. Waiting for death to release them from the misery of their uneventful lives. Not for me! What about you Steve, are you really a good man? Will you be forgotten? Who did my daughter marry? A gardener, or a giant?"

Steve was not ready for such a direct and sensitive line of questioning. He had been struggling with his own sense of purpose for some time. The questions were extremely close to the bone for him. With the baby's arrival imminent, he would often wonder what kind of example he would be for his child. He questioned what kind of life his family could possibly have with him as a karate instructor, which for all intents and purposes may as well have been the gardener of which Kumicho spoke.

He didn't like anyone directing their raised voice at him. His inclination was to meet fire with fire, but his Gōjū-ryū had taught him new instinctual reactions. He calmed and reminded himself of the penetrating questions his father used to ask him. Those uncomfortable questions which forced Steve to develop his own thought processes and helped consolidate his own belief systems. Steve took a breath and responded to Kumicho, "In all honesty, I think most people want to be thought of as good. If I try to define good in my own mind, it means to be a kind person who has the approval of others. Now you seem to have given me a choice, either be a good person or a giant. I must imagine a giant is someone powerful like you who does not feel the need to be kind or approved by others. I would like to think if you are truly good, then you will be rewarded for it. It doesn't have to be money. It can be the love of my wife and child. It can be the respect of people I interact with. I think it's heroic to stand up against evil. I think that is something powerful and noble and maybe more challenging than just trying to achieve success."

Kumicho smiled and addressed everyone, "Please let us move to the lounge so we can continue this most excellent discussion. And let's not forget that Steve wanted to see that sword again. Please come." Megumi was more than happy to leave the discussion at that. She knew more than well that her father would never be convinced of anything and this was nothing more than an exercise in mind games. "I'm tired, I think we should be leaving," she said as she looked at Steve. Kumicho had already made his way into the lounge and gestured for everyone to join him. Steve whispered to Megumi, "It's one night, let's just end it gently and then we can move on with our lives. Tomorrow we leave. C'mon my baby."

Kumicho was pleased everyone joined him as he replied to Steve's opinion, "Such wonderful ideals from the somewhat naive young man before me. Steve-san, as you become older, you will ask yourself many questions. The one you will ask the most is, 'Was it all worth it, could I have done more?' You will look at your life and then you will look around and see the world for what it is. Nothing more than resources to gather and consume. You will realise some people just want to serve and others choose to lead. There is no choice for the servant but there is for the leader. You just have to learn your true nature. Make no mistake, we all serve someone. Even Ishiganto served his god if you study his life carefully."

Sensei interrupted the discussion, "Ishiganto served the people, and by doing this, he served his god." Kumicho's eyes darted towards Sensei. He did not receive Sensei's comment favourably. He said, "Nakandari-san, when you welcomed the demons into your life and gave my most loyal servant Hiro his power, who were you serving? Who did you make a deal with? What did you receive in return? Nobody does anything for nothing, Nakandari-sensei. Tell them what you received in return", as he pointed to Steve and Megumi.

Sensei looked quite upset and unwilling to respond. Kumicho persisted, "Tell them, let them know what kind of man you are. Nakandari-sensei, tell them who you served!"

Sensei responded, "They know me. They know I created Demon Hiro. I have nothing to hide. I received your immunity. That was all. I didn't ask for it. I was ready to die. You wanted me killed and then you rewarded me with my life even though I was tortured every day with those demons of war. They know this and

they know I would gladly give my life to redeem Hiro's life."
Sensei was awash with the anguish of that traumatic moment
again.

Kumicho laughed, "Oh Nakandari-san, you think too much of
yourself. Let me tell you a secret, you didn't make Demon Hiro.
I already welcomed him into my inner circle. You only invited
the demons into your own spirit, you foolish man. You served
me very well until my daughter's husband came here. Don't you
remember?"

Sensei looked genuinely confused, "Are you saying it wasn't me
who made Demon Hiro? I have blamed myself all this time. I
have never willingly served you and I never will. And I will
take back my student and together with Ishiganto we will banish your demon from him!" Kumicho appeared bemused with
Sensei's response, "Please don't play with words. You say you
would never willingly serve me, but you did serve me. Have
you forgotten? How many times Taki returned here in the last
few years to try to kill me. You told me every time. You were
my best source of information. My best spy. Did Ishiganto banish your memory also? Or, perhaps you never told your Ishiganto and my daughter how you have been my best spy until
recently."

Megumi and Steve both looked shocked. They never really
knew what Uncle Taki was up to whenever he came back to Okinawa. He always said he had some business to attend to and they
never questioned him further about the nature of that business.
To find out that Sensei was telling Kumicho about Uncle Taki's
movements was upsetting to both of them. Steve had already
developed a knowledge of how demonic influences could mani-
fest the mind of a man. He couldn't blame Sensei for his actions
but still felt saddened to learn of his actions.

Sensei looked at Megumi and Steve with a guilty look. He said,

"It is true, I reported Taki's movements to this man. But we all know I was not myself. I made my peace with Taki-san after I was cured. My life is dedicated to fixing the errors of my past now." He looked pleadingly towards Megumi and Steve as he asked them, "Please forgive me, I already punish myself for my actions more than anyone else can."

Megumi was extremely upset. She had no anger for Sensei, his remorse for any wrongdoing was obvious and understandable. But her father was gloating and giving the impression of supreme vindication. She held her head in her hands and started to scream. She stood up and howled at her father, "We are now arguing about how bad Sensei was? Meanwhile there is no doubt you had everything to do with murdering Uncle Taki. If you are going to be completely honest, just tell me you killed my mother and then we can all accept you for what you are. Nothing more than a murdering criminal, a thug. Just another murderer in my bloodline! Admit it! You did it. You killed mother!"

Kumicho exploded in reply, "You want me to admit to murdering Taki and your mother? No. Instead of defending me, my only daughter accuses me. Taki tried to kill me many times. I chose to let him live, just so he could look after you. Yes, ungrateful you. But I have very devoted servants. Sometimes they want to help me too much. In truth, it was no great loss to lose him. And your mother should have supported me instead of working against me. She was the one behind the people who have been trying to overthrow me. You think Taki was smart enough to do that? She was sabotaging me from the inside. We could have been so successful together. But she was nothing more than a nuisance to me. She was weak and she made you weak also. Look at the gaijin you chose to marry. He will never understand our ways. He will never rise up to lead. You chose someone as weak as yourself. My little crying daughter and her little karate boy husband. If I was the man you say I am, I should kill you both right now to spare you from your pathetic lives of mediocrity."

Megumi was hysterical. She launched herself at her father and slapped him. Steve positioned himself in between them. But it was too late, her slap had already landed on his face. Her fingernails managed to scratch her father's face. "My husband is more of a man than you have ever been. You should feel ashamed just being in his presence. He is a true King and you are just a murdering thief," she said. Kumicho touched his face and found the blood. He laughed as he wiped the blood on his fingers on Steve's jacket. He glared at Steve and said, "Will you control your wife, karate boy? Or maybe you prefer to challenge me? Do you think you have any chance with me, karate boy? Or is it Ishiganto, is that your name now?"

Steve was furious, the man before him was clearly behind the deaths of Megumi's mother and Uncle Taki and he was now goading him. He looked at Kumicho with a raging intensity but managed to repress his instinctual urges to hit this man. He pulled Megumi further away from her father and said to Kumicho, "Yeah, we're done here. Stay out of our lives and don't even think about looking for us. You're nothing to Megumi and you'll never meet your grandchild and you will never see your daughter again." Steve held Megumi and guided her from the lounge heading towards the lobby area with Sensei. Sensei whispered to Steve, "I have people nearby, let's just get out of here and we can make our way back."

Kumicho had ripped his jacket and shirt off and he sniggered as he called out to them, "Stop right there! Ishiganto thinks we are done here, no, I am very sure we are far from done. In fact, I have some very unfinished business. Nakandari-sensei has lived far too long and does not seem to understand or appreciate my benevolence. I think it is time for him to meet his destiny now. And you, karate-boy, Ishiganto, don't you still want to see my sword?" Kumicho slapped his hand on the glass display cabinet, shattering the glass. He reached inside and seized the sword which Steve had admired only a few hours earlier. Kumicho held the sword up in a manner which could only be perceived as a declaration of war.

Kumicho's lean torso was rippling with muscles and his tattoos were nothing like Steve had ever seen before. Steve recalled the exquisite detail and elegance of Sensei Mike's tattoos, but Kumicho's tattoos were something far beyond that level of detail and beauty. Chrysanthemums with dragons and vipers intertwined among the petals, radiating outwards from his chest like flames. The serpents were actually moving on Kumicho's skin. They were weaving in and out of the petals, they were transfixed on Steve and he was mesmerised by them. One moved up Kumicho's arm to pounce upon a small trail of blood emanating from the hand that smashed the glass cabinet.

Steve was debating with himself, whether to engage with the madman holding the sword in front of him or to get out of there as soon as possible. He never knew Kumicho had trained under Sensei until earlier that day. As strongly as Steve believed in his own ability, he knew this was Kumicho's home and every advantage was with him. He saw all the security contingents every step of the way into the castle. He figured it was also well within reason to assume monsters like those at his tournament were likely to be nearby.

Steve turned away from Kumicho and ushered Megumi into the lobby, only to find Sensei standing there facing away from the door. He was looking upwards. Steve and Megumi turned to look in the direction Sensei was looking. Hovering menacingly near the ceiling of the palatial lobby was a winged Demon Hiro. He looked like a serpent dragonfly, jerkily suspended in the air with his all too familiar black eyes and wings spanning half the width of the lobby. He called to Sensei, "Nakandari-sensei, it is time for me to finish my job. Prepare to die!" Sensei rooted himself into the ground, he had no intention of fleeing whatsoever.

He whispered to Steve, "Please leave Steve-san, take Megumi and go far away from here. Find your path in Fujian. Remember!" Demon Hiro heard Sensei as though he was right next to them. He hissed, "I will take your Ishiganto to Fujian, in a coffin and then I will piss on Ishiganto's god!"

Steve was in an impossible situation. He needed to ensure Megumi was safe, but he couldn't let the mortal challenge continue and see Sensei killed. He looked at Sensei and took his position, Sensei immediately understood Steve's intention. Demon Hiro already sprang forward heading towards Sensei. Sensei had commenced his Luohan vortex as Steve summoned his lion energy. He unleashed his attack as Demon Hiro swooped down towards Sensei. Within an irreconcilable moment, Kumicho had entered the room and used the sword to intercept and extinguish Steve's lion energy. Kumicho looked at the sword with a sense of surprise as it began to emit a bright orange glow. Demon Hiro flew down again and Sensei blocked his attack and flung Demon Hiro to the ground. Steve powered another lion energy attack through Demon Hiro and the demon separated from Hiro. Hiro was unconscious on the floor while the demon flew around the room like a balloon losing air until it saw Sensei, then it went straight for him. Sensei recommenced his Luohan vortex technique in an attempt to trap the demon. Kumicho moved across the room at a supernatural speed. He appeared within the vortex and removed Sensei's head with Daruma's blade in one swift motion. "No time for games," said Kumicho as he turned his attention to Steve.

The demon spirit retreated and then injected itself inside Nakano. She transformed immediately. She became elongated and her facial features had transformed into a grotesque caricature of what she used to look like. She excreted a reverberating whisper directed at Megumi, "Shameful Megumi, disgusting Megumi, cry cry cry." Demon Nakano was taunting Megumi and heading towards her.

Steve saw the looming threat of Demon Nakano. He channeled his lion energy directly at the Demon. He mustered a powerful blast and the demon was ejected yet again. This time it was headed straight for Megumi. Steve had no time to waste. He knew that if the demon managed to merge with Megumi, it would potentially destroy the only things he loved in this world. He aimed another energy blast at the demon only to be slapped down on the ground by a laughing Kumicho. His energy pulse was rendered ineffective. Kumicho kicked Steve while he was on the ground. Each hit was like a brick wall had crashed down on him. Steve was losing his clarity of judgement. His sense of purpose was clouded by the physical onslaught he was enduring. He would lose everything. He remembered the Shisa necklace Sensei had given him and he powered up his hand as he ripped it from his neck. He threw it at the demon shadow flying around the room. From the medallion, two fierce Shisa sprang forth. The Shisa with its mouth open launched at the demon shadow, devoured it and quickly turned towards Kumicho. The other Shisa with its mouth closed went straight to Megumi's defence.

Steve was on the ground trying to regain his composure when Kumicho sprang towards the Shisa near Megumi. He stabbed the lion beast through the head with his sword. The blade was magical. Powerful. Too powerful. The lion dissipated immediately but the blade continued its path, straight into Megumi's throat. Steve and Kumicho screamed in unison, "No!" Steve's adrenaline propelled him towards his wife. He held his wife and summoned his energy around her throat to try to heal her. But blood was escaping too fast, she was dying. Megumi couldn't say anything but her eyes looked at Steve with the love he knew and treasured and craved his entire life. He cradled her and begged her to live as tears filled his eyes. She faded quickly and Steve roared as rage consumed him.

The other Shisa had already fiercely pounced on Kumicho's back, it tore into Kumicho's flesh as its fangs bit into his shoulder. Kumicho had transformed when the Shisa attacked him. He doubled in size and lost any semblance with the human form he had previously. His eyes had blackened and the serpents writhed upon his blackened and scaly skin. Kumicho turned and dealt the lion gargoyle an immediate death with his powerful blade. Kumicho yelled at Steve, "This is your doing. You killed my daughter the moment you touched her! And now you will die." Kumicho raised the sword and Steve immediately launched at him to ensure the blade could not gather any momentum. Kumicho swung the blade at Steve but he had already intercepted the blade near the handle. The brief contact with the blade created a power surge through Steve. He slapped the hideous Kumicho to the ground with unprecedented power. It shocked both Kumicho and Steve. Steve kicked him repeatedly until Kumicho managed to find his feet. The sword remained on the ground and Kumicho's strength had returned as the serpents on his body began to writhe. Steve seemed to have lost some momentum as Kumicho was increasingly finding his power. Steve fought for his life. He summoned all his lion energy and punched and kicked at Kumicho. It was obvious he wasn't just fighting a man, he was fighting the Demon monster in addition to each and every one of his tattoo serpents as well. His best wasn't enough. Kumicho was winning and Steve knew it. He summoned his energy and performed a take-down, it worked. He managed to negotiate a choke on Kumicho. Steve could feel Kumicho losing his life force, but then the serpents on Kumicho's chest attacked Steve's choking arm. He had to let go, the pain was excruciating. Kumicho gathered the sword as Steve quickly found his feet.

They faced each other and Kumicho said, "I tasted your rage. Now you understand true hatred. You could be of use to me. Bow to me and I will spare your life. You can easily be one of

The Few. Worthy!" Steve replied, "Your death is my only purpose in life. The only reason for my existence now is to end
yours!" Steve could hear a faint voice repeating something over
and over but couldn't understand it nor could he discern where
it was coming from. Steve concentrated and allowed himself
to tune into the voice, "........ the sword, the sword, Alexander's
sword."

Kumicho said, "Whoever is against me does not live long
enough to do anything about it." He launched Daruma's sword
directly at Steve at lightning speed, piercing straight into
Steve's heart. Steve's irises glowed a bright orange. The lobby
changed colour. It resembled a photographic negative of the
room. Except now he could see what he had only sensed previously. The white room had looked empty. But in reality, the
room was black and full of hideous demons of all shapes and
sizes. All the demons looked like they were stuck to Kumicho.
Elastic black gel strings connected to him and stretched out
in assembled formations on the walls. They were jeering and
laughing and mocking Steve until he looked each and every one
of them in the eye. He saw Temyana, she said "The sword, it was
Alexander's. His alchemy, I understand now." Then an eruption
of orange energy from Steve's chest exploded into the room.
Everything faded to black.

Interlude - The Sword of Bodhidharma

The Lion & the Priestess (4th Century BCE)

Alexander the Great was the son of King Philip II of Macedonia and his fourth wife, Olympia. His was a charmed life in his youth. Not necessarily born to rule, his mother, the serpent worshipper, ensured he was to be the next chosen King.

From an early age it was clear the young Alexander carried the divinity. He was both headstrong and of remarkable intelligence. King Philip had destroyed the great philosopher Aristotle's hometown and condemned its citizens to slavery. After summoning Aristotle to the Macedonian court, he made a deal with Aristotle to teach Alexander in exchange for the restoration of Aristotle's hometown.

As a young teenager, Alexander learned how to fight under the guidance of King Philip and his best fighters and military strategists. But it was under Aristotle's tutelage where he learned of alchemy, medicine, philosophy, morals, religion, logic, and art. By the end of his education with the famous philosopher, he had mastered the skills of rhetoric and, most importantly, justice.

By twenty years of age, he was King of Macedonia and left little room for others to question his authority and title. Aristotle's tutelage was essential for Alexander's expansionist dreams. But there was one belief where they differed, Aristotle regarded all other races as barbarians. Their natural station in this world was appropriately confined to being slaves. Alexander remained ideologically opposed to Aristotle's belief and defined his Macedonian empire as a multicultural one. Alexander had little interest in forcing his own ideas of truth or religion upon conquered populations. He embraced the differences and employed the best people and best ideas from all of his conquered nations. His leadership helped catapult human thought to the next great age.

Long after Aristotle's tutelage ended, Alexander retained his treasured gift from his teacher, a unique version of Homer's Iliad. Hidden in the texts by code was the original Secretum Secretorum. It was Aristotle's encyclopaedia of magic, alchemy, statehood and physiognomy among other topics. Such was the importance of the book, Alexander deemed it equally as important as his sword and they were both taken on all his warring campaigns. The finest sword-smiths of Macedonia were employed to forge his blade. The steel itself was unprecedented in its characteristics. Sourced from a meteorite which landed in Heraclea Lyncestis, a city founded by Alexander's father as a tribute to the god Heracles, the steel was impossibly hard and extremely light. Alexander imbued the sword with the alchemy and magic coded in the Secretum Secretorum. The magic forged into the blade magnified its power and also ensured it could never be used to kill him or anyone from his bloodline. The forged blade included the royal marks of the Macedonians, the sixteen pointed sun rosette and the lion head on the pommel.

By the time he had conquered almost the entirety of the known world, Alexander had taken a Bactrian Princess as his wife, the Zoroastrian Roxana. The man who solved the Gordian knot with the edge of his blade had almost satiated his desire to conquer. But two enemies remained that eluded him. The first was himself and the second was the underworld. Conquering other kingdoms and lands was no longer enough for the warring machine that Alexander had become. He had almost deciphered the code for immortality with the aid of his coded book. He understood he had to conquer and escape his own cycle in order for himself to become a god - then he would finally face and conquer the underworld.

A high priestess known to some as Livantia, others as Temyana, had mastered the Orphic rituals from a young age. She came from Macedonia and was feared by the Hellenes almost as much as Alexander. Her knowledge of the old ways and the threat she presented to civilised society was both feared and revered in equal proportions. Her confrontations with the new faith leaders and the relegation of women to a similar status as slaves enraged her. The Macedonians were regarded as barbarians by the Hellenes for drinking their wine undiluted. In the same way, the undiluted faith of the Macedonians who followed Livantia and her Orphic wine cult were treated as crazed, yet increasingly powerful fundamentalists.

Alexander could see the growing threat of Livantia's brand of fundamentalist faith to the civilisation he was building. He summoned her and placed her on trial in his private court. He had never met a woman with such fire in her spirit and knowledge of the metaphysical. She was beautiful, charismatic, powerful and bewitching. Roxana was becoming increasingly jealous of Alexander's infatuation with the High Priestess. The Zoroastrian Roxana had no interest in Livantia's faith and relied on nothing more than her female intuition to sense Livantia's hidden agenda. She reminded Alexander to remember what he learned from Aristotle's lectures in physiognomy and study Livantia's face carefully. The Priestess was lying to Alexander.

Alexander's lust quickly changed to bloodlust as her agenda of deceit began to reveal itself. She revealed how she had learned how to enter and return from the underworld. Nobody had managed to return from the underworld since Orpheus himself managed to persuade the gods and nymphs with his mournful tunes. She knew no army of the living could ever defeat Alexander's war machine. Instead, she was raising an army of the dead to defeat the Macedonian King and install herself as a goddess on Earth to rule in his place. He tortured her with the full magic of his blade. He placed the blade against her face and burned his royal insignia into the side of her face to be a constant reminder of whom she served. She never feared death. Livantia had already travelled that path to the underworld and re-

turned many times. But after she felt the full power and divinity of Alexander's spirit, she willingly performed obeisance to him and ended her campaign against the Macedonian King.

He commanded her to swear on Hades' immortal and infinite power to protect the earthbound souls of his rightful heirs for eternity. Upon making her oath, Alexander pierced her with his blade and condemned her spirit to permanently roam between both the living world and underworld, but never to remain completely in one or the other, until his line had ended.

The insight gained from the interrogation of the High Priestess pushed Alexander into an introspective phase. The cycle of wars had left their toll on the king. He had heard of great philosophers in the kingdoms of India and needed to find peace from the terror he unleashed on Earth in his quest for world domination. His Indian campaigns were successful, but the warring in India was insignificant in comparison with the insight gained upon meeting the Gymnosophists, also known as the Naked Philosophers, whose purity of thought challenged Alexander's belief systems.

He selected ten of the Naked Philosophers who had previously encouraged a revolt against him and threatened to put to death the first who gave an incorrect answer. Alexander was well versed in philosophical debates but was not ready to be challenged by the answers of the naked philosophers.

When he asked how a man could be most loved, "If", answered one philosopher, "he is most powerful, and yet does not inspire fear."

He asked another how one might become a god instead of man, he replied, "By doing something which a man cannot do."

Even the most innocuous and trivial questions were met with the most profound answers. Alexander dismissed the philosophers with gifts and returned to his stronghold a changed man forever. He was no longer interested in the life of gods and lost his desire for war. He knew he would be challenged for leadership and would have given it away willingly, such was his profound change. He died under suspicious circumstances but not before Livantia hid his son Alexander IV among her former followers. The boy substituted in Alexander IV's place was murdered as all efforts were made to extinguish the bloodline of the Macedonian Kings.

The Priest King (6th Century CE)

Skandar was a blue-eyed nobleman of Persian descent. More precisely, a Hephthalite or White Hun living in Bactria. He and his young family led a relatively charmed life wanting for nothing. He was a trained warrior and highly respected for both his intellect and his martial abilities.

A heaven and fire worshipper, a Zoroastrian, Skandar vehemently rejected the increasingly dominant and rapidly expanding Buddhist faith. His name "Skandar" was a family name and was an eastern variation of the name "Alexander". He was told of his ancient ties to Macedonia back when it was once a great kingdom.

His Quickening was a maddening period for him. A call to Macedonia stirred deeply from his soul. An image of a sword was driving him mad. He took his wife and young son with him on pilgrimage to Macedonia. Travelling along the well worn road of Via Egnatia, he reached Macedonia under the reign of Roman Emperor Justinian and his most successful general, Belisarius.

The Sassanids of Bactria had been a persistent and feared opposition to the Roman Empire and the painful memory of the Battle of Callinicum still lingered. Skandar was not a Sassanid, but easily could have been thought to be one due to his comfort with the Bactrian language. In fact, the White Huns were the enemy of the Sassanids. Although their power base in Bactria was diminishing, the White Huns were treated with suspicion by the Empire.

He had followed Via Egnatia to an earthquake ravaged Macedonian city called Heraclea Lyncestis. Even though the Empire had embraced Christianity, partial statues of the city's deity namesake, Heracles, remained. The impenetrable lion skin wearing Heracles was a proclaimed ancestor of Alexander the Great and imported to Bactria during Alexander's era of glory. Heracles was extremely familiar to Skandar. He was the protector deity of the venerated Demetrius the Invincible of Bactria, who was said to be an ancestor of Skandar and whose legend endured centuries later in the region.

Skandar had noticed that Heracles was the same deity which provided the inspiration for Vajrapani, a protector of the Buddha. Many generations later, one would see the likeness of Heracles in the Japanese Niō guardian gods of the Buddha and also, in a more abstract manifestation, as the Shisa of Okinawa. Vajrapani would also go on to become the patron saint of the Shaolin Monastery.

It was only two hundred years earlier when great rulers would visit the preserved corpse of Alexander the Great, in Alexandria Egypt, to marvel at the remains of the great King. The rebellion riots of the 4th Century decimated Alexandria and the corpse had been lost ever since. His sword and book were never found.

Skandar's maddening quest for the beckoning sword found him digging near the pedestal of the most prominent Heracles tribute in the once great city. The paranormal connection to that precise location was far beyond any rational thought process. He dug for two days and finally found his calling. A rusted sword inscribed with the mark of the Macedonian Royalty and a fierce lion's head on the pommel. As soon as he grasped the sword, a bright orange glow radiated from the blade and the rust fell off as though it was dust. His irises glowed a bright orange and he was reborn. The familiar apparition of the half-masked Livantia appeared before him. In line with the lingua franca of the era, she had taken to calling herself Temyana. He had been seeing Temyana in his dreams ever since his father died. She had been giving him clues about his Macedonian ancestry and his connections on a much broader scale to the world around him.

Temyana's knowledge was overwhelming. She described more completely the Empire he previously had only experienced from afar. She told him of the great demons in Europe and how the opposing resistance was being tempered to subdue their influence. She warned him the demons were gaining the balance of power in the East and his potential would be unrealised if he did not use his gift to oppose the darkness rising there. The same darkness which, if unabated, would soon consume his own people in Bactria.

With the power of Temyana's visions, Skandar's destiny was revealed. His life was immediately transformed and his bloodline would go on to suffer generationally for his sacrifice. Temyana had seen the rise of the Brahmin caste in India. Some of Skandar's own people had already found their way as great Brahmins of India. The warriors were a noble and natural enemy to the darkness preparing to consume the East and beyond. She advised Skandar to join them and find his path.

Skandar left his wife and young son behind in the comparative safety of Macedonia and, sword in hand, found his people who had entered the Brahmin caste in India. He arrived there as a warrior, but his remarkable intellect and purity of heart compelled him to engage with the Buddhist priests. He debated and exchanged ideas with the monk priests. The dialogues with the Buddhist monks challenged and nourished his soul and soon sent him into the bottomless abyss. The good thoughts, good words and good deeds of his Zoroastrian faith had been replaced with the pursuit of the four noble truths and the noble eightfold path of the Buddhists.

Such was the way with the men of his bloodline, his pursuit was relentless and his rewards divine. He spent seven years cultivating his mind and pursuing his Dhyāna, his mind training, with an extreme form of asceticism to counter his many years of hedonistic *fueled heaven and fire worship. In his eighth year, he freed himself from the desire to suffer. He had freely lost all and finally gained his enlightenment. Thereafter he became Bodhidharma, the 28th direct line descendent of the original Buddha. With the sword of Alexander on his back, he headed for China to spread the Dharma at the request of his mentor, the 27th Patriarch, Prajñātāra.*

The Blue Eyed Barbarian, as described in the Chinese Chan texts, travelled over much of Asia and shared the Dharma with all who had the mental freedom to learn from him. Some would seek to follow him while others merely begged for his blessing. He planted the seeds of his enlightenment in all corners of Asia and from them sprang forward yet another evolution in human thought. He visited the pious, yet physically debilitated praying monks of the Shaolin Monastery. They accepted his spiritual instruction and called him Da Mo but rejected his offers of physical instruction. They continued to resist his instruction in the way of Luohan. But he deemed them worthy, he persisted and finally made them immensely strong with his knowledge of the original Eighteen hands of Arhat, the way of Luohan. They were able to pursue their enlightenment with a mastery of their bodies in addition to their minds. They went on to form the entire Shaolin Kung Fu systems and used them to resist the growing evil for generations to come.

Da Mo was pleased. He had heard of great evil unfurling in the islands of Japan and decided to sow seeds of his enlightenment there. He left the Shaolin monastery and found himself on the Okinawan islands. The Ryūkyū Emperor, Agari Hachirō received the Blue Eyed Barbarian at his palace. Their conversations and debates were epic. The Emperor was most powerful, yet not feared by his people. Da Mo was pleased to meet someone who was so deeply loved, powerful and yet as humble as a beggar.

A deep intellectual bond grew between the two great men. After two years of debate and instruction, Emperor Agari threw himself at the feet of the Priest King he called Daruma and said, "I now understand, there is nothing and I am nothing." He asked for Daruma's sword so he could cut off his arm as a dedication to him. Daruma smiled upon the great Emperor, he had reached enlightenment. Daruma's dominant gift from his bloodline was his intellect. He performed a mind to mind transference and duplicated all his wisdom to the Emperor. Such was the sense of completion in his life, Daruma gifted the "Sword that Beckoned" to his protege. He left the island and returned to the Celestial Empire, China.

The Emperor decided his kingdom was unnecessary and urged his family to follow him. The Emperor's son and heir to the throne, Agari Shoto, despised Daruma's influence over his father and quickly learned his father was going to abolish his monarchy. He pleaded with his father to abdicate and allow him to rule in his place. But the Emperor had dreamt of a new and enlightened way for the Ryūkyū people. The Emperor's dream never came to pass. Agari Shoto used Daruma's sword to kill his father and claim the Crown. The Ryūkyū people soon learned of the son's filial betrayal and banished him. The murderer became a thief and the sins of his bloodline stain the world to this day.

The great Skandar, Bodhidharma, the 28th Patriarch of Buddhism, the first Patriarch of Chan/Zen Buddhism, the Patriarch of Shaolin Kung Fu, Da Mo, Daruma, the Priest King was buried by the monks in the Celestial Empire having died in his senior years. Documents revealed a man saw him walking and holding a single shoe three years after his death. He asked the master, "Where are you going?", to which he replied, "I am going home, tell no-one that you saw me or you will meet disaster." Rumours persisted of the old blue eyed bearded monk walking west, solitarily along Via Egnatia.

Book Three - The Revelators

When the Tao is lost, there is goodness.

When goodness is lost, there is morality.

When morality is lost, there is ritual.

Ritual is the husk of true faith,

the beginning of chaos.

— Lao Tzu, Tao Te Ching

Chapter 14 - Escape to China

"It's okay, don't worry. It's okay," the distant, yet familiar, voice sounded reassuring. There was too much noise. Images were only fleetingly visible. If only he could hold focus for longer than a split second. Everything was a blur as he was propelled forward at an impossible velocity. The incessant noise was getting louder. Thunderous and pulsating. His head was going to explode if it didn't subside soon. "It's okay, not much longer now," said the somewhat closer voice.

The relentless noise suddenly disappeared and the silence was even more disconcerting than the thunderous cacophony of a moment earlier. An infinite white space. "Was it Kumicho's lobby?" he thought to himself. He steeled himself and found his fighting position. The voice was clear, "That's better, now you might hear me more clearly," the blonde woman to his right said. "I sometimes forget what it feels like the first time you pass. Don't worry, there is nothing to fear here. I'm with you. It takes a little time."

Steve was fighting his disorientation. He ascertained he was somewhere else. It wasn't Kumicho's lobby. His lobby wasn't as big as the space he was in. "This is endless," he said, as he tried to make sense of the dimensions he was immersed in. Then, as if he was stabbed in the heart again, all the memories came back to him. Not just some of the memories, all of them. Literally everything. He remembered his mother's first caress when he was born. Her sweet eyes and voice. He remembered his youth, he remembered his school life, his training, the sweetest times with his beautiful girlfriend, his wife! "Megumi!" he cried while clutching at his chest. "My wife, my everything. No, no. She can't be dead. She didn't deserve to die. Our baby. How could I let this happen?"

The memories reinforced the gravity of the horror he had experienced. "A painful end," the woman said. In his mind, Steve was trying to be stoic, yet his ability to control himself was gone. The sheer vastness of his grief consumed him. He cried, he called for his wife, he whimpered and sobbed for her. The beautiful girl whom he treasured and wanted to grow old with. Gone. "It was all my fault, I should have been smarter. Stronger. I could have saved her!" he said.

The blonde woman turned to face him. Steve had never seen her before, yet he knew it was Temyana. The right hand side of her face was burned. It seemed more vivid than when he met that little girl so many years ago. He could see the outline of the Macedonian sun rosette on her right cheek. She said, "No, you couldn't have saved her. It was her destiny, the same way that sword would inevitably pass through your heart. Some things simply must come to pass. And now, you are left with a decision no man has ever made before. You can choose whether you want to live or die." Temyana proceeded to explain the significance of the sword and the magic weaved into the blade by his very own ancestor, the Great Alexander. There were gaps in her knowledge about the magic of the sword. She explained how the sword found its way to the Priest King and finally from the Priest King to the demon Kumicho.

Steve was grieving deeply, his mind returned to the horror of losing his Megumi. Temyana immediately noticed he was inside his own thoughts. "Listen! This is extremely important!" She said. "You can choose to live, but your life will be very different. The world will never look the same again. You will see the darkness. The world is full of it. It is relentless. It is inevitable and it is chaos. And, once you become fully desensitised to it, it calls you and sends its best face to beckon and tempt you. But if you choose to pass, to die, your immortal soul can finally rest and join the Infinite."

Steve stopped her, "I have nothing left, my life only brings death to the ones who love me. There is nothing there for me. I choose to die, do what you must. All the ones I love are already gone." Temyana said, "I have an oath to your bloodline, you are the last of your line. If you choose to pass, then my last obligation is to guide you through and then we can both join the Infinite. But I need you to answer me, do you choose to die now?"

"Yeah, fuck everything, make it all end," he commanded her. Temyana looked relieved, the burden of her ancient oath was finally about to come to an end. She said "I thought you might be one of the biggest of your bloodline, you burned too brightly, too soon." She instructed Steve to place his hand on her shoulder and not let go under any circumstance. Temyana gestured with her hand and they were suddenly moving at cosmic speed. The infinite white space had changed to an abstracted galaxial landscape as they rocketed inter-dimensionally through time and space. Unlike the cacophonous upheaval of Steve's immersion into the infinite white, this was silent, beautiful and peaceful.

Temyana said, "Sometimes I just want to stay here forever. Your father agreed, and so did his father. Well, actually, your entire bloodline felt the same way. This will be the last time I will experience it. I have never been this far in my full form since before the Great Alexander. It will end soon and you will find a peace you can't begin to imagine." Steve embraced the serenity of the journey. He noticed his and Temyana's physical forms were fading, yet he knew precisely where his extremities ended and where hers began. Suddenly Temyana shrieked, her physical form reappeared and she seemed tethered to a point from where they had started their journey. She was whipped back and pulled away from Steve. Steve could hear her clearly in the galaxial void as she frantically explained, "This can't be. There is nothing forcing me back. Your bloodline is finished. Wait. Unless, oh my Gods, yes, amazing! I feel it. Your son lives. My oath compels me to return to him. You are almost there, focus on your loved ones and you will pass to the Infinite. I'll see you again."

Steve's universe of serenity immediately evaporated. Every instinct told him not to pass. He couldn't leave his defenceless child in that world. His choice was immediate. But his soul was still hurtling towards the Infinite. He rejected his deceased loved ones and shouted at the Gods, "No, he needs me!" But his soul was still rocketing further away from where he began. His spirit activated without conscious thought, his life force had transformed. What recently had become transparent filled the entire celestial void. His form had become a pure orange fire and fully formed into the most majestic lion. He roared his rejection of the Infinite and saw the galaxial void consumed by his energy. As immediately as the energy pulse filled the void, it returned back to the majestic lion with the same impossible velocity. Steve saw the outline of his form, then drew his first breath after what may have been hours, or years. He clutched at his chest and saw the blur of the street lights of Okinawa.

The car stopped and Steve saw the familiar carpark lights of the hospital where Tania was recovering. "Look, look, Ishiganto! He lives! He lives! Impossible!" People gathered around the car and peered inside. One opened the door. He heard a complete spectrum of human responses. Exclamations and murmurs of shock, confusion, disbelief, joy, surprise, horror and elation. Steve looked outside the car window and saw outlines of people but, to his horror, there were demons everywhere. Similar to the ones he saw in Kumicho's lobby when the blade pierced his heart. They were clinging to the people who were looking at him. They were disgusting. Steve was in pain and horrified. He tried to muster some energy to fight what appeared to be his enemy but the pain in his chest was too intense. He couldn't move.

The people seemed sincere, but the visual reality was unbearable. Steve couldn't understand why the people weren't reacting to the obvious infestation of filthy, slithering agents of darkness. One voice rose above the commotion. "Ishiganto, I am a doctor at this hospital. I need to look at you. We are all here to help you. There is nothing to fear. They said you were dead." Steve tried to push him away but was too weak. His chest felt like it was on fire. He looked down at his chest and it was still glowing where the blade had penetrated. "My Megumi, my son?" he hoarsely groaned. The doctor replied. "We managed to save your son, we are sorry about your wife." Steve again tried to rise but his body was not functioning. "Take me to my baby," he said. The doctor stuttered in response, "Your b b b baby, your baby, is g gone, your baby is gone."

"What? Where?" Steve again tried to get up. A couple of men reached into the car to try and settle him. He saw the demons slide off them onto his arms. They looked like they touched boiling oil when they reached him. They were immediately repelled. A commanding voice boomed, "Get out of my way you idiots. Close the door and give me the keys. Don't make me ask again! We don't have much time." One of the crowd said, "Not him, he works for Kumicho. Stop him!" The man said, "I just saved his son and now I will try to save him if you can all get the fuck out of my way. Hurry, the keys! I warn you, there is no time to waste." The car started and they were moving again.

Steve was lying in the back of the car and the blur of the street lights almost looked like his celestial journey. But the persistent burning pain in his chest reminded him he had left that long behind. He tried to focus on the driver, he couldn't see any hint of those demons he saw earlier. The driver was unblemished.

Steve said, "They were everywhere. But you are clean, I don't see any attached to you." The driver said, "Some will return. They inevitably will. But you destroyed my worst one. I am grateful and indebted to you." Something about the timbre of the voice of the driver. Steve again tried to look at the driver, the silhouette was almost familiar. A tall, lean man. A sliver of clarity sliced through the haze of Steve's cognitive ability, "It's you!" as Steve tried to will himself forward from the back of the seat. "I will kill you, I'll fucking kill you," Steve screamed until all his energy was spent. He fainted as the car kept travelling at speed.

Steve woke to find himself being dragged out of the car by his nemesis, Hiro. Steve again tried to resist but he was too weak. The man tried to pacify Steve, "Stop resisting. I'm trying to help you. You said I was unblemished. It's true, my demons are gone, at least for now. I must help you get away from here. Kumicho is already searching for you. He doesn't know your baby lives. I took Megumi to the hospital after you destroyed my worst demon. I saved your baby. The baby is with your friend, Tania. Taki's people, your Ishiganto people are hiding them. They will not be safe anywhere in Japan. And you will not be safe either. You are not strong enough to help them now. Do you understand? I am not your enemy. I owe you my life."

Steve couldn't reconcile the man before him with the evil Demon Hiro that killed and created so much pain in his life. He was unblemished. A pilot in the distance was waiting on the foreshore not far from a small seaplane floating on the ocean. The pilot had some small slippery serpentine demons attached to him. Hiro said, "He is one of your followers, an Ishiganto follower. I have people waiting for us in China. They are not good people, but they follow instructions well. We must both leave Japan, if we are to have any chance. You must stay hidden. Kumicho knows people there but there are always negotiations when he deals with one of The Few over there. Time is of the essence. Quickly!" Hiro called the pilot to help him. They assisted

Steve to the seaplane.

Steve was strapped in next to his former nemesis and barely able to move. Hiro told Steve how much he regretted what his demon did to Mike. He explained how it had been many years since his spirit had been so pure. He wasn't sure how long it would last. "Everyone has their demons, if I remain in Japan, it won't be long before some demons will find me and Kumicho finds both of us. I will not be able to stay with you for long. I will make sure you are safe and able to recover, then I must move on," he said. Steve was physically incapable of moving, but he understood the Hiro next to him was a very different one from the Hiro that haunted his dreams. He offered Steve some morphine tablets to help dull his pain. Steve refused but Hiro, his unlikely ally, insisted they would dull the pain. Steve's pain was not subsiding and it was unbearable, he eventually acquiesced. He noticed the pilot's demons had disappeared just before fading into a dreamless and defenceless sleep.

Chapter 15 - Black Spice

The seaplane landed in the ocean adjacent to the Xiamen foreshore. Steve had woken from his morphine-induced sleep. His senses were still dulled from the tablets. He tried his best to elevate himself from his hazy stupor but it was impossible. He observed Hiro gesticulating and instructing a couple of Chinese men in suits. Steve couldn't understand a word.

Hiro returned to Steve, "I must not know where these men will take you. If Kumicho finds me, he will force me to tell him and I will not be able to resist. I have paid these men to hide you somewhere. You must recover. Take this money, it's all I could gather quickly. When you're better, find your way back to Australia. Do not come back to Japan. You surprised Kumicho this time. If he has another chance with you, no evil will be spared to destroy you."

Steve mustered all of his energy to find a shard of his voice momentarily and raspily whispered, "My child, I need to find my baby." Hiro grabbed Steve's shoulders and looked him in the eyes in a pleading, yet resolute manner, "I have never seen anyone fight Kumicho and live. Maybe you truly are Ishiganto. Whoever, whatever you are, you are in no condition to care for your baby or face Kumicho. Let the gods choose your baby's destiny for now. I left him with good people. I already told your people to move your child. I must not know where either of you are. He will not remain in Japan. Find him when you are stronger. You have ten thousand US dollars. It will keep you going for a while. Thank you again. For as long as I am myself, I am indebted to you."

Steve's depleted physical condition limited his ability to communicate meaningfully with Hiro. The best Steve could do was
blink at Hiro and duck his head slightly. The gestures seemed
enough for Hiro. He had found his absolution. He ran with renewed energy to the two Chinese men and barked out some instructions and handed them an envelope. The tablets had lost
their effectiveness and Steve's pain had returned in full. He was
consumed by the searing pain in his chest while noticing some
small red-eyed demons latched on at the feet of Hiro as he ran
into some back streets and out of view.

Steve witnessed the complete transformation of Hiro from
demon to human. To further compound Steve's monumental
grief and physical pain, it occurred to him that his Sensei Mike
did not have to die by his very own hands. Steve could have
saved him if only he knew more about himself. "I failed every
single one of them," he cried as he buried his face in his hands.

Hiro was right about the Chinese men. They were businesslike
in their manner. They were filthy with yellow and red-eyed demons, yet they dutifully attended to their task for Hiro and
barely engaged with Steve in the process. They kept off the
main roads as much as possible and drove for about an hour.
They finally stopped in front of an historic building that looked
untouched for the last two hundred years. It looked completely
out of place among the industrial buildings in the precinct. The
driver said something unintelligible to his associate and left the
car. The associate gave up playing with the car radio and turned
around to acknowledge Steve for the first time. He smiled at
Steve and said "Carockodel Dandi, good very good" and gestured
with his thumb up. Steve took a moment to register what he
was saying, then realised he was trying to say Crocodile Dun-
dee, the famous Australian movie from a few years earlier. The
corners of Steve's mouth turned upwards into something re-

sembling a smile and he managed to turn his thumb upwards.

The driver returned to the car with a woman walking in front of him. She was a small, old woman wearing too much makeup. Her dyed black hair abruptly changed into white at the crown of her head and her dress was flimsy and unfortunate in what it revealed of her body. She peered inside the tinted windows of the car and saw Steve slumped in the back seat. She hissed her instructions and the men assisted Steve inside the establishment.

The building looked as though it was ready for demolition on the outside but inside it was opulent and had the elegance of a much earlier era with ornate rosewood furniture, sumptuous cushions and exquisite drapes adorning the walls. It was smoke filled and dimly lit with coloured lamps. There were multiple small rooms on either side of the passageway. Partially-clothed women and boisterous drunk men were cavorting in and out of the rooms. It quickly occurred to Steve he was being ushered into a brothel. Demons were clinging to everyone. Small slithery creatures with fangs freely moving and hissing over the people inside. Even in Steve's diminished condition, he noticed the serpentine leeches had differing characteristics. Some were greyish, others were black. Their slits for eyes were different colours. Blue-eyed demons attached to the patrons and the whores with their yellow and occasional blue-eyed ones. All were repulsive and reminded him of Kumicho's lobby when the sword pierced his heart and the room changed into a filthy black pit of serpents.

The old woman was walking in front and directing the men who were assisting Steve. Her eyes were darting around the establishment in a way which made it clear she was the boss. She whispered curses at the whores as they passed her and smiled insincerely at the drunken patrons. They neared the end of the passageway and turned left into a small store room. A little girl was sitting on a pile of boxes next to the rear wall which was adorned with a luxurious drape. No more than eight years old, she was playing with her doll contentedly and seemed oblivious to all the goings on in the rest of the establishment. Steve noticed immediately that the girl was unblemished, completely devoid of demons. He had almost become desensitised to seeing them but it was jarring to see someone without the demonic affliction. The old woman, bathed in a sea of yellow-eyed demons and a few red-eyed demons, noticed Steve looking at the little girl. She shook her head and scowled at Steve. Steve gathered the old hag assumed he wanted the girl for sex but didn't have the energy or inclination to explain himself.

The little girl bounced off the boxes and quickly moved them out of the way. The old woman reached behind a nearby cupboard and pulled a lever. The drape dragged across the rear wall revealing a concealed door which opened automatically to expose a hidden room. The hag motioned for the men to take Steve across the threshold into the hidden area. Thin, semi-opaque curtains delineated the confined space and Steve was placed on a low bed furthest from the secret door. "Carockodel Dandi" laughed the men as they both left him on the dirty bed and closed the door behind them.

The only light source in the room came from a small clock radio next to his bed. Steve clutched at his painful chest while the muffled sounds of laughing and shouting continued on the other side of the hidden door. Old Chinese opera songs were playing on the clock radio. The faint orange glow radiating from where the blade pierced him reminded him of his cursed life as he drifted into a fitful sleep.

The door opened and the bright daylight from the adjoining room's window streamed into Steve's hidden chamber. He tried to sit up but tensing his abdomen muscles seemed to amplify the unbearable pain in his chest. He couldn't move. The hag dragged her slippers across the tiled floor and entered Steve's area. The same yellow-eyed demons dominated her person. She was asking Steve some questions in Chinese. He couldn't understand a word. He tried to respond but his throat was too dry and he was too weak to gesture with his hands. She left him some water and a small portion of rice with a few vegetables. Steve tried to get up, but it was futile. The clock was showing midday when the hag closed the door behind her. Steve couldn't reach the food or water and gave up trying. He fell asleep and woke up to hear the muffled laughing, moaning, shouting and screaming from the other side of the door. The clock radio showed 11pm and the faint glow emanating from his chest persisted, as did his intolerable and incessant pain.

It was just after 2am when the muffled sounds sharpened. The door had been opened and some of the lamp lights from the adjoining room filtered through into Steve's area. There was a silhouette of a small person in the doorway. The silhouette moved closer and drew Steve's curtain open. "Unblemished," Steve thought to himself, feeling oddly relieved as the little girl walked into Steve's area and stood in front of him. She noticed his food and water was untouched and pointed at them while looking at Steve. Steve was not hungry but he was parched. His blink seemed to work, she brought the glass of water to his mouth and he managed to drink some water. She brought the plate of food to him but he moved his head enough to indicate he didn't want it. As quickly as she entered the room, she left and the muffled sounds from the adjacent rooms continued to compete with the incessant Chinese operas from the clock radio next to him.

It was midday when the door opened again. The daylight pierced the misery of his darkness as the sound of slippers dragging across the floor approached him. Steve saw the yellow-eyed demons long before he even acknowledged they were attached to the hag. She had brought more food and water and noticed the food from the day before was untouched. She hissed at Steve while replacing the food and drink. She closed the door behind her and Steve was left alone in the darkness to dwell in his pain.

It was near 1am when the door opened and the noises from the adjacent rooms became clearer. He opened his eyes and was relieved to see no demons on the silhouette in the doorway. Still unable to find the strength to serve himself, he was hopeful the little girl might give him some water. She pointed to the water and said "hē" making a drinking gesture. Steve nodded and learned the word for water or drink as she helped him rehydrate. She tried to offer food to Steve but he was still unable to even contemplate the thought of eating. She remonstrated with him as though she was telling off her doll. She sat with Steve for a while and pointed around the room identifying everything in Chinese. She pointed to herself and said "Nan". Steve's pain never left him but he was grateful for the break to his wicked nightmares. He pointed to himself and said "Steve", Nan smiled, then concentrated intensely as she carefully pronounced his name as "Shidifu". She heard someone shouting her name in the next room and quickly left, looking disappointed to leave the foreigner in the hidden space.

The faint glow from Steve's chest had faded even further. But the pain continued to radiate from the same place and was his constant reminder of the immense losses in his life. His beautiful wife, the one to whom he gave himself so completely, gone in an instant. He remembered their first chance meeting. That faraway wave she gave him as she headed to her train in Shibuya, her sign and motivation for him to chase her to the end of the world. Memories of their quietest moments with no need to talk or even look at each other and the feeling of how complete they both felt just by being in each other's company.

He could still see her beautiful smile, that one especially reserved for him. Her impossible beauty and the way her smile played with her teeth. Her mesmerisingly beautiful and expressive eyes, the way they conveyed every emotion without saying a word. The way she blossomed during their time together. Her face of confidence she presented to the world when he first met her versus the woman she had become after receiving Steve's avalanche of love. She had found herself through Steve's unconditional love and told him so every day.

He had been reborn through her love. He was happy. Not happy the way a child would be with a new toy, but happy in a way that allowed him to find peace. Happy in a way that enabled him to appreciate little things, which he didn't even notice or care about before her presence enriched his life. He could feel her in bed with him there and then. He wanted to turn and see her but his pain was his only real companion in his bed. If only she could touch him again, it would surely cure him from the relentless pain. She couldn't. She was dead and Steve's punishment for letting it happen was to live. The Chinese opera streaming from the clock radio seemed to lament his loss.

Dreams and reality merged into each other as his gloomy confinement played a wicked game with his sanity. By the time it was midday, he wasn't sure if he had slept at all. The door opened and the light seemed to bounce off the yellow-eyed demons as the hag dragged her feet on the ground towards Steve. She had no interest in the foreigner hidden in her establishment. She performed her necessary tasks in relation to food, water and lodgings and quickly left Steve to his solitude.

On one occasion, Steve heard a siren and a muffled stampede somewhere in the establishment. Then the door opened and in hurried all the women working there. They were scantily clad and wearing too much makeup. Worried about being found, they remained exceptionally quiet. They had not seen Steve before and quite possibly had not seen many foreigners in their lives. It was strangely surreal as they gravitated to his dimly

lit area and peered and pointed at him as though he was a cir-
cus animal. It was the first time Steve noticed the blood on
his clothing, the same clothing he wore that horrific night only
days earlier. The door opened and the hag shouted at the women
as they promptly scuttled out.

Nan would often sneak in to talk with Steve. By the end of
the week, he could recognise some often used Chinese words.
He was grateful for her visits. Her unblemished spirit reminded
him of when he couldn't see the world's evil as plain as daylight.
She momentarily distracted him from his pain and, more importantly, from his vicious cycle of dark thoughts. The mental
torture of his painful solitude was chiseling away at whatever
was left of his former identity.

By the end of the week, the hag dragged her slippers in along
with an extra bite to her typical nasty demeanour. She engaged
with Steve more directly than ever before. A few hand gestures
were enough to convey her message. Rubbing her fingers against
her thumb, then waving her hand and finally pointing to the
door. Whatever money had been given for food and bed for
Steve was finished. Steve knew he was physically in no position
to move. He had tried the day before and remained unable to
pick himself up from his bed. He remembered the money Hiro
gave him and reached into his jacket and pulled out the substan-
tial wad of cash.

The frenzied yellow-eyed demons were teeming all over the hag
as her demeanour instantly changed. The insincere smile, usually reserved for paying patrons, was served up to Steve in all its
unimpressive theatre. She pounced upon the money and took
what she deemed was appropriate. No doubt more than what
the Chinese men paid her the week earlier. Steve's condition
was such that she could have taken all the money, but perhaps
she would have to answer to those Chinese men. In any case,
she found new motivation to care for the sick foreigner in her

midst.

He remained weak and was still barely able to move in his second week there. However, his moaning during waking hours had stopped. The hag seized upon his subtle improvement and let her greed for money be her only guide. As a retailer would seek to sell extras to a customer, the hag offered each of her harlots to Steve. Much to her disappointment, he rejected all her offers. He was disgusted at the thought and, in any case, was not in a position to even move, much less participate in coitus.

His level of disgust reached new levels when the hag threw Nan into his room. She had noticed how Nan would talk with Steve and try to teach him Chinese. She offered the little girl to him and gestured she would cost big money if he wanted his way with her. Steve's depleted physicality had zero correlation with the rage he felt internally. "How could that evil witch offer the little girl to him?" he thought to himself. He closed his eyes and turned his head away from the disgusting hag.

His mind returned to his newborn son. The thought of someone else looking after him, making decisions on his behalf. Motherless and, for all intents and purposes, fatherless. His son would not know how loved he is, nor how his father rejected the tranquility of death to come back for him. Steve's agenda was clear, he needed to find his strength and then find his son. The stabbing ache in his chest persisted and he could no longer discern between his physical pain and the ache for his parentless son.

The hag returned the following day. She brought with her a new strategy. She unveiled a small lacquered box, an ornate bamboo and silver pipe, a lamp and various knives and scissors. She pointed towards Steve's chest and proffered a thumb up and said "doctor". Steve assumed the hag had brought a traditional Chinese medicine solution to help him with his pain. He was longing to find his baby son, he needed his strength and was

eager for a remedy. His instincts shouted at him to avoid anything offered by the hag, but his son was out in the world somewhere and he needed his father to be strong enough to find him.
Steve accepted her offer immediately and had no conception of
the hell he was about to descend into.

The hag was delighted as she attended to his medicine. She
opened the lacquered box and extracted a small brownish coloured substance. She trimmed the wick of her lamp and lit the
flame. She proceeded to work the substance with the heat of the
flame until it became almost caramel coloured. She worked the
substance until she was happy with the texture and shape and
then finally transferred it to the porcelain bowl of the ornate
pipe. She instructed Steve to smoke the pipe as she lined up the
resin to the lamp flame. The medicine bubbled and released its
vapour. Steve drew the smoke into his lungs with immediate
effect.

His coughing heralded a reaction he wasn't prepared for. The
heaviness inside his chest lifted in a euphoric way. The pungent
and powerful smell from that resin sent Steve into a blurred
state of serene reality. The hag looked in Steve's eyes for his
approval while Steve consumed the last of the godly medicine.
Steve watched her demons fade as he nodded his head and continued with his pipe dream.

The hag scraped the residue from the bowl and closed the door
behind her. His medicine was fully consumed but the effects
were enduring. His mind was free and he was transported. Rec-
ollections of the celestial landscape he fleetingly experienced
with Temyana. His misery, pain and dysfunction were replaced
with a deep sense of calm. He was a bird, flying above the sense-
lessness of it all. Wordless, mindful and contemplative. He saw
it all and understood. He noticed Nan came into the room but
paid her no attention. He was on a different path and needed nobody. He didn't see the disappointment on Nan's face, nor did he

care as his waking euphoric dreams settled him into a transcendental journey and ultimately, the deepest of sleeps.

He woke in a pool of his own sweat with a stabbing pain in his chest and stomach. He was convinced Kumicho was there and twisting the blade with all his evil intent. The pain was so intense he screamed. The door opened and the daylight streamed into his area. The hag quickly rushed inside and Nan quickly followed behind her. The hag brought Steve's medicine and commenced preparing his dose. Nan was normally extremely compliant with the hag, but she argued with her and pointed at the medicine. Her reward was a slap in the face as Nan held her face and looked at Steve shaking her head in a combination of disappointment and disapproval. She left the room as the hag pointed to where Steve kept the remainder of his money. Steve nodded immediately. He was in too much pain to reach for the money, so the hag helped herself. She peeled off a few hundred dollar notes and then helped position Steve so he could take his dose.

The pain disappeared and Steve was on his celestial journey as soon as his lungs embraced the vapour from that bubbling ambrosial resin. The hag's demons disappeared and her smile looked almost sincere and benevolent as she quickly stuffed the money into her bra and left Steve in his secluded sanctuary.

Steve finished the remainder of his medicine, the vapour nectar, and found himself alone on a great desert plain. He could feel the presence of someone or something nearby, but no matter where he turned, he couldn't see anything. He heard a baby crying in the distance, beyond a desert dune. He ran towards the direction of the cries, but the baby eluded him. It seemed always beyond the next dune. The disappointment of not finding the baby after so many attempts soon eroded his serene state. His feelings of deep tranquility were quickly replaced with a sense of increasing urgency. "Is the crying baby mine?

How would he recognise it if it was? Why was it crying? Where is Megumi? Where am I? Who am I? What am I?" Questions seemed to cascade into each other as Steve tried to make some sense out of his pipe-induced excursion.

A sand storm was building around him as the baby's cries faded into a furious vortex of wind and sand. The cascading questions, unanswerable, and the relentless wind and sand lashing his face reinforced Steve's feelings of hopelessness. He was beaten down into the desert sand repeatedly. Nearing surrender, a whisper inside him became a shudder and then it transformed into an intense oscillation, shaking his entire body into a kind of mystical divination. He roared and released his lion energy into the violent vortex. His majestic and gigantic bright orange lion fiercely quelled the maddening maelstrom then turned and looked at Steve.

Hours passed as the lion and Steve silently inspected each other. Finally, Steve reached forward and touched the orange embodiment of his rage only to see the lion completely disintegrate. It fell apart and was replaced by an army of men. They were warriors. Powerful men of differing size and shape and wearing clothing of different eras. Some wearing knight's armour, others in ancient Roman style and others in nondescript peasant's garb. Poised and primed for war, they were all strangely familiar. Perhaps it was their eyes or the angle of their cheekbones, he intuitively sensed they were all of his bloodline. Steve saw the infinite stories on their sombre and purposeful faces. Among the horde, one face seemed most familiar. Steve moved closer to inspect the face of the fierce, yet familiar, warrior. The man was looking straight through Steve without giving him the slightest acknowledgement. Steve spent an inordinate amount of time examining the man before him until a spark of a memory sent him reeling. He fell to his knees in front of his father, sobbing uncontrollably. By the time he looked up to his father, the horde of his bloodline had disappeared and Steve was forsaken again, lost in his dreams.

Weeks had passed as Steve descended further into his medicated hell. One time when the police arrived to inspect the premises, one of the prostitutes hiding in his den used the English word for Steve's medication. She was pointing at the pitiful man before her and talking about him to her co-worker. He learned his medication was nothing more than opium. He had a name for what he already knew. The black spice had reduced him to nothing more than a junkie.

In the same way the British colonial empire subdued the Chinese masses well over a century earlier, he was confined to his miserly bed and lost in his wicked dreams. His only source of comfort was his next inhalation of the dragon's breath. It stung him with its venom and burned its mark on his soul. His body was barely functional and his mind was distracted with those wickedly euphoric dragon dreams. The cold sweats, stomach wrenching pain, diarrhoea and anxiety were his cue for calling for his opium confidante. His "mother witch", that wretched witch of a woman had become the most important person in his life. His sustenance, his life, his purpose .... all powerful. She controlled his happiness as she meted his rationed resin.

His money was about to run out and he knew it would only be a matter of time before the hag would cast him out of his sanctuary. He would beg her. He wasn't ready for the world. Any time he found joy in his life, it would be cruelly crushed and the people he loved would die. His Megumi was gone and the numbing effect of the black spice was his only relief. But one momentary splinter of a vision, a barely discernible question, soon became so recurring and haunting that he was forced to assess the part of himself he had been hiding from. He had succumbed to addiction and his question screamed for an answer. "What if Kumicho offered me an endless supply of opium, would I serve him?" he asked himself. He knew he could never

compromise himself for that wicked monster and yet he had
done the same thing for the pathetic money hungry hag. Ready
or not, even at his lowest point, his free will rejected the
thought of obeisance to Kumicho and he rejected the temptation of the black spice. He stood on his feet and noticed his
emaciated body for the first time as an incredible cacophony of
commotion started outside his room.

He heard the hag screaming and men shouting. Breaking glass
and furniture smashing and the sound of bodies thudding continued until his door finally opened. The silhouette of a small
unblemished human stood in the doorway. Steve whispered,
"Nan, guòlái (come here)." But a little old man laughed as he
stepped into Steve's dimly lit den of despair. He held out his
hand and said "guòlái," Steve followed without question.

Steve left the room, his safety and his jail after approximately
forty days. Led by the little old man, he crossed the threshold
into the room next door to see Nan sitting on a box. She was
playing with her doll as Steve tried to catch her attention, but
she refused to look at him. Steve felt the greatest of shame. He
was not the good man he once was. He had succumbed to the
temptations of the wicked vapour and hid from his fears and
questions. He looked down at his feet immersed in his guilt
when he noticed the filthy demons with different coloured eyes
vying for supremacy.

The old man seemed to see what Steve saw and laughed as he led
Steve outside. Everyone in the establishment quickly and fear-
fully moved out of his way. The brothel was a mess. It looked
like an explosion had been set off in the corridor. The hag approached Steve with her telltale hand gestures, clearly looking
for the last of his money. The old man did nothing more than
take a mild interest in her as she cowered and feigned a fragment
of modesty. She waved Steve forward as though she was wishing
him well.

Chapter 16 - The Three Deathbringers

The old man led Steve outside for the first time in well over a month. Steve normally didn't have enough energy to walk to the toilet and relieve himself. Yet, surprisingly, the old man's barely discernible touch on his back lightened Steve's physical burden. He left behind the den of depravity without even turning to look at it. Steve had to hold his trousers up as he walked. His emaciated body had only craved the dragon's narcotic during his time at the sinful sanctuary. Food was not even a thought the entire time he was there. It was relegated to a barely essential second place in comparison to the exquisitely intoxicating vapour which had allowed him to escape the misery of his plight.

They entered a car waiting outside as the old man spoke in a combination of Putonghua and Hokkien dialect to the driver. The driver was eager to comply and respectfully waited on every word the old man said. It was a warm evening and Steve's sweating had already drenched his clothing. He was craving his black spice and his stomach was cramping and turning over itself. The old man sat in the back seat with Steve and was examining him carefully. Steve was struggling to sit silently as he shivered and occasionally moaned. The withdrawals had set in, he craved his drug and his mother-witch was gone.

Steve was perplexed with his own actions. He somehow intuitively followed this man without question. Perhaps because he was unblemished. Not burdened or influenced, the man was impeccably free of demons. Since the sword pierced his chest and soul, Steve could see the demons on every adult as plainly as the clothes they were wearing. The different colour eyes seemed to correlate with the personalities of the people, but he never really gave that observation the attention it properly deserved. His priority was the mother's evil milk the hag provided to him. As the vapor entered his lungs, his ability to see the demons vanished and so did the reminders of Kumicho and every other miserable memory.

Whilst Steve was not under the wicked influence of the opium, he saw demons on everyone as he left the hag's establishment, yet the old man was free of the demonic afflictions. Steve looked down at his feet and saw a couple of small demons still clinging to him as he tried to fling them off his feet. He was shivering, notwithstanding the evening's warmth, and becoming extremely self conscious in the presence of the curious little old man. The old man smiled and brushed Steve's feet as though he was flicking off some dust. The demons evaporated into steam and were quickly vacuumed out of the open car window. Steve looked at the old man incredulously and asked, "You can see them?" The old man just laughed and continued to examine Steve.

Steve tried to sleep in the car but his addiction was making it impossible for him. His body was only tenuously under his control as the shakes continued to broadcast his accursed addiction. The constant movement of the car was only amplifying his nausea. Every time he opened an eye to see what the old man was doing, he would see him looking at him with an unabating and curious smile. They drove all night and by dawn they had reached the base of a mountain range. A sign indicating they were at the base of the Wuyi Mountains meant little to Steve but it was a prompt for the driver to stop and open the rear door for the old man.

The old man gestured for Steve to get out of the car. Steve had been sitting in the same position too long, he was unable to move from his sweat drenched position in the back seat. The old man's smile transformed into a look of exasperation. He reached in the car and grabbed Steve's wrist. Steve tried to move but the old man just pointed at him like he was telling a dog to sit. The old man breathed deeply and his eyes became white as a white glow began to radiate from where he was holding Steve's wrist. Steve felt a vibration through his wrist and then through the rest of his body. He looked at his wrist and saw black sweat emanating from the pores of his skin. He then noticed the sticky black sweat over his entire body as it soaked into the fabric of his filthy clothing.

The old man's eyes returned to normal and he pulled his hand away and said something to Steve in Putonghua and pointed up at the mountains. Steve took a deep breath and readied himself to try to get out of the car again. But something was very different. His tremors had disappeared, he was breathing easier and there was a lightness to his body that he never experienced before. His renewed energy belied his emaciated look as he sprang out of the car and stood next to the old man.

The old man promptly ventured off the road into the dense green foliage of the mountains with Steve following quickly behind him. The old man was inconceivably fast and deliberate in his movements as they ascended the mountains together. Winding up the mountains, they reached a beautifully farmed tea plantation on a gently sloping hill. A solitary, small cabin was situated on the other side of the plantation and the old man yelled a greeting as he neared it. A young girl, also unblemished, soon came outside with tea for the old man and Steve. She was wearing a green headscarf underneath a hat and it seemed odd to Steve that such a young person looked to be living alone in the mountains.

Steve understood little of the discussions between the old man and the young girl. The old man was pointing at the plantation and the clouds and it seemed he was talking about the weather. The girl looked to be no older than fifteen and spoke quietly with the old man. She occasionally looked over at Steve who was still processing the healing energy he received from the old man. Steve paid the girl little attention but noticed she had extraordinary eyes of green. He had never seen an Asian person displaying such a genetic trait and was somewhat surprised a teenager was still free of demons. Some girls working at the brothel were not much older than her in his estimations and were already teeming with demons.

The girl filled Steve's tea cup and gestured for him to drink. The old man seemed to be talking about the tea as he raised his cup and insisted Steve drink with him. Steve found the taste rather peculiar but found it unexpectedly invigorating. In fact, he found the environment very uplifting and a welcome change from his solitary confinement of only a few hours earlier. The old man thanked the young girl and recommenced his journey with Steve.

The climate was changing as they ascended the mountains and the humid environment at the base soon developed into a cold bite. They passed many dilapidated temples on the ascent and Steve saw some ruined lion statues which looked similar to the Shisa in Okinawa. Steve had the distinct feeling the old man would not be surprised in the least if Steve was to demonstrate any supernatural ability. The old man was moving at an impossibly fast pace and had already shown he was far from normal when he cured Steve from his addiction pains with his healing touch.

They crossed rivers and passed spectacular waterfalls and finally reached a cave adjacent to a waterfall. The cave led to a deeper cave which they traversed until reaching a statue of a fierce warrior similar in looks to the Niō he saw in Kyoto almost a year earlier. The old man held his hands in a prayer position and faced the statue. He looked at Steve and it was clear from his motions he wanted Steve to do the same. Steve held his hands in a praying position and faced the statue. His mind was wandering, he was thinking about Megumi and their precious baby, lost! The old man clapped his hands and caught Steve's attention. He pointed to the statue and insisted on more devotion from Steve. Steve focused on the statue and recalled Temyana's instructions about Bodhidharma and Alexander's journeys. It occurred to Steve that many of these statues existed because of the influence of his very own bloodline.

Steve felt a connection to the statue and was compelled to touch it. He reached out and touched the raised arm of the fierce warrior statue and the flame etchings around the statue set alight. A ring of fire surrounded the statue and the warrior moved from its fearsome fighting stance and turned to its side. It revealed a new exit from the cave. The old man looked extremely pleased. He and Steve walked through the exit and the grandeur of the mountains revealed themselves in all their glory. They were on a lush green plateau the size of ten football fields overlooking rivers and clouds. Adjacent to the plateau was an immaculate small forest. The trees of the forest were perfectly straight and in precise formation. They looked like a thousand strong army at attention. Steve took a deep breath and embraced the incredible landscape.

It was a very long journey and the sun was setting over the mountains. The old man led Steve to a small temple. Its singularly most unique feature was the fact that it was not in a state of complete ruin and was well preserved, unlike all of the others he had seen on his ascent. He showed Steve inside a small room to the side of the temple and left a robe and trousers for him to change into. Steve was left alone and watched through the window as the old man went to a nearby cave. Steve sat on the bed and, within moments, the day had caught up with him. He was exhausted and fell asleep immediately.

He entered into an extraordinarily vivid dream unlike any before that evening. In his dream he saw his Lion energy in the distance and closer to him passed a monk in orange robes. The monk turned and looked at Steve. He then positioned himself into what looked like a kata or fighting stance and moved his hands in fighting motions at a blinding pace. Circular and powerful, he stopped and then had eighteen arms attached to his torso. He then walked towards the lion and they acknowledged each other in a formal yet familiar fashion. The monk with his numerous arms saluted and the lion bowed.

Steve felt his body shaking and wondered how the dream had affected him so physically. But, to his mild disappointment, it was the old man waking him up. He slept all night and enjoyed the distraction of his curious dream. But the old man clearly had an agenda for him as he threw the clothing he left for Steve at him. Steve changed out of his filthy clothes in front of the old man. He was self conscious of his emaciated body and the old man did not help by staring at Steve and inspecting his body. Steve pulled the hood of his robe over his head wishing it could have covered more of him. The old man held Steve's arm and tapped the inside of his wrist while looking deeply into Steve's eyes. He made Steve poke his tongue out and then nodded his head whilst conversing with himself. The old man left the room and returned a few minutes later with a cup of tea.

Steve wasn't expecting this man to be his personal attendant yet he was appreciative of the hot tea. He tried to convey that sentiment with gestures but the old man just encouraged him to drink his tea. Unfortunately it tasted nothing like the refreshing tea they drank at the tea plantation with the girl with green eyes. It was absolutely vile and he couldn't keep the first sip down. The old man insisted he drink it all while Steve coughed and spluttered as he attempted to finish the putrid substance. Steve assumed something so disgusting would have had to be medicinal and persisted with the foul liquid. He remembered the last time he thought he was taking medicine and it descended him into an addicted hell. But this man was so different. All of Steve's instincts indicated there was a cocoon of safety associated with the little old man.

They went outside and walked across the beautiful green field until the view took Steve's breath away. They were high in the mountains overlooking a powerful river and some of the white water spray reached him and tickled his nose and invigorated his senses. The old man assumed a meditating stance and motioned to Steve to do the same. It was a low horse riding stance with his hands placed forward in a prayer position with the top of his thumbs level with his nose. It was substantially lower than his typical Gōjū-ryū stance and Steve's legs soon began to shake uncontrollably. He thought to himself, "I don't think I could have done this easily when I was strong, much less now."

Steve could sense the old man's placidity and soothing energy and eventually found a position for himself which optimised his body geometry such that his legs weren't screaming for mercy. They remained in their meditative stances for hours and Steve's mind wandered with the inspiration of the bird whistles and water sprays. He allowed the surrounding nature into his mind and connected with the mountains.

The location of the sun suggested it was midday when Steve heard footsteps behind him. They were light, yet purposeful. He heard the gentle voice of the girl with green eyes as she delicately interrupted the old man's meditation. The old man laughed as he sprang up from his horse stance and instructed Steve to follow him. Steve was quite sure his legs were dead. He wasn't able to spring up from his position but he managed to straighten his legs eventually. He followed the old man and girl back to the temple walking like an old cowboy.

The girl had made some more of her glorious tea. The smell was familiar enough to confirm he was not going to have to endure that vile drink he consumed earlier in the morning. Steve thought it must have been close to lunch time and was a little surprised to only have tea. His body wasn't particularly screaming for food and he thought to himself, "Beggars can't be choosers," as he drank a few cups of the hot refreshing tea. Surprisingly, the tea managed to completely extinguish Steve's faint desire for food.

He was concerned about his body. He had lost so much muscularity since he was confined to his shameful and bitter addiction in that dark room of despair. Food would help him rebuild his strength and he wondered when they might eat something. Nourishment for his body was a valid concern but Steve also gained a small insight into the state of his mind during the morning's meditation. He was not well, his mind wandered back to dark places and his spirit became paralysed when trying to address them. He quickly learned his mind needed nourishment just as much, or quite possibly even more than his body.

Steve understood very little of the conversation between the old man and the girl. He picked up a few words but wasn't able to discern anything meaningful. He found the relationship between the two of them to be somewhat peculiar. She paid him infinite respect and the old man was equally respectful to the young girl. In Japan, Steve would notice how older men received respect from younger people and often were quite dismissive to children and teenagers. Steve guessed they may well be the only two people on the mountain and had to learn to live well with each other. It was pleasing to see what looked to be a wholesome and mutually rewarding and respectful relationship between the old man and the young girl.

After the tea break and some more conversation between the old man and girl, Steve and the old man returned to the location where they meditated in the morning. The old man made Steve assume the horse stance and then corrected his posture and hand position. He then left Steve alone in his own thoughts as he returned to the temple. Steve thought about everything and nothing whilst in his meditative stance. It occurred to him that he used some of his own powers to open the cave when he touched the statue. "How did the young girl manage to pass through to us here?" he thought to himself.

It may have been minutes or hours when the old man returned. He was carrying a tiny black piglet and immediately proffered it to Steve. Steve thought perhaps the piglet was going to be dinner and he had no idea how to prepare food whatsoever. Further, "Who's gonna eat this cute little pig?" he thought to himself as he rose out of his horse stance and smiled at the piglet. The old man raised his voice and seemed to scold Steve as he instructed Steve to return to his horse stance. Steve's praying hands were now holding the piglet and, soon enough, neither Steve nor the piglet seemed particularly pleased about the arrangement. The piglet weighed almost nothing, but Steve quickly learned that 'almost nothing' could mean something quite different from 'nothing' after enduring the process for hours.

It was dusk when the old man returned and the piglet seemed as relieved as Steve to see him. They returned back to the temple with the piglet following them. The old man showed Steve where some grains and other items were stored and showed how to feed the piglet. The piglet was tiny and still on its mother's milk. When Steve saw the size of the mother pig, he couldn't reconcile how such a tiny creature could grow so big. It was surely over 150 kilograms.

Steve and the old man returned to the temple and sat together.

Steve resolved it would be a quiet contemplative evening as he copied the old man's sitting position and crossed his legs. The old man spoke in Putonghua and Steve gave the universal shrug to indicate he did not understand again. But the old man continued to speak in his little understood language as he stood up and walked towards Steve. He raised his hand and his eyes turned white and a white beam of energy enveloped Steve. The old man returned to his seated position and continued speaking. Steve had been latching on to the few words he understood from when little Nan was teaching him. But, to his surprise, he managed to latch on to every word the old man was saying. The old man said, "I have been very interested in you since you came to me in my dreams in recent times."

Steve's astonishment interfered with his ability to speak for a moment until he gathered his thoughts. He wasn't even sure what language he was using to respond with when he said, "I can't believe I can understand you. Thank you for saving me from that terrible existence back in Xiamen. And thank you for curing my addiction. I don't know how you did it, but am grateful. I am Steve Nedelkin, may I ask your name, Sir?" The old man replied, "You freely made the decision to leave that place in Xiamen. This was not foretold. You may have been Steve Nedelkin once, but we are both yet to learn your real name now. I have many names, you can call me Si-Ming. Tell me about your dreams last night? It is important I know who visited you."

Steve said, "I dreamed of an eighteen-armed monk warrior. He stood before me and ...." Si-Ming interrupted and said, "Good, I thought so. You are a warrior after all. And what did the spirit of Luohan do with your Lion spirit when they met?" Steve never mentioned his Lion Energy, nor did he assume the eighteen-armed monk was Luohan's spirit. He had heard Luohan mentioned many times with both of his Sensei. He stuttered and said, "They bowed to each other." Si-Ming said, "Of course they bowed, they are not animals. I need to know how they bowed.

Tell me how you felt about their greeting." Steve was perplexed with the man's knowledge and said, "Wait, how did you find me? .... Well, they looked like they knew each other. They had met before and it seemed as though they bowed as equals."

"Aha" said Si-Ming. "Yes, that is very interesting. You are unique in all my assessments. I will say I have never come across anything precisely like you before. You must understand, your dreams can reveal more about your present state of existence than mortal life for you now. You must study them carefully and learn from them. You will have many visitations. In fact, I was foretold about you in one of my dreams. The woman in the half-mask was very insistent! She would have been formidable in her full form in this world."

"Temyana!" Steve exclaimed. He found unexpected comfort that at least something from his past continued to exist in such a tenuously tangible way. He was also infinitely relieved to be in a situation where dialogue was possible with Si-Ming. The man was impossibly deep and timeless with his insights. Just a look from him seemed to convey the thoughts of a million wise men. He knew things about Steve intuitively and the dream connection to Temyana was further affirmation of the positivity of their coming together.

Steve asked Si-Ming if he was a Shaolin Kung Fu master. Si-Ming laughed and said, "Perhaps you missed the sign at the front of this temple. You are in the home of the Great Five Ancestors of Shaolin. This temple is the Great Southern Shaolin temple. No human will readily find it and it remains a myth to all but the truest of warriors. In a way, you can describe me as a Shaolin master. But a better way to describe it is to say the spirits of the Five Ancestors are deeply connected to me here in this Spiritual Sanctuary. If your first dream here is any indication, you will also be connected to them. We will have much to discuss but you should sleep now. You have much to learn in your sleep.

Steve retired to his room and lay on his bed and closed his eyes. He quickly fell asleep and found himself walking in an ancient Chinese city. He entered inside a grand palace and his Lion spirit was in the distance. He roamed the palace and marvelled at the beauty of the exquisite furniture and paintings and vases. He walked into the throne room and an Emperor was sitting on his throne. He was wearing the finest silks and playing with his moustache when he noticed Steve's intrusion. He stood up from his throne and cast off his robes. His thick and muscular body was somewhat surprising for an emperor surrounded by such delicate elegance. He stood before Steve and, in contrast to the circular whirlwind of the eighteen hands Luohan, the emperor proceeded to demonstrate his movements. His hands looked like knives as they cut through the air. They were linear, penetrating and decisive and his stance was low and powerful. He finished his fearsome display of martial efficiency and walked towards Steve's Lion spirit. They were also familiar with each other as they saluted each other. Steve awoke determined to remember every part of the dream.

Si-Ming was sitting in the corner of Steve's room. He was eager to learn about Steve's dream. "Who did you meet this time?" He said as he handed Steve the disgusting tea he gave him the day earlier. Steve declined the tea but Si-Ming insisted Steve drink the tea. "You are drinking this medicine to rebalance your mortal afflictions. This is not negotiable if you want to exist as a mortal in this world. Now tell me everything about your dream encounter." Steve reluctantly drank the tea and proceeded to describe his encounter to Si-Ming. Si-Ming said, "The great emperor Taizu, excellent. He also knew your Lion spirit. I am yet to understand your connection to them. Something about you intrigues me. Now you must meditate. Go and get your pig."

The little black piglet looked happy to see him but the prospect of holding the cute little creature for hours didn't particularly thrill Steve. In any case, he was absolutely sure that everything had a purpose with Si-Ming's instructions. He commenced his morning meditation while holding the piglet and was soon bathing in his own perspiration. He could have sworn the pig had put on weight since the day before. The hours passed and the light but purposeful footsteps behind him heralded some reprieve. It was time for the glorious tea with the master and the green-eyed girl.

Finally Steve was able to understand them. He guessed they were talking about the weather when he couldn't understand them. In fact, he was less sure about what they were discussing even though he could understand them. Si-Ming mentioned a dark cloud from Beijing and a Zhao something or someone and a sword of Taizu. For the first time, Steve noticed a look of concern on the master's face. Again, Steve was surprised with the weight Si-Ming gave to the answers from the young green-eyed girl. The old man seemed to have such deep knowledge of all things, yet paid great heed to the little girl's answers which were even more confusing than the master's observations.

Steve was grateful to return the piglet to its pen so he could continue his meditation in the afternoon alone. The tea was more than refreshing, it seemed to connect Steve to the mountains. He was comforted by the rushing rivers and the crisp mountain air as he meditated on the calming green plateau. He imagined his son and wondered who was looking after him, how safe he was and what he looked like. The hours passed and Si-Ming arrived to call Steve back to the temple. They drank some more of the green eyed girl's tea and Steve had many questions.

Steve said, "Si-Ming, I am embarrassed to call you by your name. If you do not mind, I would prefer to address you more respectfully as Sifu. I hope that is acceptable to you." Si-Ming smiled and said, "I have many names. Some call me the Director of Destinies, Master of Fate, Lord of the Mountains and some even call me the Big Man. But I think I prefer Sifu today. Yes, that is perfectly acceptable." The answer from Si-Ming gave Steve even more questions but he needed answers to more pressing matters. He explained the events which led him to that dark den. He didn't miss anything. He explained his experience with Kumicho and how the sword from his own bloodline pierced his chest. Even his celestial journey didn't phase Si-Ming in the slightest and the only issue which seemed to raise his interest was the sword which stabbed him in the chest. "So the sword from your own bloodline made you this way. Hmmm, it has magic I do not understand, but I certainly know what it did to you. It killed your Three Deathbringers which reside in every human's body. They dictate how long a man lives. You were meant to die at precisely that time, but instead, the sword killed the Three Deathbringers and, because of the magic in the sword, you remain in this world as a transcendent, an immortal."

Steve was bewildered and asked, "Are you saying I cannot die?" Si-Ming said, "There are much worse things than death. Imagine an eternity under the control of an all powerful evil demon spirit. You are neither alive or dead. Your only release will be to submit to the demon fully and become one yourself. You told me they called you Ishiganto in Okinawa. They received the name from a great man who conquered evil here in China. He was called Shi Dangdang here. You were able to do this in your full human form, which is remarkable in itself. But I do not know your name now. You appear to be neither human nor a god. Your purpose is best described as 'yet to be determined' and I will call you 'Warrior'. It is time for you to learn in your sleep. Go now and remember everything."

Steve retired to his room. He didn't know how to interpret the information from Si-Ming. It was not expected information nor was it anything which could be described as a human condition. It was simply too much to deal with. The notion of immortality seemed like a childhood fantasy, yet the reality was daunting. He wondered what he lost or would continue to lose of his humanity. He thought about his newborn son and what purpose or function he could possibly have in his child's life. He thought about the evening when his beautiful wife and his life were taken away from him. Si-Ming and Temyana and even Baba Rada spoke about destinies to him, yet he was lost and not even able to understand who or what he was. He missed his wife. His confusion and deep sadness were his only companions as he eventually faded into a sleep.

Steve's dream found himself walking near a lake. His Lion spirit was inexplicably walking on the water. A majestic White Crane flew from the water next to Steve and changed into a young woman. The woman charged at Steve in an attacking manner and Steve tried to push her away. Her defensive arm changed back into the crane's wing and she used her wing to block Steve's arm as she evaded his push. The woman smiled and then saluted Steve. She reverted back into the White Crane and flew to the lake whereupon the Lion spirit and White Crane greeted each other in familiar fashion. The White Crane then launched into the sky and flew off into the sunset.

The following morning Si-Ming expressed surprise that the White Crane feigned an attack on Steve. The smile and the greeting to the Lion Spirit were significant to him. "It seems you might be ready for instruction soon," he said. Steve drank more of the terrible medicine in the morning and went to his morning meditation with the piglet whom he had named "Pig". Pig had seemed to accept his role in Steve's morning meditation. He would sleep while Steve's mind wandered beyond his physical location. He watched his timeline unfold and dissected traumatic moments in his life in endless loops. He kept searching for better answers in his mind and was surprised the entire morning had already disappeared when Si-Ming and the green-eyed girl called him to tea.

Steve was increasingly curious about the interactions between Si-Ming and the green-eyed girl. It appeared she was his source of news and he placed great importance on her observations. She spoke of someone called Zhao Duyi and Si-Ming immediately insisted on every detail. Zhao Duyi was moving higher up the ranks of the Chinese Communist Party (CCP) and had recently become the director of a provincial commission for National Defence Mobilisation. The national newspaper was talking about his meteoric rise and the prospects of him becoming the Commander-in-chief of the Armed Forces of the People's Liberation Army. "This demon will rule the Celestial Empire if he continues unabated. I cannot believe I didn't see his intentions. You were so little and yet you warned me." said Si-Ming. The girl just nodded as she topped up Steve and Si-Ming's tea cups.

Steve still didn't know the girl's name. He told her how much he enjoyed her lovely tea and introduced himself. The green-eyed girl responded, "I am Ling, you are welcome." Steve was still perplexed with the relationship between Si-Ming and Ling. It was obvious she was intelligent beyond her years. She had a quiet confidence which belied her youthful years and Steve wondered if Si-Ming had been instructing her in any way similar to him.

It was time for afternoon meditation and Steve was becoming more accustomed to letting his mind roam freely and allowing himself to truly relax. He was finding ways to process his grief and realised how fruitless the time he spent in the opium-induced stupor was for him. He could feel the mountain's energy and immersed himself deeply into his own consciousness. He had entered into a dreamlike trance and found himself in the nearby little forest. It was noisy. The wind was blowing through the trees and he was acutely aware of every insect and creature in the forest. Through the perfectly-aligned trees he could see his Lion spirit on the field. He then heard a shriek from above as a Golden Monkey jumped from the trees and stood in front of Steve. The monkey picked up a rock and threw it at Steve. He could feel the sting of where the rock hit his forehead even in his meditative state. The monkey then jumped at Steve and he quickly blocked a fist the monkey was aiming at his head. Monkey let his arm collapse around Steve's block and then hit Steve with its elbow. Steve went to strike the monkey but it hooked its hand around Steve's arm and twisted him off balance. By the time Steve found his balance, he looked up and the Golden Monkey had transformed into a monk who saluted Steve. The monk walked onto the field and called out to the Lion spirit. They both looked pleased to see each other and proceeded to bow to each other. As the Lion spirit lowered its head, the monk transformed again into the Golden Monkey and jumped on top of the Lion spirit shrieking in laughter. The Lion spirit shook its head and Monkey fell on the ground laughing. They both seemed to find the interaction amusing and Steve arose from his meditation with a chuckle.

Steve told Si-Ming about the events of his afternoon meditation and Si-Ming was astounded. He said, "Golden Monkey couldn't wait for your dreams, he found you in your meditation. Remarkable! And he was joking with your Lion spirit? Monkey will never follow protocol!" Si-Ming was very impressed with the visit from the Golden Monkey in Steve's meditation. "Soon you might be able to see them in your waking hours, but you still have one more to meet," he said.

Steve retired to his bed and recalled the events of the last few days. His dreams were significant and the visitations were positively palpable. There was much to learn in his dream and meditative states. He practised his deep nasal breathing and eased into his sleep determined to open his mind to any visitations. His dreams were upon him as he saw his Lion spirit in the distance. He was not on the mountain, he was back in Okinawa. It was Kumicho's castle grounds where his Lion spirit was pouncing on imaginary targets. Steve was walking to the castle entrance and next to him was a monk of similar height to his own. He was a barrel-chested man, perhaps a little overweight but in no way unhindered by his paunch. His movements were effortless as he glided alongside Steve. From the top of his head radiated a bright orange energy and it contrasted greatly with the brightest blue eyes he had ever seen. The monk walked straight into the castle and headed straight for the display cabinet with the sword that pierced Steve's chest. Steve watched as the monk retrieved the sword and held it in the air. The castle shook and turned to dust around them as they found themselves back on the mountain near the temple. The monk threw the sword at Steve's feet and then stood in a standing meditation position. Steve synchronised his breathing with the monk and they meditated together for the entire night.

The monk arose from his meditation and walked towards the Lion spirit. Even in Steve's sleep, he was paying particular attention to the expected salute and watched every minute detail of the interaction. However, the monk did not salute the Lion spirit at all. As he reached closer to the Lion, he gained pace and then ran full speed at it. When the two finally met, there was no impact at all. The monk merged with the Lion spirit and the Lion expanded into a larger version of itself. The Lion spirit then charged at Steve until it was right next to him. Steve felt compelled to touch the Lion, as he had done once before in one of his poisoned dreams of the opium pit, but this time the response was indeed different. Instead of collapsing into the horde of warrior ancestors, his hand seemed to merge with the energy. He became one with the Lion spirit as he walked completely into it. He was himself, yet he was linked to the energy in a way that was automatically obvious and natural to him yet completely unknown to him before that moment. He awoke feeling energised.

Si-Ming was eager to learn of the dream. He was elated with the information and interpreted it for Steve. He explained, "This was your most powerful dream. It confirms what I had already seen yet could not fathom. It confirms what you are but cannot see. Your own bloodline, Bodhidharma, the spiritual ancestor of all the Shaolin great ancestors has reached you. He led you to your Lion spirit and the power of one of the greatest bloodlines resides in you and deems you worthy. He threw his own sword at your feet! The sword is important to you. You must retrieve it. You have now met all of the Shaolin Five Ancestors and your own bloodline is the one who the other four look to for spiritual guidance. The four are obligated to you as you are to the five. Your path is singular."

Steve was processing Si-Ming's interpretation of his dream. His anxiety increased tenfold when he was reminded of the sword. In order to retrieve it, he knew he would need to be ready for combat with Kumicho. A confused combination of resolve and fear in relation to the sword and Kumicho began to wrestle in Steve's mind. The intense emotion of what that evil monster had taken away from him lingered in his mind and influenced his every action. Not only did he lose everything he loved, but his own connection to humanity was also lost because of him. The thought of battling Kumicho gave Steve a genuine sense of dread as he recalled the ferocity of Kumicho in his full demon form. Steve understood he needed to learn much more about himself before he could consider confronting Kumicho again.

Chapter 17 - REN-SHEN

Steve's meditation was better described as a waking-sleep. His dreams over the next few months were periods of great instruction. Through his deepening meditative guidance from the one great ancestor, Bodhidharma, he became immersed in the styles of the four fighting ancestors via metaphysical interactions. Real in every way except from an externally viewed perspective, the spirits would demonstrate movements which were representative of their martial specialty. The ensuing months saw Steve being tested in physical combat by these powerful spirits. Anyone watching would have seen Steve standing in contemplative meditation, yet within the blurred confines of his rapidly expanding conscience, he was in constant battle.

The morning meditation sessions were still dedicated to his physical development. The presence of Pig was always confirmation of the importance of physical conditioning. After half a year, Pig had reached a weight of approximately 100 kilograms and remained contentedly perched over Steve's praying arms as he meditated every morning. What started as a small nagging reminder became an outright test of strength every morning. Steve was transformed physically. He was leaner than he had ever been in his late teens. He quickly learned food was no longer necessary in this new condition. His meditation and breathing routines learned from his very own ancestor had enabled him to nourish his body with nothing more than the air he breathed.

Si-Ming had only been momentarily present each day after the first few months. Rising tensions within China were causing great unrest, necessitating frequent consultation with other gods and immortals. Indeed, Steve learned Si-Ming was an extremely powerful god of the highest order, being in charge of the life spans of humans. As with all gods in his realm, his power came from a connection between primordial mystery and collective human beliefs. Si-Ming's power was immediate, absolute and native to the Chinese region. Yet the collective beliefs of humans were never quite the same since China's Cultural Revolution of the 1960s had gained momentum. Factors including the diminution of faith were impacting Si-Ming's predominant ability as the arbiter of human life. Another force was interfering with his powers. Something was also happening with the spirits of the deceased. Many were not passing to the Infinite and even the ones who did were tarnished in ways never seen before.

These were very concerning times for Si-Ming. His demeanour had changed such that his uplifting energy and air of positivity had transformed into one of grave concern. From an outsider's perspective it would have been easy to question how the "Director of Destinies and Taker of Lives" could have had such a light hearted or jovial personality. But it was obvious to Steve something had changed about him. The name of Zhao Duyi had been mentioned more frequently. He was consolidating his power politically and there appeared to be no stopping his ascension. Steve had asked Si-Ming about this powerful man. Si-Ming seemed quite disappointed in himself as he explained how Zhao Duyi entered into his sacred sanctuary. "He was not unlike you. He had exceptional ancestry. From the line of Emperor Taizu himself! He found this sanctuary by himself and entered without difficulty. He is now one of The Few. He sought instruction from the great Five Ancestors, but I did not see his true agenda. His star shone brightly and I allowed fate to prevail. Such was his power and knowledge of the Infinite, I came to believe he would be the prophesied 'Twice Born' who had lived both lives. First as human and second as a god. The Twice Born will relieve me of my earthly duties. He deceived me. I didn't know the Five Ancestors rejected him. Even his own bloodline, the great Emperor Taizu, would not come to him. In fact, he was not here to learn their ways. He only wanted to learn my ways. How to control the Three Deathbringers and take the lives of his enemies without even engaging in battle. Such power can only be wielded justly.

"There is talk of how he has gained the power of the sword of his own ancestor, the great Emperor Taizu, and now he seeks to usurp my power and promises to destroy every child except for the first born here in the Celestial Empire. The one child policy here in China makes him out to be a hero but, in fact, he is a genocidal maniac. He is indeed one of The Few, not unlike the Kumicho you spoke of, and ... in truth ... not unlike something you have the potential to become. He must be stopped.

"I initially thought you may be the Twice Born but I am presently feeling less sure of this. Even Ling believes there is a chance you may be him. The corruption true power brings will always be a risk to a potential candidate of one of The Few such as you, Warrior. The closer you reach the gods, the more you must reach for the essence of your humanity."

Steve felt the doubt and concern in Si-Ming's voice. The threat was real and of worldly importance. He had no idea how but immediately offered his help to the god before him, "Sifu, you have all of my dedication. Just tell me what to do and I will fight for you. I can try to find Zhao Duyi and destroy him before he takes the lives of so many innocents. I have been learning well from the Five Ancestors and I know I have improved."

Si-Ming replied, "Warrior, I feel your sincerity and potential. I do not believe I have made a second mistake with you. You are indeed a warrior. I can see your spirit is bound to justice and war. You are not yet ready for battle. You have not found your sword and you are not even ready to face my best student. I still see great potential in you, but potential is never enough. Where is your sword now, Warrior?"

Steve wasn't sure if this was a rhetorical question from Si-Ming. He answered, "The sword is with the Kumicho of Okinawa. I will find it, I promise. Sifu, please tell me, you have always placed great importance on Ling's opinions. I am confused why you, a god, heed the advice of a teenage girl. Why do you value her thoughts so highly?"

Si-Ming laughed in his familiar and comforting way. He said, "Ling is the third daughter of a third daughter. She was abandoned in a cave in these mountains as a baby. Placed next to the bones of the Immortals as a sacrifice to the gods of the mountains and rivers. You think she is a teenager? She is in fact a "leftover", thirty years old and already undesirable for marriage in the Celestial Empire. Why do I pay heed to her advice? I cannot say. In truth, she confounds me. I will say that from the first time she spoke as a young child, her thoughts were timeless and beyond her age and time. She found her own way into this spiritual sanctuary. She moves freely between the natural and spiritual regions of the mountains. Her tea is the most expensive tea in the world and is consumed by only the richest and most powerful people of the world. She lives modestly and has more money than she needs. In truth, I do not yet know her name as I am yet to learn yours, Warrior."

Steve resolved to learn as much as he could from the Five Ancestors. It seemed battle was imminent and, in any case, he would need to learn more in order to defeat Kumicho. He continued to train in his meditations. The mornings with big black Pig strengthened his physical condition. Steve learned the character of Pig indeed aligned itself with the nature of humans born in the Chinese year of the pig. Diligent, compassionate, realistic and generous. Pig knew it was assisting and tried its best to help Steve's progress by not moving or farting too much when perched over his arms.

The afternoon mind battles were intense. Steve was immersed in every nuance of the Five Ancestor spirits. The wings and beak of the White Crane and the way to trap and attack became second nature to him. The powerful circular movements of Luohan. Like a steel ball on the end of a chain, with energy summoned from his Qi centre and bounced off the ground to be infinitely multiplied through his body as it reached his opponent. The powerful strikes from the Emperor Taizu as his shortest attacking paths sliced the air and defeated his enemy. The surprise of the Golden Monkey as he evaded every attack and then pounced on his assailant after hooking and using every part of his body for attacks. Steve learned to summon the power from the ground and take the energy from the Infinite. His power was multiplying.

His Lion spirit remained ever present during these meditative training exercises. Steve had gained an understanding of the spirit in a way that only a few of his bloodline had ever fully comprehended before they passed to the Infinite. He could move inside the Lion spirit and use the power of his bloodline to assist against the four fighting Great Ancestors. After meditation sessions, he would summon his Lion spirit and repeatedly move inside it. An orange glow developed around his entire body on those occasions which was a phenomenal spectacle to behold in the evenings.

Steve had taken to meditating inside the forest in the afternoons. The perfectly-arranged trees felt as though they were standing together in meditation with him. Si-Ming would often come to inspect Steve's progress in the afternoons and say, "Where is your sword now, Warrior?" Steve would always reply, "The sword is with the Kumicho of Okinawa." Si-Ming would laugh and shake his head. He said, "You are almost ready to face my best student soon." Steve remained permanently perplexed with the suggestion of another student. He had never seen anyone else being taught by Si-Ming. The only person he could think of was Zhao Duyi and he was very sure Si-Ming was not referring to him. He wondered if Si-Ming might summon a spirit to fight with Steve one day and continued to train his mind and spirit in anticipation.

Ling continued to perplex Steve. Perhaps even more than before Si-Ming explained her age and the curious way she came to the mountain. He once asked her how she found her way into the spiritual sanctuary. He recalled his own way of entering with the warrior statue's permission. She shrugged her shoulders and said, "I just always knew where to go. The warrior in the cave has always stood aside for me." Steve was becoming increasingly aware of her unique nature. She remained unblemished of demons at thirty years of age. She moved between the spiritual and normal parts of the mountains effortlessly and, most importantly, confounded Si-Ming.

Steve had been on the mountain for two years when Si-Ming asked, yet again, "Where is your sword now, Warrior?" Steve gave his standard response about Kumicho and Okinawa. Si-Ming shook his head and advised it was time for Steve to fight his best student. The following day, Steve had completed his morning meditation with Pig and heard Ling and Si-Ming's footsteps reach him. It was always a relief to put down Pig's 150 kilogram frame. After five hours of holding Pig every morning, Steve's body was conditioned beyond normal human levels. Both Steve and Pig were quite accustomed to the ritual of the exercise. Notwithstanding the obvious fondness they had for each other, it was always a relief to end the gruelling sessions.

Si-Ming asked yet again about the location of his sword, much to Steve's exasperation. Si-Ming didn't even wait for an answer when he thrust Ling in front of him. "It is time for you to fight my best student now," he said. Ling removed her hat and took off her green head scarf as her long black hair crashed over her shoulders. Steve had barely even thought of Ling as a woman before and most certainly never thought of her as a fighter in any way whatsoever. Steve looked incredulously at both Si-Ming and Ling. He said, "Sifu, I don't think it would be fair or appropriate to fight with Ling." Si-Ming genuinely considered Steve's statement and replied, "Yes, I understand and agree with you. It would not be fair to fight with Ling. You have not trained as long as her. But I think you can still learn something from the battle. Hurry now."

Ling had assumed a fighting stance and Steve hesitantly moved into a fighting position. By the time his feet locked into the ground, Ling had already launched an explosive kicking attack at Steve. He blocked her easily and paid attention not to hurt her with his blocking motion. In fact, it occurred to him that he never even touched her at all. She evaded his block entirely and landed a stinging strike to his face in the process. Steve smiled and was genuinely surprised, and slightly embarrassed, with her agility and precision. He went to punch her and she used the White Crane technique to trap his hand and then Golden Monkey to attempt an elbow strike at Steve's face. Steve blocked the elbow just in time and returned with the piercing attacks of the Emperor Taizu. Ling jumped backwards as the Golden Monkey and evaded his attack.

Si-Ming clapped and told them to stop. Ling saluted in Shaolin style to Steve and he returned the salute along with a look of complete surprise. He had never fought a woman, or anyone, with such precision and speed in his life. Steve scratched his head in a combination of awe and bewilderment. They drank tea together and discussed the latest activities of Zhao Duyi. Steve went to sleep that evening still thinking about Ling's fighting prowess. His face still throbbed where she had struck him and he decided he would be a fool to underestimate her abilities next time.

Over the ensuing months, Steve and Ling fought with each other every day. She used her lightness and small physical frame in the most amazing way. She gravitated towards the Golden Monkey in her physical style but her mind projected all the Ancestors. They had tested all of their physical fighting strategies against each other and Steve found his rhythm quickly.

One night Steve was awoken from his sleep by a loud explosion. He rushed to Si-Ming who kept appearing and disappearing in front of him. Si-Ming was concerned. He told Steve it was Zhao Duyi's minions trying to enter the spiritual sanctuary. "I have fortified the sanctuary. They have tried and failed this time, but they will try again," he said. Steve realised he had not stepped outside of the sanctuary for well over two years. During the night, Ling found a chance to enter the sanctuary. She shakingly told Si-Ming and Steve, "I had to wait and hide until they gave up. If I tried to enter the sanctuary while they were near, they would have found the way in. There were demons of all shapes and sizes. I would have destroyed a few but there were too many." As always, Si-Ming carefully considered Ling's observations. He said, "You must stay inside the sanctuary from now on. Zhao Duyi already knows you and I suspect he would have an awareness of some of your abilities. It was nothing more than luck that the demons did not try to attack you and use you to enter the sanctuary. This must not happen."

Ling's continued presence meant Steve had more opportunity to train with her. During one particularly arduous session, Steve summoned his Lion spirit for the first time. He immersed himself in the Lion spirit and with his orange glow launched at Ling. She instinctively reacted and immersed herself in a green glow he had never seen before. Their battle was epic with both of them stopping short of lethal attacks. Steve's abilities had multiplied exponentially and Ling's abilities had also improved dramatically with the constant testing of wills. Si-Ming would continue to ask Steve where his sword was when he bothered to watch their battles. Ling would sometimes laugh as she could feel Steve's exasperation with the repeated question.

Steve and Ling grew to enjoy keeping company together. He eventually confided in the greatest loss of his life, his one true love, Megumi. He wondered about his son and tried to imagine what his three-year-old child looked like. Ling reminded Steve how far his life had been displaced from that of a conventional existence. She dispassionately questioned his ability to be a loving father in addition to being an immortal. Steve attributed her own abandonment as a child to the coldness she displayed about his ache for his son. After feeling somewhat put-out by her response, he accepted her opinion as one based upon practical realities. He continued to pine for his dead wife and lost child but eventually acknowledged his path was not a normal one.

Ling and Steve would talk long into the night and discuss numerous issues ranging from politics to the healing arts. Steve would learn geopolitical trends from Ling and they would discuss issues relating to their unique energies. Ling had developed great skills in the way of healing. She reminded him that if one can truly hurt an opponent, then one should also be able to heal.

In battle, Steve's Lion spirit would be met with Ling's Bird spirit. She never understood it, but it came to her from a very young age. She had only recently been exploring her Bird spirit during their fighting exercises. Unlike Steve's Lion spirit which was fully formed, Ling's Bird spirit still appeared to be blurry on the edges and it was difficult to discern what kind of bird it precisely was. Steve had the edge when he employed his Lion spirit, but Ling's physical mastery remained incredibly challenging. Her skills in the way of the Golden Monkey were particularly complimentary to her smaller physical frame. Steve found the combination of directness of the Emperor Taizu in addition to the wing defences of the White Crane helped. Naturally, the circular motions of Luohan were also helpful. In fact, any attack other than Golden Monkey was advantageous to him. She had complete control when they both engaged the way of the Golden Monkey.

During one particularly violent tussle they both wrestled in an attempt to gain advantage. For the first time in many years, Steve experienced a very human reaction. He realised there was a sexual attraction to Ling when they both looked at each other in the tight embrace. He quickly flung her off of him and tried to process the sense of guilt which immediately washed over him as he thought of Megumi, his wife and one true love.

Ling came to him that evening. She wore a thin, loosely fitting nightgown and the candlelight behind her showed the silhouette of her petite body. She climbed into his bed and caressed his body. She kissed the scar on his chest and straddled him. She looked deeply into Steve's eyes and said "Sex is the battle of stealing and strengthening. I give you my energy." Her eyes glowed an even brighter green colour as Steve reached forward and touched her legs and brushed his lips against hers. Her tongue briefly touched his bottom lip. Steve was surprised with the explosion in his physical desire for her. He no longer required food, yet his body's reaction was nothing more than primitive in its urges. There was little tenderness in their actions. Their lustful interaction was hungry, desperate and intense. Both had desires and the meeting of their bodies created a hue of green and orange inside the entire temple. They explored each other all night and Steve stole every part of Ling and strengthened his energy with their joining of essences.

Steve awoke the next day feeling invigorated and the closest to being a human being for the first time in well over three years. Ling later explained the Taoist theories in relation to sexual alchemy. How the union of essences created "Jing" which could be converted by the man into Qi and replenish his life-force. Whatever it was, it reactivated Steve's life-force and the lustful joining of energies and essences over the ensuing weeks instilled a new strength inside Steve so his command over his Lion spirit was becoming more nuanced in unexpected ways. He could snap the Lion spirit into action instead of summoning it. The activation of his energy was more immediate. It felt such that the reconnection with his humanity had inexplicably given him more control over the energy forces within.

Si-Ming had noticed the change in Steve and was well aware of the energy and essence exchanges taking place between the pair. During one training session where Steve had activated his Lion spirit, again Si-Ming asked, "Where is your sword now, Warrior?" Steve had reached the end of his tether on the persistent question. It reminded him of his helplessness with the things he had loved and lost. It reminded him of the questions he was still unable to answer. He engaged his Lion spirit and drew the great Five Ancestors in his mind in an incoherent rage. The orange glow around him began to flash intermittently and then the colour changed into the colours of the Fighting Ancestors; yellow, white, red and gold until an explosion of orange energy shot out of Steve's chest scar. Steve turned to Si-Ming with his eyes now emitting a fiery orange glow and said in a terrifying voice which thundered throughout the sanctuary, "The sword is here," as he pointed to his heart.

Ling was visibly shocked and Si-Ming appeared almost drunk in surprise. Steve had transformed. His eyes were not human and the boom of his voice shook them both. Steve noticed the quizzical looks on their faces and settled his spirits so he could assume his normal form again. Ling had her hand over her mouth. It was clear she had never encountered such a transformation before. Si-Ming was euphoric as he seemed to absorb the new energy source emitting from Steve. He laughed and then disappeared from where he stood. He reappeared directly in front of Steve and placed his hand on Steve's shoulder. He looked Steve in the eyes and said, "I was wrong about you. I said you were neither man nor god. But I can see now you are in fact both man and a god. Your Lion spirit is also so completely linked to you that it is difficult to distinguish between you and your spirit. The spirit of the Great Five Ancestors are now also wholly inside you and at your command. I now know your name. You are Ren-Shen, Half Spirit."

Chapter 18 - Breach

Steve was fully aware of the difference between himself as a man and the god who could channel his Lion and the Great Five Ancestor spirits. He was a different entity as Ren-Shen. Everything was more vivid, his feet felt as though they had sprung roots into the ground and his breathing transformed into vibrations which presented an awareness of the space around him in a way which was far beyond the ability of humans. Ren-Shen could feel traces or essences of spirits, both past and present through these vibrations. He could feel where they had been and even sensed where battles had been fought. His Lion spirit had also transformed. It had become even more ferocious as a consequence of his deification in the Spiritual Sanctuary. When summoned, it now presented characteristics similar to the Shisa.

In truth, Steve knew nothing more about Ren-Shen than he knew about himself before his transformation, but the change was all consuming. Incredibly powerful sensations were ever present and rippling beneath his human exterior. He had much to learn about himself.

Steve had come to appreciate the visceral connections he had made with his own sense of humanity thanks to Ling. She was a reminder of what he once was. However, since the emergence of Ren-Shen, her interactions with him had become stilted and awkward. Steve was disappointed to lose the stolen moments of intimacy they had shared. Another part of his life had been cut short again due to his own actions. It particularly affected him because, as Ren-Shen breathed his vibrations, he became immediately aware of Ling's pregnancy. As Ren-Shen, it was simply a factual observation with an immediate assessment of the potential for immortality attached to the female foetus in her womb. But as Steve, it was something impossible to process devoid of emotion. His son was already fatherless somewhere in the world and the chance of a normal upbringing for his future daughter also seemed extremely unlikely.

Steve finally was able to approach Ling and discuss his concerns. He said, "I don't understand what is happening to me. But I am still a man. I've cherished the intimacy we've shared and I honestly don't know what our future can be....." Ling interjected, "You are not human, you were already an immortal and now you are a god. I literally watched you become a god! Our life can never be normal and I do not even know how to talk with you. I am nobody and your destiny grows every day. How can I look at you? Gods have their own problems and I'm not able to help you even if I was able to understand your problems."

Steve understood her confusion and said, "I feel the same way about myself. I don't know how to deal with my nature. I know I've changed. I feel things differently and I see the world in a way that I never did before. But I am still a man and I care about you and our baby. Can we try to find a way?" She glared at him with her blank matter-of-fact expression, "Of course you know about the baby. You know everything now I suppose. I stole some happiness with you. But I cannot see a future for us. At least I can love our child and have some company on these mountains. I was thrown away as a child. I am ready to be a mother and I will love my child, it's enough for me."

"I don't even know where my son is, what kind of father can I be to our daughter?" Steve said. Ling's piercing green eyes lit up with excitement, "Daughter? We will have a daughter?" She quickly calmed herself and extinguished any trace of excitement and said, "Do you think your destiny is to tend to our

child? Maybe read books to her? No! Evil in the world is building and you, Ren-Shen, with your warrior powers are destined
to meet them. You are a good man, now be a good god. Fight for
the Infinite and defend on the side of humanity. I will raise our
daughter!"

Steve knew he had lost his chance for normality. His destiny
was unknown but Ling was correct, yet again. Her logic was
difficult to refute and although Ren-Shen's purpose was yet to
be fully realised, Steve could feel a resolve building within himself. His energy was coming from that resolve. He spent many
evenings discussing his transformation with Si-Ming. Both Si-
Ming and Ren-Shen understood the necessity to answer questions of the Infinite with riddles and questions. This was Ren-
Shen's destiny and his supernatural existence came about from
the pool of humanity who were calling for him. Si-Ming could
not answer much about Ren-Shen's destiny but was confident
of the purpose of his deification. Ren-Shen was a call for justice. Just as Ren-Shen looked at Si-Ming and immediately fully
understood his purpose as the Director of Destinies. Si-Ming saw
Ren-Shen as a god of Justice. Ren-Shen knew the time was nearing to find his destiny outside of the spiritual sanctuary.

Steve had never felt as peaceful as he did during his time in the
spiritual sanctuary. He spent some time with Pig who seemed
to know Steve was leaving soon and kept trying to climb into
his arms. Steve was crestfallen as he realised he was looking at
yet another casualty of his destiny. "Am I destined to be alone
forever?" he thought to himself as he lifted the very fully-grown
Pig into the air.

That evening he again discussed his path with Si-Ming. The importance of the sword was again stressed to Ren-Shen. "It is part
of the reason why you are now a god. Think what it can do in the
hands of someone who truly understands the magic in it. You
must claim the sword and learn its power at all costs. The sword

is inside you but it also remains in the hands of evil. There are many like the Kumicho you describe. Zhao Duyi has now truly embraced his evil form as one of The Few. He has chosen darkness, but the darkness has chosen him also.

"You have a curious existence. Your human nature is linked to your divine nature. It will not be easy to manage your duality. First you must explore your powers as a god, but you must also ensure you do not lose what makes you human. Your duality is what makes you remarkable. As a man, you will be able to go anywhere unnoticed and your divine purpose as arbiter of justice is best served among mankind."

Ren-Shen walked throughout the entire spiritual sanctuary that evening. His eyes pulsing their orange glow. His breathing vibrations revealed much about his home for the last three years. Great powers had tried to claim the sanctuary for thousands of years. He sensed the enormity of their demonic energy and also the power of the resistance which kept the celestial oasis sustained. He walked among the perfect trees in the forest and realised even they held a defensive power in the sanctuary. Everything had a purpose in the sanctuary and the preconditions for forging Ren-Shen's divinity were plain to see from a god's perspective. The energy of the sanctuary was tied to the power of the Earth's creation. The mountain formation and rivers and trees and orientations were all tributes to the Infinite. "A great place of connection," Steve thought to himself as he emerged from the perfect little forest. He smiled as it occurred to him that the literal translation of "Shaolin" meant nothing more than "little forest", yet he could not find the words to describe the magnificence of the Great Five Ancestors of Shaolin.

Steve rested his body that night. He thought about what Si-Ming said about the duality in his existence. Holding on to his humanity was beginning to feel like nothing more than holding on to his self-doubts and his suffering. His humanity was his weakness and yet Steve also understood where the call for justice came from. He always had a sense of justice, a desire to right wrongs. Those very human doubts and losses he had suffered were the precursor and the sword and spiritual sanctuary were the catalysts in Ren-Shen's creation. But still, answers to questions he couldn't even articulate continued to evade him.

He knew he had no choice, he needed to find his way back to Japan. It was essential to claim the sword. He knew absolutely nothing else about what he would do after that. A return to the sanctuary to examine the power of the sword with Si-Ming seemed logical. The idea appealed to him. He would quickly return and spend time with Ling. Perhaps he would sense something about the sword as Ren-Shen and determine his destiny thereafter. Among all his fears and doubts, the call for justice within him was absolute. He could feel that call to justice as Steve, but as Ren-Shen it was something more. It was his divine energy, his purpose, and he was resolute. He would destroy Kumicho.

He settled and found his dream. His fighting and lion spirits had converged and stood before him. Ren-Shen had to choose which energy he required; The power of Emperor Taizu, the nimbleness of the Golden Monkey or perhaps his ferocious Lion. He awoke to an intense vibration. Si-Ming had appeared before him, "Breach," he said. "Hurry, they have found a way inside!"

Steve's eyes pulsed to their orange glow as he became Ren-Shen. He dashed through the temple looking to ensure Ling's safety. Ling was already standing outside in a fighting stance. She was already emitting her green glow by the time Ren-Shen and Si-Ming had reached her. They all embraced the magnitude of the army of demons filtering through the breached cave entrance. The wrathful red demonic eyes were all the same, but the creatures were of all shapes and sizes. Many were human-like, some were serpentine in character and others were gruesome dogs.

The most hideous were human shaped with claws and black batlike wings the span of small houses.

There was no doubt about the demonic horde's trajectory. They were all headed for the temple. As if to shine a beacon for them, the white, orange and green respective glows of Si-Ming, Ren-Shen and Ling in front of the temple gave the army a precise focal point. They were drawing closer and the noise was intensifying. The cacophony of growls, barks, hisses and shrieks combined to send a message of nothing less than a declaration of war.

Ren-Shen's vibrations revealed the presence of a powerful dark energy. It was something more than the army of demonic creatures. Si-Ming said, "You can feel his presence. He has grown." The evil orchestra of noise ceased abruptly and the demonic horde stopped their march and stood eerily still. A man emerged from the evil throng. Ren-Shen saw how many of the demons were tethered to the man as he confidently walked towards them. He was a different man but was surprisingly familiar. He was precisely the same type of evil monster as Kumicho. He was carrying a sword and smiling wickedly as he called for Si-Ming. "Si-Ming, it is your time of reckoning. I have come for you and demand nothing less than all of your powers from the Infinite. Offer yourself and I will spare the sanctuary, otherwise I will destroy every part of this, your holiest of places," he said.

Si-Ming whispered to Ren-Shen, "Zhao Duyi. His power is totally different. He carries the entire darkness of Chaos within him now. The sword he carries has also given him new insight and abilities." Zhao spoke as though he was right next to Si-Ming, "Yes, old man of the mountains. I do have a new insight. I see your powers and I know how to take them. Offer yourself freely and I will not do any more damage than is necessary."

Si-Ming turned to Ren-Shen and Ling and said, "Expect the

unexpected," as he disappeared then reappeared directly in front of Zhao quickly touching him on the chest. He sought to command Zhao Duyi's three deathbringers. It was pointless, the man was an immortal and the three deathbringers had long been destroyed inside the powerful demon. Zhao sliced his sword straight through Si-Ming's neck. The blade did nothing. It looked as though it merely went through a holographic representation of Si-Ming. Ren-Shen was relieved to see Si-Ming unharmed. Even though he was becoming increasingly aware of his own powers, he was completely unaware of any weaknesses he had. It was comforting to see Si-Ming survive the attack without consequence.

Zhao-Duyi began to roar with laughter. The throng of demons joined in as Si-Ming's white glow began to fade and then his image began to flicker like a faulty light bulb. Ren-Shen looked at Ling as they both attempted to digest the impossible outcome. Si-Ming was extinguished. Zhao-Duyi led the demonic horde closer to the temple when both Ling and Ren-Shen heard the concerned voice of Si-Ming, "I cannot find my physical form. It is unavailable to me. You must not allow this force of evil to claim the spiritual sanctuary."

Ren-Shen sprinted towards Zhao. He quickly reached fighting range. Ling was already alongside Ren-Shen glowing green and poised to fight, she shouted at Zhao, "I never trusted you. I warned Si-Ming and expected your betrayal the moment I met you." Zhao looked bemused. He was cautiously looking at Ren-Shen and listening to Ling. He laughed and focused his glare on her. "The little leftover girl speaks. Look at her now, she glows green and maybe has learned magic tricks from Si-Ming. I should have killed her when I left this pigsty last time." He returned his focus to Ren-Shen and said, "You look interesting to me. You saw how quickly I disposed of Si-Ming, do you think either of you have any chance against me? Prepare to die!" Zhao Duyi stepped forward but was immediately taken aback when he heard Ren-

Shen respond. Ren-Shen with his deep, vibrating voice said, "I make no empty promises about death. You tried to destroy a god and now you must face justice. You will pay for your actions."

A demon dog leapt at Ling. She quickly evaded it with her Golden Monkey movements. Serpents slithered towards her feet while she launched her bird spirit at them and disintegrated them. Ren-Shen remembered Si-Ming saying that Zhao's sword was possibly linked to the great Emperor Taizu. He recalled how much more powerful he became when he touched the sword of Bodhidharma with Kumicho. He summoned the spirit of Emperor Taizu so he might harness the energy of the sword. The Emperor's glow surrounded Ren-Shen.

Zhao almost doubled in size and transformed into a hideous caricature of himself. He shouted at Ren-Shen, "You dare to threaten me with the spirit of my very own ancestor?" Ren-Shen did not hesitate as he launched his attack with the spirit and directness of Emperor Taizu. He went straight for the hand holding the sword in an attempt to minimise the blade's swinging potential. Zhao responded immediately, but his hand only managed to move a few centimetres before Ren-Shen reached the blade.

Ren-Shen immediately realised the wrong choice had been made. Selecting the spirit of Emperor Taizu against his own blade created an explosive event. Instead of multiplying his power, the collision of forces triggered a reaction creating a powerful blast of energy. Ren-Shen was repelled over fifty metres and Zhao stood defiantly unaffected by the blast as he roared with wicked delight. Ren-Shen had converted back to Steve. His disorientation and physical pain clouded his ability to flash into Ren-Shen. In the distance he saw Ling fighting furiously against the horde of demons. Her green bird energy looked almost fully formed for the first time. It was the outline of a bird Steve had never seen before. Glorious in its magnitude and fierce in its intent. The demons were quickly dealt with but they were building around her. He calculated she would soon be overwhelmed. Steve needed Ren-Shen immediately but could not connect himself to the other side of his duality.

A number of winged demons took flight and hovered above Ling while other demons headed for the forest. There were too many. Ling was fighting and defending the spiritual sanctuary on her own while Steve was still trying to find his feet. Zhao raised his hand at the winged demons hovering above Ling. He gestured towards Ling and then the winged creatures blasted fire from their fanged mouths at her. She sent her bird spirit into the air and it created a barrier against the flames. More winged demons gathered until she was surrounded by flames.

Steve was helpless to assist. He managed to find enough of his human strength to stand up. He attempted to summon his Lion Spirit but he had lost his connections to the Infinite. Ling's bird energy was fading. She would be overpowered soon. The more he tried, the worse it became. His spiritual centre had escaped him and he was at his lowest ebb when he felt a jarring thud against his legs. He looked down and focused his eyes in the darkness to see his ever faithful black Pig looking up at him with an impassioned plea. Pig was nudging Steve forward towards the battle and his display of loyalty and justice registered strongly with Steve. Something about the loyal creature of Earth gave Steve his much needed immediate connection to humanity. Steve found the necessary gateway to the Infinite and welcomed its eternal power. He had found his spirits and Ren-Shen finally returned from the Infinite.

Pig had already charged towards the battle. Ling's Bird spirit had faded into the faintest of barriers against the flames raining down upon her. Demons were still trying to attack her at ground level and Zhao was walking purposefully towards Ren-

Shen. His focus was singular and his intent was nothing less than annihilation. In the darkness, Zhao failed to see or care about the black 150 kilogram mass charging towards him. He was bowled over by the determined and loyal Pig. Ren-Shen sent his lion spirit towards Zhao and sprinted towards Ling, but it was too late. The flames had finally reached and engulfed her. She had succumbed to the relentless fiery attacks of the winged demons. Left in her place was a charred statue of that mysterious little woman with the power of one thousand men. She was kneeling towards the temple. Her head bowed down with hands held high in prayer position. She was praying to the Infinite in her death and maintained her mystery even until her final moment. Pig stood by her charred remains and defended the burnt tribute to her greatness from the gloating serpentine demons near her.

Ren-Shen's Lion spirit returned to him after pummeling Zhao. The image of Ling trapped in her final moment and carrying Steve's child was soul destroying for Steve. For Ren-Shen, it invoked a calling from deep within . He summoned Ling's green Bird spirit. It was familiar to him. Steve and Ling had often shared their spirits during their fighting and lovemaking. When Ren-Shen summoned the Bird spirit, it was red instead of green. He sent it towards that beautiful woman with the green eyes as a protective shield to encase her blackened form. As it reached her remains, the red glow disappeared and the glowing red energy shield was absorbed into the blackness of her charred tributary pose.

Ren-Shen turned his attention to Zhao. His wrath manifested itself as the brightest orange glow from his eyes and his breathing vibrations were causing ripples in the air which were troubling to the network of demons within his proximity. They were all connected to Zhao and the look on his demonic face indicated he could feel their confusion. Ren-Shen would not make the same mistake by summoning Emperor Taizu's spirit. He embraced the Luohan spirit and the outline of sixteen energised arms joined his two existing arms to engage in combat with Zhao. He created a vortex of interdimensional magnitude spinning the nearby demons around him and Zhao.

Zhao's use of Taizu's sword was precise and logical. The sword was indeed powerful. Ren-Shen could feel the majesty of its power as he generated the circular vortex of the eighteen hands of Luohan. Zhao didn't waste time attacking arms. He went straight towards Ren-Shen's heart with his blade. One of Luohan's spiritual arms intercepted the blade and was severed in the process of diverting it away from Ren-Shen's body. The momentary diversion was enough time for Ren-Shen to bridge the distance between them. He reached in and grabbed Zhao by the throat. Ren-Shen was compelled to feel the powerful demon's energy. Zhao's black eyes glared back at Ren-Shen's orange, luminous eyes. "You can join us, you know, or you can be destroyed. The Few can never be destroyed!" Zhao said in a choked and guttural voice. Ren-Shen contracted his fingers tighter around Zhao's throat while curiously noting how the demon reacted to the immensity of his power. Ren-Shen was squeezing the human life-force out of his opponent. It wasn't enough, he wanted Zhao to fully grasp the justice he was delivering. He dragged Zhao closer to the burned remains of Ling in her ultimate and solemn pose. He would destroy Zhao in front of her charred remains.

Dragging Zhao towards Ling, Ren-Shen surveyed the spiritual sanctuary. The demons were innumerable and unleashing their devastation on the temple and surrounding tributes. Punctured and bleeding, Pig was still defending Ling's corpse from the many fanged serpentine and dog demons trying to reach her. Ren-Shen stomped on a vicious dog demon with its fangs firmly embedded in Pig's hind quarters. He turned to Zhao and said in his low pitched growl, "Everything dear to me has been taken by monsters who seek their glory in exchange for the suffering of humans. Your punishment is my justice." He used his grip on Zhao's throat to slam him on the ground. He kneeled down and continued to crush his throat while the demons tethered to Zhao attempted to attack Ren-Shen from behind. Their attempts were futile as Ren-Shen's energy was too strong for the lowly servants of evil.

Ren-Shen began to feel the pulse of another god in the spiritual sanctuary. The vibrations were intoxicating, immediate and were connecting him to his celestial identity in a way he had never experienced before. The cosmos was being further woven into himself. He assumed Si-Ming had found a new physical form. But it was different and he was reacting to it in an unprecedented manner.

As the pulses increased in frequency and loudness, Ren-Shen realised Ling's charred body in prayer was the source of the powerful oscillations. The energy being generated pleased him. More than the opium at his weakest moment and indeed more than any natural phenomena he had ever experienced as a human. What was, until a few moments earlier, a source of pain for Steve somehow gave Ren-Shen an intoxicating pleasure. He was absorbing the radiation from the new energy source with an almost drunken joy. The feeling was so intense he had to let go of Zhao's throat. Steve opened his arms and legs to feel the incredible energy pulse through him.

Zhao was also feeling the impact of the radiation sourced from the Infinite. He tried to turn his disgusting head away from Ling's remains. It was slowly forcing him back into his human form as he writhed in pain.

Ling's charred solemnity was interrupted with what commenced as a subtle red glow. It very quickly became so intensely bright that even Pig had to move further away from the powerful energy source. Her burned remains were no longer discernible. The charred corpse had been replaced with a bright volcanic red egg-shaped monolith. The light energy emanating from the glowing monolith was impossibly hot and the oscillations increased in volume and frequency until the entire moonlit sanctuary began to pulse in synchronisation. Ren-Shen intuitively understood the energy generating from the monolith was celestial in nature. The celestial pulses were anathema to the demons as they ceased their trails of destruction and attempted to steady themselves against the celestial forces of the Infinite. Suddenly the monolith exploded and a powerful and relentless stream of red energy shot upward into the heavens.

The powerful beam unified Earth with the Infinite and set the sky on fire, turning night into day. The horde of demons throughout the entire sanctuary looked sickened by the event as lightning bolts from the sky of fire energised the spiritual space. Suddenly, a deafening shriek echoed throughout. Piercing the fiery heavens and descending on the back of a giant red phoenix was a woman in a green dress with eyes of pulsing green light and a streak of green through her long black hair. It was a deified Ling and Si-Ming's voice could be heard by Ren-Shen, "A goddess has been born. The Mysterious Woman of the Nine Heavens, Lady Jiutian Xuannu, goddess of war and sexual alchemy. The twice born. I cannot believe I didn't foresee it, such is her mystery."

The goddess reached closer to Ren-Shen and the demonic fray which was beginning to reanimate. Ren-Shen was able to communicate with Xuannu without even talking. "The trees," he revealed to her cosmic awareness and she acted immediately. She pulled on the clouds which appeared to be her phoenix's reins and her sublime phoenix changed its path and headed towards the forest next to the temple. Her green eyes flashed a bright green light over the entire forest. The rows of perfectly arranged trees began to shudder violently. The leaves were cast off and the bare trees transformed into a thousand strong army of impeccable orange-robed Shaolin monk warriors.

The monks immediately entered the battle with the ground level demons administering their perfectly-honed techniques of the Shaolin Five Ancestors. Xuannu exacted her justice on every single one of the winged demons using clouds of red fire to destroy them. Ren-Shen returned his attention to the demonic Zhao Duyi. Zhao tried to reach his sword but Ren-Shen was too fast. He kicked away the sword and roared with his internalised Lion spirit as he flashed through all his available spirits instinctively while fighting a reinvigorated Zhao. Ren-Shen realised he was fighting an extremely powerful force yet his powers from the Infinite had every answer he needed for as long as he allowed his celestial connection.

Zhao tried everything to distract Ren-Shen. "Agari should have killed you when he killed your wife," he said. Ren-Shen flashed into Steve and wondered how demon Zhao knew about his loss. Zhao used the talon which replaced his hand to strike at Steve. Steve pulled his head back in time and the talons broke the skin on his chest. Steve's eyes flashed orange and Ren-Shen spared no quarter to the vicious demon. His White Crane spirit trapped his talon and he summoned the Grand Emperor to spear his fingers into Zhao's throat. He roared as he ripped off Zhao's head and crushed it under his stomping foot. The demons tethered to him immediately evaporated as Ren-Shen turned to survey the spiritual sanctuary.

The army of monks had already destroyed the demons and had begun restoring the temple. One monk approached Ren-Shen and respectfully collected Emperor Taizu's sword and saluted Ren-Shen as he ran to place the sword inside the temple. Xuannu had destroyed every last one of the winged demons and landed her phoenix near the temple. She was walking towards Ren-Shen with her eyes glowing green. Ren-Shen looked down at the remains of the demon Zhao who had returned to his human form with his head detached. He noticed a black smoky gel on the ground leaking from the severed head. It was being absorbed into the ground, Ren-Shen reached down and dipped his finger in the last of the gel before it disappeared. He tasted the bitter black substance and instantly understood the full breadth of the demon's evil as it caused his body to briefly convulse and temporarily lose connection to the Infinite.

He heard the familiar grunts of Pig who limped over to him and affectionately rubbed his bloodied face on Ren-Shen's leg. He patted Pig on the head and walked towards the Mysterious Woman of the Nine Heavens. "That was interesting. You still carry our baby you know," he said to her. She replied, "I know .... everything."

They watched the army of monks restore order to the spiritual sanctuary with the same precision they used in battle. When they finished, they arranged themselves in formation and silently reverted back to the perfectly-arranged trees they once were.

Ren-Shen surveyed the spiritual sanctuary one last time and then beheld the glory of the goddess in the green dress before him, the ever mysterious Jiutian Xuannu, "Fly me to Okinawa," he said.

The End (and Beginning)

"Hold on to the centre."

— Lao Tzu, Tao Te Ching

Acknowledgements

It was indescribable fun immersing myself in the world of REN-SHEN. I spent countless hours researching, planning and writing this, my first novel. After coming up for air, it was always a joy sharing my ramblings with my family.

My beautiful wife Tania supported my obsession and tolerated my isolation. She offered wonderful suggestions sourced from the inspiration of millions of books she has read in the past.

My sons, Mitchell and Paul, would immediately advise me if my streams of consciousness had the potential to be cool! Their encouragement was a special joy to me.

The proofreading and editing suggestions from Eda Payne and Mark Manuel were gratefully embraced. More importantly, their enthusiasm for the story gave me further fuel.

Kylie Fleming's precision and professionalism in editing my manuscript was essential. Her excitement with the story as it progressed gave me infinite joy and motivation.

They say an artist never finishes his work, rather, he abandons it. This was not the case for me. Your help removed any doubts about the completion of this story and I remain eternally grateful.

Thank you so much, my dear family and friends.

About The Author

Chris Milanko

 Chris Milanko has enjoyed martial arts for much of his life. He previously held a national Australian all-styles fighting title and has been teaching Shaolin Five Ancestors Kung Fu for over 30 years.

He runs a very busy Chartered Accounting firm in Australia and consults to all sizes of business in matters of taxation and business logic.

An overwhelming response to a tiny story he wrote as a YouTube comment surprised and motivated him to create the world of REN-SHEN.

He enjoys writing, making music, martial arts, travelling and spending quality time with his family and friends. He is madly passionate about the world of REN-SHEN and is resolutely committed to the development of the REN-SHEN series of novels and beyond.

Join him in the Infinite!
www.ren-shen.com

More to Come!

Stay tuned for the next instalment in the REN-SHEN series. **REN-SHEN Secret of Secrets** sees our hero learning more about the consequences of his duality as both man and a god.

We learn about The Few and their multi-generational agenda for the glory of Chaos. The Watchers and their divine relationship with the god of Yeqon.

The stage is being set for the battle of good versus evil on a celestial scale. Stand for the Infinite and resist the evil abound!

'We, the Twenty Three.
  From the many, The Few.
  Will find the way to the Infinite.
  And the gods will bend their knees.
  Crushed in hope and spirit,
  We will end humanity.
  As black as our eyes,
  Will be the skies.
  We will take what is rightfully ours.
  For the glory of Chaos.'

The Infinite needs YOU!
www.ren-shen.com